Cover Design and Interior Format

© **KILLION**
GROUP, INC.

Falling for TENDER HEART

A TENDER HEART TEXAS NOVEL

KATIE LANE

"'Thank you, but I don't need any help,' Etta said with a slight lift of her chin. 'I can certainly get down from a stagecoach all by my—' Her foot slipped on the step, and she landed face-first in the muddy street. The irritating cowboy chuckled. 'Yes, ma'am, you sure can.'"

—Tender Heart Book One

CHAPTER ONE

❦

"EXCUSE ME, MA'AM."

Emery Wakefield looked up from the book she was reading—more like rereading for the hundredth time—and was disappointed that the man speaking wasn't a handsome cowboy with a sexy smile. He was just the businessman sitting next to her on the plane.

He was nice-looking, but not nearly as nice-looking as Rory Earhart. Although few men could compare to her favorite fictional hero—the key word being *fictional*.

Emery had a wee bit of a problem keeping fiction separate from reality. As an editor and avid reader, she loved to get lost in the fantasy worlds of her characters, which sometimes caused her to lose sight of her own life. Her two older brothers teased her about having her head in the clouds. And her close friends Carly and Savannah were always reminding her to live in the real world. In the real world, there were no perfect heroes. Just regular guys like this businessman who had ignored her the entire trip to play video games on his phone. But if she ever wanted to be in a relationship again, she needed to lower her standards and make an effort.

She smiled. "Yes?"

He nodded at the aisle. "The plane's landed."

She finally noticed that people were out of their seats and collecting their luggage from the overhead compartments. "Oh! I didn't even realize." She pulled her laptop bag from beneath the seat in front of her and placed the tattered paperback in the side pocket.

"So you like those naughty romance novels?" When she glanced over, the businessman winked.

Emery felt her spine stiffen, but she quickly reminded herself that few men understood romance—books or otherwise. Romance to them was all about the sex. It wasn't about the first prolonged glance. The first heated touch. The first breathless kiss.

She blinked. *Reality, Emery, reality.*

"Yes," she said. "I like those 'naughty' romances. What genre do you read?"

"I don't do a lot of reading. I usually just wait for the movie."

Okay, she was willing to lower her standards, but not that much.

Since the conversation was pretty much dead, she busied herself by straightening the pages of the manuscript she'd been reading earlier. While most of the other editors at Randall Publishing did their reading and editing electronically, Emery preferred to have a hard copy. There was something about holding the pages in her hands that made the reading experience so much better. Although it hadn't made this particular manuscript any better.

After talking to the writer's agent and reading the first few chapters, she'd had high hopes for this book. The author had a fresh voice and a great ear for dialogue. Unfortunately, the entire plot had crumbled midway through, and there was little hope of salvaging it. Which meant that this wasn't the book that was going to give Emery job security and make her boss overlook the other books that had flopped. But hopefully, she had the key to the one novel that would. She looked at the zippered pocket where she'd carefully tucked the envelope she had received a month ago.

She was a firm believer in fate, and there was no other explanation for her having received the envelope. When she'd first opened it, she felt like Harry Potter getting his invitation to Hogwarts. And even if her boss was convinced it was a hoax, there was no way Emery could ignore it. That would be like ignoring destiny.

The Tender Heart novels were her favorite books of all time. The ten-book series about mail-order brides in the old West had gotten her through her horrific puberty years. The pimples and braces wouldn't have been so bad if she'd been a genius like her brothers and could've fit in with the geeks. But she wasn't a genius. She was horrible at math, couldn't have cared less about science, and hadn't gotten through one *Star Wars* movie without falling asleep. In school she'd been labeled the homely, weird girl who walked around with her nose in a book.

It was in those books that she'd found refuge from school bullies and the fact that she didn't fit in with the rest of her family of geniuses. And she was still struggling to fit in. She had yet to find her place in New York City and was only months away from losing her job.

Unless what was in the envelope turned out to be authentic.

"So what brings you to Austin?" The businessman pulled his briefcase out from under the seat.

She got to her feet. "I'm meeting my two best friends for spring break." It wasn't a lie. She had roped her two unsuspecting friends into joining her on this trip. They thought they were checking out the setting of their favorite series. They knew nothing about the letter Emery had received . . . or the chapter.

Something about her reply made the businessman's eyes light up. Probably the prospect of spring break with three naughty romance readers who were only interested in sex. "Really? I live here so I'd be happy to show you and your friends around if you'd like. Austin is an exciting town."

"I'm sure it is, but we're not staying in Austin. We're staying in Bliss."

He looked confused. "Bliss? Why would you want to go there? It's practically a ghost town."

She glanced at her laptop case, and a smile bloomed on her face. "In a way, that's exactly what I'm looking for. Ghosts." She didn't wait for him to ask any more questions before she moved into the aisle.

Since Carly and Savannah's flights didn't get in until much later, Emery planned to meet them in Bliss. Excited to get to the small town, she wasted no time picking up her luggage and renting a car. The entire drive from Austin, she couldn't help feeling like she was on the Hogwarts Express headed to a place that had only existed in her dreams.

Unfortunately, that excitement fizzled when she drove into Bliss and reality hit. She knew a modern town wasn't going to be like an old western town—especially a fictional western town—but she had expected to find something that reminded her of Tender Heart. A quaint knick-knack shop that sold souvenirs. A bookstore with the entire series displayed in the window. The 1950s diner where the author Lucy Arrington had plotted her famous stories. The pretty little chapel where all the mail-order brides had found their happily-ever-afters.

Instead, the two-lane highway Emery drove into town on was lined with vacant brick buildings that had fading signs and cracked windows. Rusty grain silos stood like aged sentinels, and weeds filled every empty lot.

The businessman had been right. It did look like a ghost town.

There were few cars on the road. So when a muddy pickup truck passed her going the opposite direction, Emery couldn't help but stare. The old guy behind the wheel stared back with a suspicious look. Or maybe it was her clean Hyundai that he found suspicious. The few vehicles parked along the street looked as dirty as his truck. It was hard not to feel disappointed. She had arrived at Cinderella's castle to find a hovel nothing like her fantasies.

She glanced at her laptop bag on the front seat next to her. The town might not look like what she expected, but there was still hope that her fantasies would be realized—if not in the town, then on paper.

Pushing her disappointment down, Emery searched for the Bliss Motor Lodge where she'd made reservations. It was the only place to stay in town, and she hoped she hadn't booked the Bates Motel. If she walked into the lobby and spotted a bunch of stuffed birds, she was out of there.

Since Main Street was only a couple of blocks long, she easily found the motor lodge. But before she pulled in, she couldn't help driving a little further to see if she could find a little white chapel with beautiful stained-glass windows. She didn't, but what she did find was a gas station that wasn't boarded up. In fact, two men sat at a table in front. And she couldn't help pulling in to see if she could get some information.

The old guy with the balding head looked at her just as suspiciously as the man who had driven past her on the street. She couldn't tell how the other man looked. He wore a brown felt cowboy hat that was tugged low on his forehead and shaded his face. But the hat turned in her direction when she got out.

Since she couldn't just start asking questions without adding to their suspicions, she decided to get gas. The pump didn't have a credit card slot, so she topped off her tank, then leaned into the car to get her purse from the front seat. That's when she heard one of the men speak.

"You gonna gawk? Or are you gonna play?"

She straightened and peeked around the pump in time to see the cowboy hat turn away. She had assumed he was the same age as the old guy. But on closer examination, she realized her mistake. The hard chest and broad shoulders that filled out the western shirt belonged to a much younger man. As did the dark hair curling on the back of his strong, corded neck.

She watched the muscles in that neck tighten as the old guy continued, "I thought you just got finished telling me that you didn't have time for women."

"Would you keep it down, Emmett?" the cowboy hissed as he picked up a domino. His hands were big, but agile enough to manipulate the small white tile into place on the table. Something about those long fingers made Emery's heart skip and her stomach feel all light and airy. The empty stomach she could blame on being hungry. She'd only had a bagel at the airport and a Cranapple and peanuts on the plane. The skipping heart was a little harder to explain.

"Now that was stupid." Emmett positioned a domino on the table, then picked up the pencil next to the notepad to put down his score. "Almost as stupid as wasting your time gawking at a woman who's just passing through. That's a rental car if ever I saw one, and no woman from around here wears heels that high unless it's Easter Sunday." He glanced over at Emery and noticed her watching. He smiled, revealing a chipped front tooth. "Howdy, ma'am."

Emery stepped around the gas pump, and both men stood up from their chairs. But it was the cowboy she couldn't look away from. If she'd thought his body was nice sitting down, it was nothing compared to how he looked fully stretched out. He had to be well over six feet tall with long, muscled legs that were emphasized by the fit of his well-worn blue jeans.

And his legs weren't the only things they emphasized.

Her gaze zeroed in on the bulge beneath the zipper. Not a small bulge, but a long, hard one. Before she could blink, his cowboy hat blocked her view. She lifted her gaze. Everything inside Emery went very still as reality collided with fantasy.

She had been searching for some sign of Tender Heart. Some small piece of the series she loved so dearly. And she'd finally found it. From the lock of raven black hair that curled over his forehead to the intense eyes as blue as a Texas sky at twilight, the man standing in front of her looked exactly like her favorite book boyfriend.

Her hero Rory Earhart had come to life.

"Rory Earhart didn't like the woman. He didn't like the haughty way she lifted her nose in the air whenever she looked at him and he didn't like the snooty way she talked . . . he did, however, like the way her dress hugged her breasts and trim waist. He liked that a lot."

CHAPTER TWO

❦

COLE COULDN'T REMEMBER THE LAST time the mere sight of a woman had given him an erection. Maybe when he was sixteen and Miss Jenkins the school librarian had taken off her glasses to clean them. But that was only because he'd just watched a porn flick at Jimmy Watson's called *Sexy-Assed Librarians*. But he was no longer a wet-behind-the-ears teenager who fantasized about sexy librarians. He was a month away from being thirty, three decades, with more than a few notches on his bedpost. Not that any of his past lovers had eyes the color of a freshly mowed pasture. Or breasts the size of hill country peaches. Or long chestnut hair he could wrap around his fist twice. Or a shapely ass that would fit perfectly snugged up against his—

He cleared his throat and nodded a greeting. "Ma'am."

For the briefest of seconds, those clear green eyes widened as if she felt the same sexual awareness that he did. But it must've just been wishful thinking because the next second, she completely dismissed him and addressed

Emmett.

"I couldn't find the credit card slot on your gas pump."

"That's because there ain't one," Emmett Daily said.

"There isn't one," the woman corrected. The contrite look that quickly entered her eyes made it obvious that she hadn't meant to speak the words aloud. But she had. And Cole's erection softened as if he'd been dunked head first into a chilly horse trough.

If there was one thing that frosted his butt faster than a panhandle blizzard, it was watching a woman make a fool of someone he loved. Cole's father had spent his life being made a fool of by his mother. And Cole flat refused to let some uppity out-of-towner do the same to his good friend. A friend who had given Cole a job when he'd most needed it. But before he could let her have it, she spoke.

"I apologize, sir. I spent my four-hour flight correcting grammar, and sometimes I have trouble shutting that side of my brain off."

Emmett got to his feet. "No need to apologize. My wife Joanna was a school teacher and has spent our entire marriage correcting my grammar—of course, it didn't do no good. You can't teach an old dog new tricks. And speaking of my school teacher, I better get on home for lunch." His eyes twinkled at Cole. "I'm sure you can hold things down here." He limped around the corner of the station.

Cole wasn't as forgiving as Emmett. He smoothed back his hair and slipped his cowboy hat on. "Yep, that's right," he said in his thickest Texas twang. "There *ain't* no fancy credit card slots on them there pumps. Here in Bliss, we believe in interacting with our customers and being polite to strangers—even ones who are disrespectful to our Vietnam War heroes." He nodded at the open door to the office. "Now if you head right in there, I'll ring you up so you can be on your way."

She didn't look apologetic now. She looked about as perturbed at him for pointing out her rudeness as he was at her for pointing out Emmett's bad grammar. It was a standoff of sorts. Each one waiting for the other to blink. He would've come out the winner if she hadn't crossed her arms. The action pushed her breasts higher, and damned if his eyes didn't lower to those sweet peaches outlined by her sexy white blouse like iron filings to magnets. He quickly jerked his gaze back up. But it was too late. The triumph in her eyes was easy to read.

"Your friend is right," she said. "You are just wasting your time gawking at something you can't have."

There was only one woman Cole hated, but this woman was fast becoming the second.

"Well, since I don't like to waste anybody's time," he drawled, "how about I just pay for your gas so you can be on your way."

"That won't be necessary." With a sassy little twitch of her hips, she turned on her heel and walked into the office. She wore one of those skinny business skirts that caused women to take smaller steps. Which, in turn, caused her hips to wiggle enticingly. But Cole was through being enticed. Once inside, he wasted no time ringing her up and giving her a total.

She rummaged through the large bag that hung on her shoulder. The bag was made of expensive leather and was the size of one of those totes women took with them to the grocery store. Which might explain why she couldn't find her wallet and had to start taking things out: a pile of papers with red marks all over them, a half-empty plastic bottle of water, a small notebook, two red pencils, a package of tissues, another red pencil, a small zippered bag with a smudge of red lipstick, two more red pencils, and a red case for glasses that brought back the fantasy of sexy librarians.

He pushed down the images. "So you like red, do you?"

She stopped rummaging and glanced at the clutter on the counter. "Oh, these." She started to collect the pencils. "I didn't realize I had so many. And yet I never seem to be able to find one when I need it."

So she was a teacher. If he'd had a teacher who looked like her, he never would've made it through high school without a major case of blue balls.

"Where are you from?" he asked.

"New York City." The pride in her voice told him a lot. She was one of those people who thought New York City was the only city worth living in.

"Ahh, New York. Went there once . . . and once was more than enough." He nodded at her purse. "You sure you don't want to take me up on my offer? You've pulled a lot of stuff out of that Mary Poppins bag of yours, but nothing that would pay for gas."

She started digging again. "I'm sure my wallet is in here some—" She froze, and her head slowly lifted. Her eyes were wide enough to swim in. Not that he had any desire to take a dip. Okay, maybe he had a little desire. "Oh. My. God. I left my wallet at the rental car counter in the Austin airport."

Before he could comment one way or the other, she quickly pulled out a cellphone and thumbed it expertly. Cole didn't use his cell phone much. If he had something to say, he preferred to say it in person.

The woman held the phone to her ear. "Yes, this is Emery Wakefield. I just rented a car from you and I think I left my wallet—you do?" Her shoulders wilted with relief. "That's wonderful. If you can just hold on to it, I'll pick it up." She paused. "On second thought, two of my friends arrive later today. They can pick it up. Carly Hanover and Savannah Reynolds. Yes, you can call when they get there to verify. Thank you. Thank you so much."

She hung up, then redialed. When she noticed Cole watching her, she turned and walked a few feet away. "Carly? Thank God I caught you before you got on the plane. I left my wallet at the Hertz rental counter." She paused and laughed. "No, I was not lost in a book. I was just excited to get here." She walked over to the old-fashioned Coke machine. She dug through the side pocket of her bag and pulled out some change. He had a hard time keeping his mind from going down a raunchy sex road as she leaned over the freezer-style Coke machine to put the money in and pointed her sweet ass in his direction.

Shit. He squeezed his eyes shut and recited some Texas Ranger pitching stats. When he opened them, she was looking at him with exasperation and pointing at the machine. He stepped from behind the counter, then lifted the lid of the freezer and pulled out a bottle.

She lowered the phone away from her mouth. "Do you have Vitamin Water?"

Ignoring the stupid question, he used the opener on the side of the machine to pop off the cap before he held out the bottle. Her fingers with their neatly trimmed nails brushed his grease-stained, calloused ones with more heat than he expected. Their gazes collided for a fraction of a second before he pulled back, and she turned and continued her conversation.

"No, I saw no sign of it. I saw only one church. And it wasn't a cute little white one with stained glass windows." She paused. "Oh, you're right. The chapel isn't going to be in town. It's going to be on the Earhart Ranch."

Cole stopped in mid-stride on the way back to the counter, and the last of his desire fizzled out like a snuffed candle. The conversation went on, but he was through listening. He grabbed his hat off the hook and walked out the side door that led to the garage. He needed to finish replacing the serpentine belt on the Chevy half-ton pickup that sat in one of the bays—something he'd been working on when Emmett interrupted him for a game of dominos. Then he needed to pick up some horse feed and get home. He had chores to do, dinner to make for Gracie, and a stack of hospital and therapy bills to try to figure out how to pay. Emmett was right. He didn't have time to waste on a woman looking for something that no longer existed.

He had just leaned under the hood to loosen the serpentine belt tensioner when the click of heels echoed on the concrete floor. A white shirt and nice breasts appeared in his peripheral vision.

"Unfortunately, I won't be able to pay for the gas until my friends bring me my wallet. So if the loan offer is still good . . ."

He continued to work. "No problem."

She lifted the bottle, and from the corner of his eye he watched her lips pucker against the rim of the bottle as she pulled in a long sip of Coke. When she lowered the bottle, one topaz drop of cola quivered on her full bottom lip. He redirected his attention to removing the belt.

"So how long have you lived in Bliss?" The question was punctuated with a soft burp. She covered her mouth. "Oh, excuse me."

He kept his answer short. "All my life."

She took another sip, but he didn't watch this time. "So you've read the books?" When he didn't answer, she continued. "I guess that was a stupid question since the author lived here and based the stories on the town." She paused. "Although Bliss isn't anything like Tender Heart."

The note of despair in her voice had Cole glancing over. She stared out the open bay door with the bottle of Coke clutched in her hand. She had the same look that every other person got when they discovered that their favorite fictional book series was just that . . . fiction.

And what did they expect? Did they expect to find acres of ranch land filled with cattle all carrying the Earhart's heart-encircled *E*? Dust-covered cowboys slumped over their saddle horns after a long day of riding the range? A group of virginal, starry-eyed mail-order brides fresh off the stage?

The spark of disappointment in Emery's spring green eyes said that's exactly what she'd expected. It's what all the tourists who traveled to Bliss expected. They expected to find Tender Heart: The general store with its old men playing checkers and gossiping on the front porch. Miss Loretta's saloon with its G-rated cancan girls and advice-giving bartender. And the little white chapel where all the mail-order brides had married their true loves.

It was ridiculous.

Cole was an avid reader and had gotten caught up in more than a few series. But he didn't believe that Jack Reacher would show up one day and kill all the bad guys or that James Bond could wreck as many company cars as he did and still have a job. There was fiction, and then there was reality. And Cole dealt in reality. He had ever since his mother ran off when he was a kid, crushing all his childhood fantasies of a happy family.

"Sorry." He went back to work. "There's no Tender Heart here. Never has been. Never will be."

"Etta expected the boardinghouse to be run by a woman. She did not expect it to be run by a little man with a white beard longer than Rip Van Winkle's. 'Well, don't just stand there starin' like a darn blamed fool,' the man said. 'Get in here so I can close the door before all the heat gets out and my arthritis acts up.'"

CHAPTER THREE

SINCE EMERY HAD NO IDENTIFICATION or credit cards, she worried she wouldn't be able to check into the hotel where she'd made her reservation. But the owner of the small motor lodge wasn't concerned about identification or credit as much as she was about finding out why Emery was in town. And after the reaction she'd received from the mechanic cowboy at the gas station, Emery was hesitant to give away too much information.

"It's just a girlfriend road trip," she said. "My two friends and I love the Tender Heart series and thought it would be fun to see the place where Lucy Arrington wrote the stories."

Mrs. Crawley visibly relaxed. "Well, there might not be a ton of fun things to see in Bliss, but we do have lots of history if you're willing to listen."

Emery knew the history, but she played along. "I'd love to hear about Bliss."

Mrs. Crawley took a room key off a hook and moved out from behind the desk. "The town was built in the eighteen hundreds by a man named Gustav Arrington. He was a scrawny Englishman who had inherited money from his father and decided to invest it in the Wild West he'd been reading about in dime novels. Of course, he learned soon enough that the reality of raising cattle is a lot tougher than in fiction. Still, he stuck with it, and at one point his ranch covered 525,000 acres in six counties with thousands of head of cattle. Of course, with all that land and all those cows, you need people to work it. And you can't keep cowboys without women."

Emery couldn't help the excitement that sizzled through her veins. The town might not look like Tender Heart, but Mrs. Crawley was right. The history was here. Emery followed the woman out the glass door and prompted her to keep talking.

"Which is where the mail-order brides came in."

"Exactly. Gus put ads in numerous Eastern newspapers asking for 'strong, determined, tender-hearted women to help settle Texas and some wild cowboys.' He was flooded with responses. He picked an even dozen to start things off, and all but one showed up that year." Mrs. Crawley led her down a sidewalk to four flat-roofed stucco bungalows. Each one had two rooms with a carport on either side. They weren't fancy, but quaint with a hitching post–style railing that ran in front and bright turquoise doors.

"Thus the eleven brides that Lucy Arrington wrote about in her epic series," Emery said.

Mrs. Crawley stopped in front of a room with a horseshoe and a number 7 on the door. "Yes, the eleven brides. Although we only got ten stories before Lucy died in the late 1950s." She shook her head. "It's a shame."

It was a shame, and something that Emery was hoping to fix. But first she needed to move Mrs. Crawley up about six decades. "So what about her descendants? Do any Arringtons still live around here?"

"Lucy didn't have any kids, but her brother's descendants are still living on the same ranch—although it's no longer one big spread. In the 1970s, after a bad drought and the oil crisis, the three brothers who owned the ranch got into a terrible fight over how the ranch should be run and ended up splitting it three ways. If you ask me, that was the true ending of the Tender Heart series."

Mrs. Crawley unlocked the door and opened it. "Here we are. All the other rooms are mostly the same, but lucky number seven has an extra big tub and one vibrating bed. The vibrator doesn't always work, but when it does . . ." She placed a hand on her chest and looked up at the sky. "Lord have mercy." She smiled and winked at Emery. "And since you're here first, I figure you have first dibs on that bed. So when do your friends get here?"

"Tonight some time." Carly and Savannah would be as disappointed as Emery when they realized that the town held nothing of Tender Heart.

An image of the mechanic cowboy popped into her head. Okay, so maybe there was something of Tender Heart. The man was the spitting image of Rory Earhart. Same coal black hair. Same deep blue eyes. Same tall, lean, muscled body that had made the heroine's heart skip a beat when he'd first tried to help her down from the stagecoach.

Emery's heart had skipped a beat and certainly picked up its pace when those hungry blue eyes had settled on her. But she wasn't here to be some cowboy's feast. Even if it was an extremely tempting thought.

"You okay?" Mrs. Crawley asked. "You look a little flushed."

Emery fanned a hand in front of her face. "I'm fine. It's just a little hotter than I thought it would be."

"It has been a hot spring. Which means that summer's going to be a real scorcher." Mrs. Crawley stepped into the room, and Emery followed.

The room wasn't anything like the modern hotel rooms Emery was used to staying in when she traveled. The furniture was old and the décor western. The curtains and bedspreads had a vintage cowboy-and-lassos print. A rustic horseshoe lamp sat on the center nightstand. Framed pictures of cowboys riding the range hung over the two double beds. There was even a pair of old cowboy boots with spurs sitting on the dresser next to a Mr. Coffee machine.

"The air conditioner will cool things off soon enough," Mrs. Crawley said as she clicked on the window unit. "And there's an ice and soda machine by room five. But I'd stay away from that room if I were you. Dirk Hadley is good lookin' as sin but he's a no-account drifter and that spells trouble with a capital T. And believe me, I know about drifters. My first husband was one of the worst." She set the key on the dresser next to the coffee machine. "I leave at five o'clock. If you and your friends need anything after that, you'll have to wait until morning."

Emery got the key and followed Mrs. Crawley back to the office, hoping to get more information. "So what happened to the Arrington Ranch once the brothers split it up?"

"Nothing much. There are still three smaller ranches owned by Arrington cousins, but none of them compare to the big spread it once was."

"Are any of them married? Is there a Mrs. Arrington?"

Mrs. Crawley stopped in the process of pushing open the office door and turned with narrowed eyes. "Why do you ask?"

Worried Mrs. Crawley would clam up like the cowboy

at the gas station, Emery hedged. "I just thought that one of them might've married a mail-order bride like their ancestors." She forced a giggle that sounded ridiculous.

"They could do a lot worse," Mrs. Crawley said. 'Those mail-order brides were strong, determined women who saw a way out of their unhappy lives and took it. My great-great grandmother was one of them, and she went through hell to achieve her dream of coming to live in America. In her diary, she talks about the horrible conditions on the boat trip from Ireland, being herded through Ellis Island like cattle, and living on the streets of New York for months before she read Gus's ad for mail-order brides."

Emery felt a rush of adrenaline. "You read an actual mail-order bride's diary? Is it in a museum here?"

Mrs. Crawley laughed. "We don't have any museums in Bliss. I keep it in an old butter cookie tin in the top of my closet. If you want to see it, I'd be happy to let you take a look."

The thought of a priceless nineteenth-century diary being kept in a cookie tin was alarming, but her excitement about getting her hands on the diary of a mail-order bride eclipsed her concern and made her feel slightly lightheaded. Of course, that could've just been from lack of food.

"I would love to see it," she said.

"Then I'll bring it tomorrow." Mrs. Crawley walked into the office, and the door closed behind her with a soft whoosh.

Emery didn't follow her. She had interrogated Mrs. Crawley enough for one day, and she would have to be subtle if she wanted to get the answers she needed.

After pulling her car into the carport, she grabbed her suitcase from the trunk and laptop case from the front seat, then unlocked the door to her room. The air conditioner had made the room much cooler, and as soon as she set her things down and dead bolted the door, she slipped off her heels and fell back on the bed closest to the window. Immediately, the mattress started to vibrate. Once she got over her shock, she laughed. Maybe the town wasn't exactly what she'd expected, but she was here. She was here where it all started. And with any luck, she would find a happy ending for Tender Heart . . . and success for Emery Wakefield.

☾

EMERY WOKE TO HER STOMACH'S loud grumbling. The vibrating mattress had stopped and late afternoon sunlight spilled in through the window above the air conditioner. She rolled to her side and looked at the analog clock on the nightstand. Thinking it must be wrong, she got to her feet and grabbed her purse from the chair. But her cellphone verified the time. She'd slept for more than two hours, and she was starving.

After dumping the contents of her purse on the bed, she found over two dollars in change and went in search of a vending machine. But all she found were the soda and ice machines . . . and a half-naked drifter sitting in a metal lawn chair in front of room number five.

Mrs. Crawley was right. Dirk Hadley looked like trouble with a capital T. His long, narrow bare feet were propped arrogantly up on the hitching post railing and a beat-up straw cowboy hat covered his face. It was impossible not to stare at the tan naked chest and rippled muscles of his abdomen above the faded jeans.

"Howdy."

She looked up to find the hat tipped back and the sparkling gleam of youthful cockiness in his bluish-gray eyes. If he had a role in the Tender Heart series, he would be Rory's little brother, Johnny. He looked like he enjoyed getting into mischief of one kind or another. But Emery didn't have time for mischief. She merely lifted a hand in greeting before she turned to the soda machine. If she couldn't eat, at least she could fill up on sugar, caffeine, and carbonation. Unfortunately, once she got her two dollars in the machine, it refused to spit out a can.

"It's a little fussy." The drifter leaned against the soda machine. "It doesn't like dimes or nickels." He reached in front of her and pushed the eject button.

She collected the coins that clinked into the holder. Four quarters and no dimes or nickels. While she stared down at the money in her palm, her stomach growled again. She glanced over to see if he'd heard. He cocked one eyebrow, and his smile deepened. Then, without a word, he turned and disappeared inside the open door of his room.

Emery put the money back into the machine and tried again, with the same results. She was about to give up and return to her room when the drifter reappeared wearing scuffed cowboy boots and an unsnapped western shirt that flapped around his ripped abs.

He stopped next to her and snapped his shirt. "Come on, I'll buy you a burger and a beer."

"Thank you, but I'm fine." She punched the soda machine button once more before she headed to her room.

She needed to check her email to see if she had any from work and text her parents. Even though they were busy with their medical practices—her father's psychiatry and her mother's gynecology—they got nervous if she didn't text or call at least once a day. Her parents still viewed her as the helpless baby of the family who needed to be watched over, and they weren't happy about her living so far away in New York City. To be honest, Emery wasn't all that happy about living there either. Since she hadn't fit in on the West Coast, she had hoped she'd fit in on the East. But she still couldn't manage to hail a taxi and had yet to make one friend in her apartment building.

She stopped to unlock the door to her room and realized that the drifter had followed her. If he seemed dangerous, she would've been a little nervous. But he looked like Scott Eastwood before he needed to use a razor. And his smile was impish and contagious.

"From the sound of that tummy growl, I don't think you're all that fine," he said. "And since you lost your wallet, it looks like I'm your only option for satisfying that hunger."

Her brows knitted. "How do you know I lost my wallet?"

He held up his hands. "Don't get jumpy. I stopped by the gas station to see if Emmett had any odd jobs for me, and I overheard him talking about a pretty tourist who lost her wallet. And since you're new in town and as pretty as they come, I figured you were the woman he was talking about." He held out a hand. "Dirk Hadley."

She stared at his hand for only a second before she took it. "Emery Wakefield. So you're trying to get a job at the gas station? Mrs. Crawley acted like you were just passing through town."

He laughed. "That's just her wishful thinking. Her daughter Winnie has developed a bit of a crush on me and I think her mama wishes I'd up and leave town so she could get back to her housekeeping chores—although Winnie seems to clean my room pretty well." The dimples in his cheeks deepened, and Emery had a hard time not smiling.

"Mrs. Crawley also said you were trouble with a capital T. And I think she was right about that."

"Now, why would you think a thing like that?" Dirk innocently blinked his long eyelashes. "I'm just a harmless country boy looking to feed a penniless stranger a burger and maybe some extra crispy fries." His eyes twinkled as if he knew she was salivating. "The Watering Hole is just up the street. We can walk if it will make you feel safer." He glanced down. "Although I'd change into something a little more casual if I was you. That skirt and those heels don't look like they're made for walking."

It only took Emery a second and another grumble of her stomach to make up her mind. "Fine. But I'm paying you back as soon as my friends get here. And I want to make it perfectly clear that I'm not interested in a one-night stand with a cute cowboy. I just want food."

His smile broadened. "Cute? Well, thank you, Emerald Eyes."

The Watering Hole bar was small and dark with a strong scent of onions and beer. Being that it was a Saturday night and the only bar in town, Emery had expected it to be crowded, but only two men sat at the bar. They both turned on their stools when they walked in and openly stared as Dirk led her to a booth with torn vinyl seats and a sticky table. A jukebox played a country-western song, but there was no dance floor. Unless it was in the same room as the pool tables she could just make out in the back.

"What can I get y'all?" The bartender called from the bar.

"We'll take a couple beers and cheeseburgers with plenty of onions and extra crispy fries," Dirk said as he took off his hat and tossed it onto the back ledge of the booth.

Emery corrected the order. "Water for me and no onions on my cheeseburger. And could I exchange the fries for fruit?"

The bartender snorted. "Would you like strawberries and blueberries or a melon selection?" Before Emery could answer, the men at the bar broke out in laughter.

Dirk's smile slipped. "Lay off, Hank. Just bring her a burger without onions and no fries."

"Fine. But I'm not putting this meal on your tab. You won't get any more credit until you finish those cabinets in the back."

"I'll finish your cabinets. I've just been busy with other things."

Hank's gaze flashed to Emery. "And I know what those other things are." He turned and grabbed a glass from a shelf and started filling it with beer from the tap.

"You're a carpenter?" Emery said. "I thought you said you were looking for a job at the gas station."

"A carpenter, a mechanic, a plumber. Whatever odd job I can find to pay the bills."

"I guess a steady job is hard to come by in a small town."

He waited for Hank to deliver their drinks and leave before he spoke. "I've been offered steady jobs, but I'm not interested. I don't want to be tied to this town—to any town, for that matter. The jobs I take, I take for no more than a week or two. That's as far as I want to see into the future."

She took a sip of water. "So why Bliss? I would think that you'd have more job opportunities in a bigger town."

He paused with the frosty glass of beer halfway to his mouth, and for a split second, the twinkle left his eyes. He took a deep drink of beer, and by the time he lowered the glass and wiped the foam from his top lip, his smile had returned. "Just random luck," he said.

She didn't believe him, and she had to wonder if there wasn't more to Dirk Hadley than met the eye. But since she wasn't sharing all her secrets, she figured he didn't have to share his.

The Watering Hole's cheeseburgers left something to be desired. The meat patty was thin and burned and the processed cheese cold. There was no lettuce or tomato, just a few curled up sliced pickles. But Dirk's French fries were crispy, greasy, and yummy.

"What is it with women?" Dirk asked as he watched her munch a fry. "You don't order fries, but then you steal all of ours."

Emery finished off the fry. "I did not steal all of yours. I've just taken a few. And if you didn't want to share, all you had to do was say so."

"I don't mind sharing. I just want to know why women don't order their own. That way you wouldn't have to reach so far."

Since he had a good point, Emery acquiesced. "It probably has to with diets and bad self-image. We can feel good about ourselves if we don't order them, even if deep down we really want them."

He dipped a fry in catsup and held it out. "And I say do what feels good. What's life for if not to enjoy?"

It was hard to deny his philosophy with a salt-sprinkled, crispy French fry dipped in sweet catsup staring her in the face. So she didn't even try. She leaned in and took a bite. As she chewed, her gaze shifted over to the poolroom.

A cowboy stood in the doorway. Even in the dimly lit bar, she recognized him immediately. She recognized the fit of the plaid western shirt on his broad shoulders and the way the faded jeans hugged his long, lean legs. The brim of his brown felt cowboy hat hid most of his face, but if the angle of his body was any indication, he was looking straight at her.

"Who is that man standing in the poolroom?" she asked.

Dirk popped the rest of the fry in his mouth and glanced over his shoulder. When he turned back, his eyes held no twinkle at all. "Arrington. Cole Arrington. And if you think I'm trouble, sweetheart . . ."

"It seemed that half the men in Tender Heart wanted Etta Jenkins as their bride. Rory couldn't figure it out. He'd rather be bit by a rattlesnake and left in the desert to die than to be chained to that woman."

CHAPTER FOUR

(*

"WHAT THE HELL ARE YOU looking at, Cole? Either play or let's call it a night."

Cole turned away from the bar and back to the pool-room where his cousin Zane was leaning on his cue. His words might be gruff, but the smile on his face ruined the effect. Zane was the easygoing cousin, the one who always found the silver lining in every situation. Of course, it was easy to find the silver lining when you were one of the wealthiest people in Bliss.

Unlike Cole's and his cousin Raff's fathers, Zane's father had had the foresight to invest in something other than the unpredictable cattle business. Those investments had seen Zane's family through drought, disease, and low prices. Subsequently, their ranch still prospered, while Cole's and Raff's were close to bankruptcy.

Cole might resent Zane for that, but it was hard to resent a man who had been his best friend since kindergarten. The three fathers had started a feud and split up the Arrington ranch, but their three sons had bonded in grade school and sworn to remain friends.

"Are you in that big of a hurry to get your butt whupped?" Cole asked as he moved back into the room and studied the balls on the table. Or tried to study them. He was having trouble concentrating. His thoughts kept going back to the couple in the bar.

Just what did she think she was doing hanging out with a no-account drifter? What happened to her friends? What happened to her finding Tender Heart? What happened to her not being interested in a Texas cowboy? Maybe that was what ticked him off the most. She'd turned him down cold, but ate French fries out of the hand of a kid who had probably used a fake ID to get into the bar.

Zane snorted. "As if you could whup my butt."

Colt took his shot and knocked the six ball into the side pocket. "I believe I've whupped your butt on more than one occasion, cuz." It was the truth, but only because Colt was competitive while Zane just enjoyed playing the game. The only things Zane took seriously were women and money. He'd been successful at both—doubling his family's money and marrying his high school sweetheart right out of college.

"Are you talking about riding Black Bart?" Zane asked. "Because I didn't realize that was a competition or I would've held on longer."

Colt took his shot and dropped another ball into a pocket. "You're kidding, right? That bull only bucked once before you went sailing through the air. Even your sister Becky stayed on longer than you did."

Zane sat down on a barstool and shook his head. "Because that girl loves anything dangerous. I've got my eye on a new bull, and she better stay away from it or I'll paddle her butt."

"Good luck with that. Becky wouldn't stand still for a paddling, and we both know your father wouldn't allow you to harm his little princess."

"Princess?" Zane snorted. "More like Medusa. She's been putting Rachel through hell ever since she graduated from college and came back to the ranch. I don't know why she didn't want to move to Austin with Daddy and Mama."

"Because you know Becky isn't a big city girl. That girl is country through and through."

"Well, I wish she'd be country in Austin."

"I thought she was looking to buy the Reed place. That would get her out of your house."

"She's too damned wild to live that far away. She needs to be close enough where someone can keep an eye on her."

It was a perfect opening for the business proposition Cole wanted to discuss, but for some reason he couldn't bring himself to take it. They talked about a lot of things during their pool games, but ranch business wasn't one of them. The ranch was what had caused the feud between their fathers. The three cousins had ended the feud, but only because they refused to talk about their ranches. They talked about religion, politics, and women, but never about the three ranches that had once been one . . . and were soon to be two.

"So who's winning?"

The question had Cole missing his shot and knocking one of Zane's balls into a pocket. He turned to find Emery standing there with an overly bright smile on her face. She had changed into skinny jeans that showed off her mile-long legs. The high heels were gone, and in their place were flat sandals that displayed pretty toes with light pink frosted nails.

"After that shot, I'd say it isn't Cole." Dirk stood behind her with the usual cocky grin on his face. Cole didn't know the kid that well, but he'd never trusted a man who smiled so much. Especially when it was easy to read the touch of annoyance in his eyes. No doubt, he'd rather be back at the table feeding Emery fries. For some reason, the thought made Cole a tad bit snappy.

He glanced at Zane. "Did you realize this was junior high night?" He looked back at Dirk. "Or did you steal your big brother's ID before you ran away from home?"

Dirk's smile never wavered. "I don't have a brother. And I didn't run when I left home. I just strolled right out the front door."

"Maybe you should do the same now."

Dirk continued to stare at him for a long moment before he took Emery's arm. "Come on, Emerald Eyes, how about we let these boys get back to their game and head to the motor lodge. I'll buy you an ice cream on the way."

Cole wasn't sure if it was the cute little nickname or the fact that they were staying at the motor lodge together that turned his annoyance to pissed off in three seconds flat. But whatever it was, his hand tightened on the pool cue and he took a step closer. "She can stay. You're the only one not welcome."

Dirk opened his mouth, but when Zane moved next to Cole, he closed it and shrugged. "Maybe we should let the lady decide." He winked at Emery. "You ready, darlin'?"

Since she'd only had smart-assed remarks for Cole, he figured she'd leave. Instead, she surprised him.

"I'm afraid I've had enough calories for one night, so I'll have to pass. But thank you so much for dinner." She patted his hand before she removed it from her arm. "I'll pay you back as soon as my friends get into town."

Cole had to hand it to the kid. Dirk was much better at hiding his emotions than he was. His eyes registered shock at getting the brush off for only a fraction of a second before they twinkled with humor. "Well, if your friends are as pretty as you, I'll look forward to meeting them." He tipped his hat at Cole. "Gentlemen, enjoy your game."

When he was gone, Cole should've introduced Emery to his cousin. Instead, he chalked up the end of his pool cue while Zane walked over and introduced himself.

"Zane Arrington." He held out a hand. "And it sounds like you know my ornery cousin Cole already."

Emery shook his hand. "Emery Wakefield. And yes, Cole and I met at the gas station earlier today." She flashed Cole the overly bright smile he trusted about as much as he trusted Dirk's. "He was nice enough to buy my gas when I discovered I'd left my wallet at the rental car counter in Austin."

"Well, that's a piece of bad luck," Zane said. "I'd be happy to buy you a drink."

Cole didn't know why he butted in. It wasn't his business if Zane bought her a drink. And yet, it felt like his business. Even if Zane was happily married and only being nice, there was such a thing as dibs, and Cole had seen her first. "I'll buy her a drink."

"Thank you, but I'm not thirsty." She flapped a hand at the table. "Don't mind me. Just continue with your game."

Except Cole couldn't continue with his game. Not when she sat down on a barstool and crossed those long legs, then started bouncing a foot. Every time it was his turn and he leaned down for a shot, all he could think about was taking a taste of those pink icing toes. He missed his next shot, and his next, and when Zane finally won, Cole was more than a little pissed.

He leaned on his pool cue and looked at Emery. "So what exactly do you want? I thought I made it clear that there's no Tender Heart here."

Her bright smile finally slipped, and she became the sassy little thing he'd met at the gas station. "You didn't mention the fact that you owned the Arrington Ranch."

"I wouldn't exactly call it a ranch."

"But it's the same land where Tender Heart was written. The basis for the Earhart Ranch."

Zane looked at Cole. "She's one of them?"

Cole nodded. "This fanatic came all the way from New York City."

Zane whistled through his teeth. "Well, at least she's more reserved than the last one. I thought that woman was going to sexually assault you right in the middle of the street."

Emery's gaze slid over him from hat brim to boot toe. And damned if he could control the blush that heated his face. "So I guess I'm not the only one who thinks you look like Rory Earhart."

It was hard to keep from gritting his teeth. "I don't understand how I can look like a fictional character that no one has ever seen."

Emery suddenly looked like he had just called her mama a bad name. "What do you mean? Of course people have seen Rory. They've seen him through Lucy Arrington's words. His black hair that rippled in the wind like a river on a moonless night and his eyes that looked like the sky at twilight—"

Cole cut her off. "And no matter how thoroughly Lucy described him, he's still just a made-up character like Mickey Mouse. Now why don't you head on back to the motor lodge and Little Boy Dirk and let us get back to our game?"

Her features scrunched with annoyance as she got to her feet. "Does your hostility have anything to do with me rejecting you when you were looking at my boobs? If so, then you need to grow up."

Cole's anger sizzled, and Zane hooted with laughter. "I think I need to hear this story. What happened at the gas station?"

"Nothing. Not a damn thing." He tossed his pool cue down on the table. "I'm calling it a night." Without another word, he headed to the bar to pay his tab.

"You're leaving early," Hank said as Cole handed him money. "Is Gracie doing okay?"

"She's fine. I'm just done playing is all."

Hank glanced over Cole's shoulder. "She's a city girl, that one. What's she doing in town?"

Cole didn't even have to guess who the bartender was talking about. "She's looking for Tender Heart."

Hank snorted. "Aren't we all?"

Cole dropped a few bucks into the tip jar. "Not me. I wouldn't waste my time." He nodded at Mike and Orville who sat at the bar, then walked outside. He had made it to his truck when Emery called his name.

"Cole!"

He ignored her and climbed in. But before he could do more than start the engine, she was sitting on the bench seat next to him with those long legs stretched under his dash.

"Okay, so we got off on the wrong foot," she said as she slammed the door. "But there's no need to run off all mad."

"I'm not mad. I just don't have time to play your little game. And since you're out here with me, I guess Zane wasn't willing to play it either."

"He wouldn't answer one question." Emery turned to him, spearing him with her direct green gaze. "And I don't see what the problem is. What do you have against

Tender Heart?"

The list was long. Tender Heart had never done any-thing for him. His childless great-aunt had willed all the royalties from the books to the Texas library system. And while Cole thought it was a worthy cause, he also believed in the old adage that charity begins at home. Lucy could've willed her family something. Even a small portion of the millions the series had made, and still made, would've helped Cole with all the medical and physical therapy bills that filled his desk. But he hadn't seen a dime of the money.

And to top it off, thanks to his aunt using her ancestors as templates for her heroes, Cole had to deal with the townsfolk's expectations. Like the tourists who confused him with Rory Earhart, the people of Bliss expected all Arringtons to be bigger-than-life heroes with amazing super powers. Zane had met all their expectations. He had been the star quarterback. Class president. Graduated with honors from Texas A&M. Married the homecom-ing queen. Gone to law school. And become a successful rancher and businessman.

Cole wasn't a hero. He had been an average football player. A mediocre student. He preferred horses to cows. He rarely dated. And he sure as hell wasn't a businessman. He was just an ordinary man who'd had his fair share of bad luck. And he was ready to put that bad luck behind him. If that meant leaving Texas and all its expectations, then so be it.

"Just a few questions," Emery cut into his thoughts. "Then I promise I'll leave you alone."

Since it didn't look like she was getting out of his truck unless she got her answers, Cole took off his hat and tossed it on the dash. "Fine. What do you want to know?"

"Was Lucy your relative?"

"Yes."

The look on her face was awe mixed with respect. And Cole had to admit that it was a nice change from the annoyed, superior look she usually gave him. "That is so cool," she breathed. "You're related to the great Lucy Arrington."

"I don't know how great she was. She was an eccentric recluse who dressed in long gowns even in the 1950s and wore veiled hats whenever she went out in public. That just sounds weird to me."

"She was a genius. All geniuses are a little weird." She looked at him. "Do you write?"

"Are you saying I'm weird?"

She laughed. "No. I just wondered if you'd inherited the writing gene."

"Nope. That gene seems to have bypassed the present-day Arringtons completely—or at least the male side. Gracie writes a little—" He cut off. He hadn't meant to bring up Gracie. He didn't talk about his sister with the townsfolk, let alone complete strangers. But there was something about Emery that made him let down his guard. Which wasn't good. Letting down your guard only exposed you to hurt.

"Gracie?" Emery's eyes sparkled with interest. No doubt she thought she would be another Tender Heart look-alike.

Cole quickly brought an end to the conversation. "I'll drop you by the motor lodge." He popped the truck into reverse, then placed his arm on the edge of the seat as he backed up. It was merely an accident that the tips of his fingers brushed the strand of silky hair that hung over her shoulder.

"Pardon me," he said as he dropped his arm. But he didn't want to be pardoned. He wanted to wrap that chestnut strand of hair around his fist and tug her closer. So close that he could count the flecks of gold in her green eyes. So close that he could feel her breath against his lips. Instead, he concentrated on backing out. Once they were on the road, he kept his gaze straight ahead.

"You aren't going to tell me anything else, are you?" she said.

"There's nothing else to tell that the entire town doesn't know. Lucy Arrington wrote a series about some mail-order brides and then she died. End of story."

"But it isn't the end of the story. She never finished the last book in the series . . . at least, she never published it."

Suddenly, Cole knew exactly why she was so determined to get her questions answered. She wasn't just a fan. She was one of the nuts who believed that his aunt had written the ending to the series and hidden it for someone to find after her death. Which meant Emery wasn't an avid reader consumed with the Tender Heart story as much as a greedy fortune hunter looking to make money on something that, if it did exist, belonged to his family. That annoyed him even more.

He pulled into the parking lot of the motor lodge and cut the engine before he turned to her. "So you're one of those treasure hunters who believes my aunt wrote the final book and hid it." He laughed. "Funny, but I didn't take you for a crazy loon." He opened the door and hopped down from the truck. When he reached her side, she was already out and slamming her door.

Her eyes flashed. "Why would it be crazy to think that your aunt wrote the last book? From what I've read, Lucy knew she was going to die for months. That would have been plenty of time to finish the series." She headed toward one of the rooms, and he followed.

"But why would she hide it?" he asked. "Why wouldn't

she just send it to her publisher for the world to read?"

She stopped at the door of number seven and turned to him, her brows knitted and her lips pressed into a slight frown. They were tinted the same color as the smudge on the little bag she'd had in her purse. Not a dark red, but a light, cheerful red that reminded him of the poppies that grew in a field on his property. "I don't know. Maybe she died before she could. She never talked about her manuscripts until they were finished and completely revised. Maybe she intended to send it in and couldn't."

He pulled his gaze away from her mouth and leaned on the doorjamb, crossing his arms. "Or maybe she just didn't write it."

"Maybe, but I think otherwise."

He snorted. "You and every other fortune hunter who has come here looking for the book. But as far as I'm concerned, it ended like it should've ended."

"With all those loose ends?"

"Exactly," he said. "Life doesn't always have a happy ending. Some people never find love. Some people never find happiness. Some people just live loose-ended lives until they die."

He was only being truthful. Cole's life was one loose end after another. But the disappointment and hurt that entered her eyes made him feel like he'd just stepped on a kitten. With those big green eyes, she reminded him of a kitten. An innocent kitten who it appeared wasn't looking for money as much as an ending for her beloved characters.

"Look," he said, "I'm sorry. You shouldn't listen to me. I didn't even finish all the books in the series. In fact, truth be told, I only leafed through the first one looking for sex scenes. When I only found one pathetic kiss, I tossed my aunt's stories for *Playboy*."

Her eyes widened. "Pathetic? There was nothing pathetic about the way Rory kissed Etta. It was one of the best kisses ever written."

"But all he did was kiss her."

"And sometimes that's more than enough." Her gaze lowered to Cole's mouth, and he felt the burn of those eyes like a red-hot brand that seared his lips, then spread through his entire body.

Cole clenched his fist as if to tighten the reins on his desire. But when her tongue flicked out and wet her plump bottom lip, the reins slipped right out of his hand. And he did what he'd wanted to do since he'd first laid eyes on her.

He kissed her.

Her lips were as warm and lush as they looked. And once he touched them, the soft brush he planned soon turned into a deep, hungry slide as he devoured her sweet poppy mouth. Before he knew it, he had her shoved against the door with his hands tangled in her hair and his aching hardness pressed into her soft sweetness. If she had shown any kind of resistance, he would've been able to pull back and apologize. Instead, she released a sexy moan and melted into him.

He didn't usually have sex with strangers. Especially weird Tender Heart freaks who were a little too big for their britches. But she wasn't acting too big for her britches now. Those britches fit her just fine and he wanted to see her out of them. Like now.

"The key?" he muttered against her mouth.

"Hmm?" she asked in a deep, husky hum that made his knees weak. He untangled his hands from her hair and slid them into her back pockets to search for the key. But he got distracted. With his hands full of sweet ass, he stopped worrying about finding the key and started maneuvering her toward the dark carport. But before they could reach it, they were interrupted.

"And here I thought you would be lonely without us, Em."

Cole pulled away from Emery to find two women. One was a petite blonde who looked like that Peter Pan fairy and the other was a beautiful redhead who looked like Jessica Rabbit. He figured it was the fiery redhead who had interrupted. He was wrong. The petite fairy surprised him by continuing in the same sarcastic tone.

"All this time I thought Rory Earhart was just a fictional character." She looked at Emery and smirked. "When you're finished, Em, you think we can have a turn playing Tender Heart?"

"The way Rory looked at her made Etta feel like she'd felt the first time she'd gone up in a hot air balloon—excited, breathless . . . and terrified that she was about to plummet to her death."

CHAPTER FIVE

𝒞

E VEN AFTER COLE RELEASED HER, Emery didn't have enough firing brain cells to answer Carly. All she could do was watch as he reached for his cowboy hat, which had obviously been knocked off in the same wave of lust that left Emery feeling like a tsunami victim. Once he tugged the hat on, he tipped it at Carly and Savannah before heading for his truck. He didn't glance at Emery once as he backed out and pulled away.

"Sweet Baby Jesus," Savannah said in her breathy, southern voice. "He looks just like Rory Earhart."

Carly dropped her duffel bag. "Which probably explains why Emery was only moments away from getting her brains fu—"

Savannah cut her off. "Don't you dare drop the f-bomb, Carly Sue Hanover! You know that word grates on my nerves."

Carly rolled her eyes. "How many times do I have to tell you that my middle name isn't Sue? And everything grates on your nerves. I spent the last hour listening to you worry about me going over the speed limit, if the hotel Emery booked would have five-hundred thread-count sheets, and if the mole on your butt is cancerous. I thought southern belles were supposed to be cool, calm, and collected. Not pains in the ass."

"I am not a pain in the bottom. Although you're thinking of South Carolina and Louisiana southern belles. Georgia southern belles are as high-strung as a badly tuned fiddle." Savannah maneuvered her two designer roller suitcases closer to Emery, who was still feeling like a limp lump of lust. "Do you think she's okay? She looks like Aunt Pitty Pat the kitty cat after that horrible tomcat jumped in my garden and sexually assaulted her."

Carly shouldered her way next to Savannah. Not only were the two complete opposites in personality, they were also complete opposites in looks. Carly was a petite blond with big brown eyes, a cupid bow mouth, and short spiky hair. Savannah was a statuesque redhead with startling blue eyes, a wide, generous mouth, and long hair that that swooped over one eye. She looked deeply concerned. Carly not so much.

"If Aunt Pitty Pat looked like this, she enjoyed every second of Mr. Tomcat's visit," Carly said. "That look is pure, unadulterated lust if ever I saw it. You don't recognize it because you've never experienced lust with that pantywaist you're about to marry."

"Miles is not a pantywaist," Savannah huffed. "He's just a southern gentleman who confines his acts of lust to the bedroom. Unlike the Neanderthal men you hang out with, who think fondling a woman in public is the appropriate way to woo her."

"Woo? Who uses the word 'woo' unless they're playing trains with a kid? And as far as my boyfriends go, at least they don't—"

Before things could escalate and feelings get hurt, Emery snapped out of her lustful fog and pulled her friends into a hug. Carly and Savannah resisted for only a second before their arms came up and the three shared a long group hug.

It had been almost a year since they'd met in Atlanta for Savannah's engagement party. It was the longest they had been away from each other. They'd met in college, and since graduation they usually hooked up every five or six months. But in the last year, they had been too busy to meet and had only communicated by group texts or live chats. Carly had gotten a new job as head chef for an exclusive restaurant in San Francisco and worked seven days a week. Savannah was busy with her interior design business and planning her wedding. And Emery was busy trying to keep her job and prove to her family that she wasn't an underachiever who walked around with her nose in a book.

Carly pulled back from the hug first and glanced at the street. "You weren't lying when you said it doesn't look like Tender Heart. This place isn't much more than a grease spot on the highway."

Emery couldn't deny it. "I know. And I'm sure after seeing it, you wished you had gone to a sandy beach in Mexico for your spring break."

Carly and Savannah exchanged looks that said she'd hit the nail on the head, but instead of voicing her disappointment, Savannah gave her the sunny smile that had won her a Miss Georgia title and the wealthiest man in Atlanta. "Nonsense. You always let us pick our meeting places. It's only fair that we let you pick one. Besides, I'm anxious to see the birthplace of the great Lucy Arrington. Did you find the little white chapel? Is that the surprise you were telling us about?"

Emery had yet to tell her friends about the letter. Not only because she didn't want them telling anyone else before she had a chance to prove it wasn't a hoax, but also because she wanted to be there when she sprung the surprise.

They loved the Tender Heart series as much as she did. All three of them had taken the same class together their sophomore year in college. After discovering their common love for the series, they spent hours reading and rereading each book and discussing them—and even more time arguing over how the series ended. If the pages in the envelope were real, they'd all find out soon enough.

Not wanting to tell them where anyone could overhear, Emery took the key from her pocket and unlocked the door. Savannah's face when she saw the cowboy motif could only be described as horrified. Carly, on the other hand, didn't seem to notice. She walked right in and flung her bag on the bed. It started to vibrate, and she jumped back.

"What the hell?"

Emery laughed. "It's a vibrating bed."

"Sweet Baby Jesus." Savannah stared at the bed with her hand pressed to the strand of pearls around her neck. "Just what kind of sinful den of iniquity did you book for us, Emery?"

"Well, if it's sinful, I need to try it out." Carly spread her arms and freefell back onto the bed. "This feels gre-e-e-at." Her voice vibrated along with the bed. "I call di-i-ibs on this one."

"You can have it. I like my mattresses to remain still at all times." Savannah placed a suitcase on the other bed and started to unpack. She hated wrinkled clothes as much as she hated mussed hair and crooked eyeliner. To say Savannah was a perfectionist was as much of an understatement as saying that Carly was a little outspoken.

"I'm sure you do-o-on't have to wor-r-ry about that."

Savannah stopped in the process of pulling out a silk shirt. "And just what do you mean?"

It was pretty obvious what Carly meant. Not only did she dislike Savannah's fiancé, she disliked the entire idea of matrimony. As Savannah's wedding grew closer, Carly's jabs at Miles had gotten worse. It was her way of trying to stop Savannah from making a mistake. Unfortunately, it had only caused a rift between the friends, and Emery wasn't sure how to fix it. Having grown up the only girl in a family of boys, Emery had always been the peace-keeper. She had taken the same role in their friendship.

"I'm sure Carly just meant that Miles is a stable kind of guy," Emery said. "Isn't that right, Carly?"

The bed stopped vibrating, and Carly sat up. "As stable as a statue." She looked at Emery. "So are you going to tell us about Rory and the kiss, or not?"

Emery took the chair by the window and perched on the edge. "His name is Cole, not Rory. Cole Arrington, a relation of Lucy Arrington." She paused for only a second to let that sink in before she shared the secret she'd been keeping for months. "I think I've found the last book in the Tender Heart series."

Savannah exchanged looks with Carly before she sat down. "Start from the beginning."

Relieved to finally get to share the story with her friends, Emery wasted no time. "About two months ago, I received a letter in the mail from a woman saying she had found the last book in the series and wanted to know if I'd be interested in publishing it. At first, I thought it was a hoax. I mean what were the odds of the last book in my favorite series of all time landing in my lap? But then I read the first chapter she sent with the letter."

Emery grabbed her laptop case and unzipped the side pocket. She pulled out the manila envelope and handed it to Carly. "Go ahead and take a look for yourself. It's just a copy so you don't have to worry about damaging the original."

Carly opened the envelope and pulled out the chapter while Savannah peeked over her shoulder. It was hard to wait, but Emery wanted their opinion so she held her tongue until they were finished.

"So what do you think?"

"It definitely Lucy's style and voice," Carly said.

Savannah nodded. "And it starts exactly where the last one left off. Although someone who loves the series could've done that."

Emery joined them on the bed. "True, but they couldn't have used the exact same typewriter as Lucy to write it." She pointed to the first page. "See the way the lowercase *t* drops below the type line? That is consistent with all of Lucy's original copies. It was a funky little mechanical problem with her 1950s Smith Corona typewriter. As is the fading tail of the lowercase *p*."

"And how do you know this?" Carly asked.

"I discovered it when I did the research paper on Lucy Arrington in college. Which is exactly how Gracie Arrington found me. She found my paper online."

"So have you talked to her?"

Emery shook her head. "The only contact information she left in the letter was a post office box here in Bliss. I replied to her letter numerous times requesting the full manuscript, but she never answered. I wanted to come here weeks ago and check it out, but I couldn't convince my editor-in-chief that it wasn't a hoax. And I couldn't blame her when Gracie never wrote me back. But I can't let it go. Not until I talk with the woman face to face. Cole mentioned a Gracie, but when I asked who she was, he clammed up. And I wasn't about to tell him about the letter when he doesn't even believe that there is a final book."

"If he doesn't know about it, then his Gracie can't be yours," Carly said.

"Unless she kept it a secret from him. I don't share a lot of things with my family."

"And I don't understand why." Savannah went back to hanging her shirts on hangers. "Your family is so cool. You should be thrilled to be part of such a talented and respected family of doctors."

Emery should be thrilled. But being in a family of overachievers when you haven't achieved anything wasn't thrilling as much as depressing. Which was why the last Tender Heart book was so important to her. It would be the literary find of the century and, if she could edit it, her one chance to claim a little respect for herself. But leave it to Carly to find the holes in Emery's plan.

"I don't know, Em. Are you sure this isn't just wishful thinking? Since Lucy Arrington died, there have been numerous people who have claimed they have the last book in the series, but none of them have turned out to be real. And if this Gracie wanted to sell the book, why didn't she answer your letters? Or leave you a better way to contact her? We aren't talking about a little money here. We're talking about millions."

"You're right. It doesn't make sense." She paused. "But I have this gut feeling that this isn't a hoax. I have a feeling there's a reason she hasn't contacted me again."

Carly studied her for a moment before she nodded. "Okay. Just don't expect your gut to always be right. I went with my gut when I took the job at Sauce and I've been miserable ever since."

"You were miserable at the last three restaurants you worked at too," Savannah said. "Which probably explains why you keep getting fired."

"I didn't get fired from all of them. I quit two. Owners and I seem to disagree on how a restaurant should be run. That's why I'm saving to buy my own place."

With the way Carly keep losing jobs, it would take a while. Emery wished she could help her friend, but her salary didn't leave much extra. Although if she found the last Tender Heart book, that could change.

Savannah closed her suitcase and stowed it with the other in the bottom of the closet. "Speaking of restaurants, I'm starving. Is there some place to eat in this one-horse town?"

"There is," Emery said. "But the food is pretty bad."

Carly got to her feet. "I'll be the judge of that."

As it turned out, Carly never got the chance to taste a Watering Hole burnt burger. By the time they got to the bar, the doors were locked tight.

"What kind of bar closes at ten o'clock on a Saturday night?" Savannah asked.

"The kind that doesn't have any customers past nine-thirty." Carly scowled at Savannah. "And if we hadn't had to wait for someone to fix her hair and makeup, we would've gotten here before they closed."

Savannah shrugged. "A woman should never go out in public looking like she's been in a tornado. Something you need to learn." She licked her fingers and reached toward Carly's spiky hair.

Carly slapped her hand away. "Don't you dare put your saliva on my head."

"If you would've let me make you an appointment with my stylist when you were in Atlanta, you wouldn't have wild-thing hair. Raphael's haircuts fall beautifully."

"They should at a hundred dollars a pop." Carly glanced around. "So there has to be somewhere else to eat. Or at least a grocery store."

They walked down Main Street, but the entire town was locked up tight. Which was completely baffling to three city girls who were used to getting whatever they wanted to eat whenever they wanted it. The one restaurant they did find looked like it had been closed for years. But there was something about it that struck a chord with Emery. Once she looked inside the large window, she understood why.

"Oh my God. This is the diner where Lucy plotted her books."

Carly cupped her hands around her face and peered in the window. "Hey, I think you're right. It's too dark to see much, but I can make out the 50s-style jukebox and mile-long counter. And I bet the cooktop in the kitchen is one of those old cast-iron ones that heats to the perfect temperature." Without one word of warning, she headed around to the back of the diner.

"Where's she going?" Savannah asked as she and Emery followed.

"I don't know, but knowing Carly it can't be good."

They rounded the corner in time to see her disappear through the back door. When they got inside, she had the light on and was leaning over looking at the dials on the stovetop.

"What are you doing?" Emery asked. "Besides breaking and entering?"

"I didn't break. The back door was open." She turned the dial and felt the top of the stove. "I'll be damned. It still works."

Savannah looked around anxiously. "Would you quit messing around and let's get out of here before the cops come."

Carly opened the huge refrigerator and walked in, then

reappeared with a carton of eggs and a big smile. "I just found us dinner."

"Oh, no," Savannah said. "I'm not eating eggs from the 1950s."

"They aren't from the fifties. The expiration date is a week away." While Emery and Savannah watched in disbelief, she pulled a bowl off a shelf. "Obviously, someone is still cooking in this kitchen. It's as clean as mine." She took two eggs out of the cartoon and expertly cracked them into the bowl. She grabbed a whisk from a hook, twirled it once, and whisked the eggs to a frothy yellow. Within minutes, she had the eggs cooked, seasoned, and plated.

Savannah didn't say another word of complaint as Carly handed her the fluffy eggs. She just started opening drawers until she found a fork.

"You want some, Emery?" Carly asked as she dished up another plate.

"No, someone has to bail you two out when they discover the egg theft."

Carly dug into her eggs. "I'll return them tomorrow. But a woman shouldn't have to go to bed hungry."

The click of boots on tile startled all three. Savannah dropped her plate and it shattered while Carly ducked behind the prep counter. Before Emery could look for a place to hide, Dirk appeared. He didn't look as clean as he had earlier. Both his torn beer logo t-shirt and faded jeans were speckled with sawdust. But his smile was still cockily impish as his gaze took in the scene.

"You ladies have the right of things. No woman should ever have to go to bed hungry." He lifted a six-pack of beer. "Or thirsty."

"The only thing worse than Rory figuring out he was attracted to one of the mail-order brides was when his ornery siblings found out."

CHAPTER SIX

❦

"GOOD MORNING, COLE."

Cole looked up from the newspaper spread in front of him as Gracie wheeled into the kitchen. The sight of his pretty blond-headed sister in the wheelchair never failed to cause his stomach to clench with guilt. It had been over five months since the accident, and he thought the guilt would lessen, but it only seemed to grow worse. He looked back at the newspaper and reached for his cup of coffee.

"Mornin'." He took a sip. "Did you sleep well?"

"I stayed up a little later than I should have."

"Texting with Becky?"

"No, I was just writing in my diary." She rolled over to the lower cabinets and took a glass out.

After he'd brought Gracie home from the hospital, Cole had moved all the glasses and plates from the top cupboards to the bottom so it would be easier for her to reach. He had thought about redoing the entire kitchen—lowering the range and countertops, getting a special refrigerator with pull-down shelves—but if they were going to move, it would be a waste of money and make it harder to sell the house. And they were going to move. The only reason he'd stayed this long was to give Gracie time to recover. She was as attached to the ranch as their father had been and had dreams of bringing it back to its former glory. The only dream Cole had was leaving Texas and all the bad memories it held.

Gracie rolled to the refrigerator and pulled open the door, wrangling her wheelchair around as easily as she had wrangled her horse around the barrels at the state fair rodeo. She had been a champion barrel racer. One wall of her room was covered with ribbons and trophies. Cole had been too busy working his way through college to pay much attention to his little sister's abilities. But one summer he had come home and caught her practicing in the corral. The image of her sailing around the barrels as if she was one with the horse, her cowboy hat pulled low and blond hair whipping behind her, was an image that would never leave him. Especially now.

He closed the newspaper and got up. "How about pancakes this morning?"

"No, thanks. I'll just have a bowl of cereal."

Cole started for the pantry where they kept the cereal, but she stopped him.

"I can get it, Cole."

He opened the door and grabbed the box of her favorite cereal. "Maybe I'm not getting it for you, Brat."

She took the orange juice out of the refrigerator. "Since when do you like Cinnamon Toast Crunch? You usually don't like anything sweet."

"That's not true. I like you, don't I?" He ruffled her hair before grabbing the carton of milk. "Now pour me a glass of OJ, and I'll pour you a bowl of cereal."

When they were seated at the table with their juice and cereal, she took up the same conversation they had every morning.

"So I was thinking. What about if we restored some of those old trucks that are rusting out in the south pasture? I was watching this car show and a truck like Granddad Henry's went for close to one hundred thousand dollars. If we sold all three for that much, we would make a fortune."

He took a bite of his cereal and tried not to grimace at the sweetness. "And exactly when am I going to do this restoring? Between fixing cars for Emmett, taking care of Brandy, and trying to fix up this place so we can sell it, all the hours of my day are pretty spent."

Gracie took a bite of cereal and crunched it. "You still have time to go to the Watering Hole and hook up with a girl."

Cole set his spoon in his bowl and narrowed his eyes. "And just who told you that?"

She smiled like a cartoon cat holding a mouse beneath its paw. "That's for me to know and you to find out."

"It was Becky, wasn't it? Zane probably texted her as soon as we left the bar."

He realized his mistake when her eyes widened. "So it's true. You did hook up with a girl." She leaned closer. "Who? Please don't tell me it was Sissy Miller. I refuse to have that snobby girl who thinks her poop doesn't stink as a sister-in-law."

"It was not Sissy Miller. That girl is the same age as you, for Christ's sake."

Her chin came up. "I'm twenty-two. Which is plenty old enough to marry and have the daylights kissed out of. Which seems to be what you were doing last night."

At the mention of the kiss, Cole realized that it hadn't been Zane who squealed. He hadn't known about the kiss at the motor lodge. Which means that someone else was

Gracie's snitch. Someone who had seen him "kissing the daylights" out of Emery. And he had kissed the daylights out of her. Once he'd touched her lips, he'd never wanted to stop. It was unfortunate that her friends had shown up when they had. He'd been only moments away from seeing if other parts of her were as soft and sweet as her lips.

"Are you blushing, Cole?" Gracie asked.

"No, I'm just a little angry that my sister is butting her nose into something she has no business butting her nose into."

She leaned her elbows on the table. "So who is she? My informant was too far away to see."

Cole grabbed his bowl and got up. "Her name is Nona Your Beeswax." He took the bowl to the sink and dumped the sickeningly sweet cereal down the disposal.

"You know I can find out." She continued to crunch her cereal. "I've got all day to investigate."

It was the truth. His little sister did have all day. She had become a homebody since the accident and rarely left the house. And he couldn't blame her. The people of the town had yet to get used to seeing her in a wheelchair and couldn't seem to help gawking. It annoyed him as much as it embarrassed his sister. The stab of guilt made him cave. What did he care if she knew the woman's name? After seeing that the town was nothing like Tender Heart, Emery was probably long gone by now.

He turned on the disposal and waited for it to clear before he turned it off and answered Gracie. "You don't know her, Brat. Emery Wakefield is just passing through."

The crash of glass hitting porcelain tile had Cole whipping around to find Gracie staring down at her broken glass of orange juice. Cole was at her side in an instant.

"Are you okay? What happened? Is your hand feeling numb?" It was an irrational fear of his that the paralysis in her legs would spread to her entire body.

"I'm fine," she said. "The glass just slipped from my hand." But when she lifted her head, she didn't look fine. She looked flushed and feverish.

Cole didn't hesitate to lift her from the chair. "You're going back to bed and I'm calling Doc Sanchez."

"Put me down, Cole." She slapped at his shoulder as he carried her down the hallway. "I don't need Doc Sanchez. It was just a clumsy accident is all. And we can't afford to call the doctor out."

It was the truth. Cole was still making payments on Gracie's huge hospital bill. "Fine, I won't call the doctor. But I want you to rest today. And if you're still feeling weak tomorrow, you're going in to see him. I don't care what it costs." He carried her into her room and almost fell over all the boxes in the middle of the floor.

"What's this?"

Gracie's face got even redder. "I was just going through some boxes from the attic."

"The attic? How did you get up to the attic?"

"I flew on my magic carpet, what else?" She laughed. "Becky helped me bring them down. I was looking for things we could sell."

Cole stepped over the boxes and placed her on the bed. "I wouldn't waste my time. If there was anything of value up there, Mom would've sold it when she lived here."

"She wasn't that bad, Cole."

Ava Arrington had been worse than bad. And if anyone should know it, it was Gracie. After leaving Cole and his father, she'd hooked up with a trucker from Albuquerque. Two years later, she showed back up at the ranch with Gracie. Not even a year after that, she ran off again— leaving his father with a huge credit card debt. Cole had never forgiven her. But Gracie didn't hold a grudge against anyone. Even a good-for-nothing mother who hadn't contacted either one of them once in the years that followed.

"Well, good luck looking through all this junk. But not today. Today, you just rest." He set her on the bed and adjusted her legs under the covers. Usually, she got herself from her wheelchair into bed so it had been a while since he'd helped. Was it just wishful thinking or did her legs feel like they had more muscle tone?

"What about Pastor Milford's wife?" She asked. "You know coming out to see me every Sunday makes her feel like she's doing her charitable duty."

He pulled his gaze away from her legs. "I'll call her and tell her that you don't feel well."

Gracie fluffed her pillow before sitting back. "You go right ahead and do that. Then she'll relay the information and we'll have everyone in town bringing us casseroles— and you know how you hate casseroles."

"Then I'll tell her that you've become as big a sinner as your brother and don't want to listen to her bible verses."

She laughed and swatted at him. "Then you'll have her preaching hellfire and brimstone." Her face grew serious. "Besides, you're not a sinner. You have the kindest heart in Texas."

That was the thing about Gracie. She should hate him. Or at least blame him for the part he'd played in the accident that had ruptured a disk and bruised her spinal cord, causing paralysis in both her legs. But she never did. Not once. She viewed him as her perfect big brother.

Cole was far from perfect. And he would prove it when he took her away from everything she loved. But he couldn't stay here anymore. Gracie had forgiven him, but he needed to forgive himself. And he couldn't do it in Texas. Once they were away from the pressure of being

Arringtons, of meeting the expectations of the townsfolk, they could just concentrate on being happy

He adjusted the covers over her lap. "The kindest heart in Texas is right here looking at me. Now get some rest. I'll check on you later."

He had almost reached the door when she asked, "So what is this Emery Wakefield doing in Bliss? Did she say?"

He didn't even turn around when he answered. "She's a school teacher looking for the final Tender Heart book."

&

AT ONE TIME, THE ARRINGTON Ranch had owned some of the best thoroughbred horses in the country. Now there was just Brandy, a skittish ten-year-old mare with a sweet tooth as bad as Gracie's.

"Get out of here," Cole swatted the horse's nose away from his shirt pocket. "You're not getting another peppermint."

The horse continued to badger him until Cole pushed her head out and closed the top half of the stall so he could finish mucking it out. It took a while. He should've gotten to it sooner. His daddy had always taught him that a clean stall made for happy, healthier horses. But with his schedule, it was hard to get to everything.

After filling the bucket, he opened the door so he could empty it into the wheelbarrow sitting just outside. He expected to see Brandy waiting for another peppermint. Instead, she was in the stall across the walkway, receiving a thorough grooming.

Dirk Hadley nodded his head at Cole as he stroked Brandy's back with the curry comb. "Good mornin'. Feels like it's gonna be another hot one."

Cole dumped the bucket of manure in the wheelbarrow before he stepped out of the stall. "I don't know how they deal with trespassers where you come from, but here in Texas we usually shoot first and ask questions later."

Dirk went back to grooming Brandy as if he hadn't heard. "She's got a bad swollen tendon that needs wrapping."

Cole hated know-it-alls about as much as he hated trespassers—especially when they were right. He'd been meaning to wrap Brandy's leg for a good week and just hadn't gotten around to it. But he wasn't about to tell this cocky kid that.

"Thanks for the advice, but I handle my own horses."

"Horse. Unless you keep a couple in your house." Before Cole could do more than drop the bucket, Dirk held up a hand. "Hey, I'm not here looking for trouble. I just stopped by to offer my services. Not only am I good with horses, but I can fix that fence that needs mending in your north pasture, paint the trim on your house, and rebuild that chicken coop." He glanced around. "Although I don't see any chickens."

"Because we don't have any."

"No chickens. What's a farm without chickens?"

"This isn't a farm. It's a ranch. My ranch."

Dirk stroked the comb over Brandy's withers and damned if the animal didn't close her eyes as if she was at the day spa getting a massage. "The way I see it, a ranch has cattle and more than one horse. Now a farm, on the other hand, can have only one horse, but it definitely needs chickens."

It was almost like the kid was trying to piss him off, and after spending a sleepless night thinking about a kiss he had no business thinking about, Cole was happy to oblige. "Farm or ranch, get your ass off my property."

"Fair enough. But if you ever change your mind, I'm

staying at the motor lodge." Dirk set down the comb. "I'd even be willing to trade work for that car parked out front."

The car he was talking about was Gracie's. Cole should've sold it months ago, but he still held out hope that Gracie would be able to drive it one day. After the surgery to reduce the swelling on her spinal cord caused by the ruptured disk, the doctors had been hopeful that she would walk again. And Gracie had shown great signs of improvement in the hospital. She had feeling in her legs and the physical therapists had even gotten her up on the parallel bars. But once Cole had brought her home, she'd regressed. The physical therapist Cole took her to three times a week in Austin had trouble getting her to do anything. Which meant that keeping the car was stupid.

"I'll sell it to you," he said.

Dirk shook his head. "Sorry, but I don't have money to buy it."

"Then I guess this conversation is over."

Dirk studied him for a moment before he shrugged. He expertly unhooked Brandy's lead rope and led her out of the stall. And damned if the horse didn't nuzzle his ear, which had Dirk giving her a good pat. "She's a pretty horse. I'd get to that leg real soon if I was you. You don't want to have to deal with a lame—"

His words cut off when Gracie rolled in on the ramp Cole had built over the threshold of the door. "Before you go all ballistic on me for getting out of bed—" She stopped when she saw Dirk. "Oh, I'm sorry. I didn't know you were busy." She started to back up, but with her gaze still on Dirk, her angle was crooked and one wheel went off the edge of the ramp, causing the wheelchair to tip to its side.

"Gracie!" Cole would've rushed to her rescue if Brandy

hadn't blocked his way as she searched his front pocket for a peppermint. By the time he'd ducked beneath the horse's neck, Dirk had already righted the chair and was kneeling in front of Gracie.

"You okay, miss?"

Cole hurried over and knelt on her other side. "Are you all right? Do I need to call an ambulance?"

"I'm fine, Cole," Gracie said. "I just feel like an idiot."

Dirk reached out and pulled a piece of straw from her hair. "I wouldn't. I've never been real good at backing up either. Once, I backed right into a sheriff's car with the most popular girl at Riley High sitting right there in the seat next to me. Now you talk about feeling like an idiot."

"I'm sure it didn't stop her from going out with you again," Gracie said.

Dirk grinned his annoying grin. "As a matter a fact, it did. The sheriff just happened to be her daddy. After that, I wasn't real high on his list of suitors."

Gracie laughed. Not just the giggles she gave Cole when he teased her, but an out-and-out laugh that he hadn't heard in months. The sound should've made him happy. Instead, he just felt sad that he hadn't been the one to bring it out of her.

Cole got to his feet. "So I believe you were just leaving, Mr. Hadley."

Dirk glanced up at him before he looked back at Gracie. "Your brother is right. I do need to get going." He stood, then took off his straw cowboy hat and held out a hand. "Dirk Hadley."

Gracie cheeks turned bright pink as she took his hand. "Gracie Arrington."

He lowered his head and kissed the back of Gracie's hand. "Nice to meet you, Gracie. If your pigheaded brother ever changes his mind about needing some help around here, have him give me a holler." He walked out of the barn.

Gracie's gaze remained on the doorway. "So who is he?"

"Just some cocky drifter who wanted to stop by and tell me what needed to be fixed around the ranch." He snorted. "As if I don't already have a list a mile long." He went and got the wheelbarrow and headed for the door. After he dumped the manure, he came back to find Gracie sitting outside the barn, staring off at the road.

"You could use some help, you know," she said. "Especially with a useless sister like me."

He grabbed the hose and sprayed off the wheelbarrow, then washed his hands. "You're not useless." He paused. "In fact, why don't you help me feed and water Brandy?"

He had been trying to get Gracie back with Brandy ever since he'd brought her home from the hospital. Brandy was Gracie's horse, a gift from Cole's dad when Gracie had turned fourteen. At one time, his sister had been as spirited as the horse, and together they had won most of the ribbons and trophies in her room. She had loved Brandy with a passion—even sleeping out in the stall with her during thunderstorms. But after the accident, Gracie wanted nothing to do with her.

Gracie hadn't blamed Cole, but she had blamed Brandy. Even if the horse had only reacted as she should've to a fast truck almost running them over.

"I can't," Gracie said. "Becky is coming to take me into town for lunch."

Cole turned to her. "You're going to go into town?"

Gracie studied her lap and shrugged. "Yeah. I thought it was time for me to get out a little."

Hope bloomed in Cole. Maybe with time, Gracie would heal.

Maybe in time, he would too.

"Etta didn't want to think about Rory. She didn't want to think about his black hair that rippled in the wind like a river on a moonless night. She didn't want to think about his eyes that held the intense blue of the sky at twilight. And she certainly didn't want to think about the way the muscles in his chest felt when she'd run into him in front of the general store . . . and yet, that was all she could think about."

CHAPTER SEVEN

"THERE'S A GRACIE ARRINGTON LIVING there all right." Dirk took a big bite of the French toast Carly had made and closed his eyes. "Mmm, now this is what I call breakfast."

"Just wait until you taste my strawberry crepes," Carly said. "I would've made them this morning if the grocery store had fresh strawberries."

Dirk took another bite. "You pretty much bought out the store as is. But I'm not complaining. It's been a long time since I found a decent meal in this town. Which is exactly why I had to use this kitchen and start cooking for myself." He winked at Carly. "Although I'd much rather have a beautiful woman cooking for me."

Carly rolled her eyes and looked at Emery. "What do you think, Em? Should I tell him about the last guy I poisoned for assuming that I'd be his personal chef?"

Emery wasn't interested in being part of Carly's teasing

or Dirk's flirting. She was interested in finding out more about what had happened out at Cole's ranch. She had paid Dirk good money to do a little investigating and she expected some answers.

"So who is she? His mother? An aunt?"

"She's his sister."

Her shoulders relaxed. She had already spent the night tossing and turning over almost having sex with a man she'd just met. If that man had been married, her guilt would have been even worse. Although if she were honest, it wasn't just guilt that had kept her awake. It was lust. Never in her life had she wanted a man as much as she wanted Cole. She wanted to believe it was all because he looked like Rory Earhart. But while Cole looked like Rory, he didn't act like him. He was quieter. More reserved. Almost like he had a secret that he didn't want getting out. Which of course made him even more intriguing . . . and lust-worthy.

Emery shook her head and tried to get her mind out of the gutter. "Did you get a chance to talk to his sister about the book?"

Dirk took a big bite of the chicken sausage patty Carly had also made for their late breakfast. The woman was unstoppable when she got in a kitchen. She was now working on some kind of braised beef for dinner. "I couldn't talk to her about the book. Not when her big brother was just looking for a chance to kick my ass." He shook his head. "I've never met a man with a bigger burr up his butt. All I did was offer him a little help in exchange for a beat-up Chevy Malibu, and he acted like I wanted to burn his barn to the ground. Although it would only be an improvement. That is one rundown ranch."

The fact depressed Emery. She had hoped that Cole's ranch would be more like Tender Heart than the town.

She had pictured a large ranch house, a big red barn, and miles and miles of cattle roaming the range. Obviously, that wasn't the case.

Dirk squinted at her. "Don't look so sad, Emerald Eyes. Just what's the big shake about this book, anyway? And why can't you just waltz out there and ask Gracie yourself?"

"I've been wondering the same thing." Carly shoved a foil-covered pan into the oven just as Savannah hurried into the kitchen.

"Sweet Baby Jesus! I was keeping watch out the front window and I just saw a sheriff's car drive by. I swear they know that we're in here. They're probably surrounding the building as we speak. Any second now, an entire SWAT team will be busting in through the windows."

Dirk grinned. "You're a worryin' little thing, aren't ya, Red? Pretty as a southern peach, but as high strung as a skittish colt. Like I told you before, no one gives a darn if we're hanging out in the diner. In fact, they'd probably be tickled pink if we opened the doors and let them get some of Miss Carly's cookin' rather than the crap they serve at the Watering Hole."

"We are not opening the front doors." Savannah started stacking empty plates and taking them to the sink. "The sooner we get out of here, the better. Breaking and entering is not something I planned to do on my vacation. We should've stuck to Mexico where we'd be lying on a beach right now getting massages."

"Well, why didn't you say so, darlin'?" Dirk set down his fork and stood up. "It just so happens that I made a little money in Tulsa giving women massages." He walked over to Savannah and placed his hands on her shoulders and started kneading. "Just tell me when it feels good."

If the euphoric expression on Savannah's face was any

indication, Dirk was as good at massaging as he was at flirting.

"Oh my, that does feel good," she moaned.

"It would feel much better if you were naked."

Savannah's eyes flashed open, and she pulled away. "Why you little gigolo! I am not taking my clothes off for you. I'm almost a married woman."

Dirk's smile got even bigger. "Hey, you can't fault a man for trying."

Carly closed the oven and turned. "Man? How old are you? You look all of seventeen."

"Twenty-four and counting." He winked. "Old enough to know a few things, and young enough that I'm still willing to learn. Want to play teacher and naughty student?"

Carly tipped her head and smiled a smile that Emery had seen before—usually when she was about to put the hammer down on some unsuspecting guy. "Sweetheart, if I pull out the paddle, you won't sit for a week."

Unlike most guys, Dirk wasn't intimidated. "Good thing I've never been much of a sitter."

"Okay, enough flirting," Emery said. "None of us are going to play sex games with you. What else did you find out at Cole's?"

Dirk's disappointed puppy dog look was almost comical. "Not even a quick foursome? I don't even have to participate."

Carly laughed and looked at Emery. "You have to admit he's pretty cute. I think we should keep him. Even if it's just for amusement's sake."

"Please don't egg him on." Emery picked up her plate and carried it to Savannah, who was furiously washing the dishes. It showed just how nervous she was about being tossed in jail for breaking and entering. Savannah didn't do dishes. Taking pity on her, Emery started rinsing the plates. "So tell me about Gracie."

Dirk grabbed a dishtowel and took the plate from Emery. "She's beautiful."

"Then I'm surprised you didn't know her until this morning," Carly said. "I can't believe you'd let a beautiful woman slip past you."

Emery glanced over at Dirk, expecting to see his impish grin. Instead, a frown wrinkled his forehead. "She's not the kind of girl you can flirt with—I mean, she's beautiful and all, but I would never play her."

"Play her?" Emery asked.

Carly moved behind them and handed Savannah a dirty spatula. "He means he would never try to flirt her into bed like he's been trying to do to us. Isn't that right, Lover Boy?"

Dirk placed a hand over his heart. "Why, I'd never do any such thing, ma'am. I merely enjoy making friends." Carly laughed and started cleaning the cooktop.

"So what's so different about Gracie?" Emery asked.

"She's special." When Emery looked confused, he continued. "When I was looking around, I wondered why there was a ramp on the front porch and one that led into the barn. It all made sense when I saw her in the wheelchair."

A wheelchair? That explained why Cole got so defensive when she'd asked about Gracie. It also might explain why Gracie hadn't written Emery back.

"What happened?" Emery asked.

"I'm not sure. Cole wasn't exactly the welcoming committee."

"Okay," Savannah said. "The dishes are all done. Now let's get out of here. And I don't care what you're cooking in that oven, Carly. I'm not coming back."

"Oh, stop being a wimp," Carly said. "I'm not going to eat at the Watering Hole for dinner. Especially when Dirk and Emery say it sucks."

"Then we can drive into Austin." Savannah herded them toward the door. "I'd like to do some shopping anyway."

"I'd love a trip to Austin with you lovely ladies." Dirk held open the door for them. "I'll even use the money Emery paid me to buy you lunch."

Emery didn't want to go to Austin. She wanted to find the last book in the Tender Heart series. And if that meant she had to go out to Cole's rundown ranch and talk with his sister, then so be it. She was through with the subtle approach. It was time to get straight to the point of her visit to Bliss—even if that meant getting over her embarrassment at almost having sex with Cole. Who cared if he thought she was a slutty big city girl with loose morals?

Okay, so maybe she cared a little. It was hard to remain professional when you'd tongue danced with someone the way she and Cole had. In fact, she couldn't remember ever having been so thoroughly kissed in her life. And while she hadn't kissed much in high school, she'd made up for it since.

Of course, none of those guys had looked like Rory Earhart. And who wouldn't enjoy thoroughly kissing the book boyfriend she'd fantasized about for years? But regardless of how much she had enjoyed the kiss, she needed to pull her head out of the fictional clouds and stay focused on the real world. In the real world, she was here as a professional editor. An editor who was going to lose her job if she couldn't pull a rabbit out of this hat.

"You guys go on to Austin. I'm going to go to Cole's ranch and talk to Gracie."

"It's about time," Carly said. "This waiting around is bull—"

"Hockey," Savannah finished the sentence. "And I do agree that the time for stealth is over. Besides, I'm dying to get my hands on that last book and see what happened to Dax Davenport."

"You need to get over your infatuation with Dax," Carly said. "Dax is the villain. And we all know what is going to happen to him. Rory or his brother Duke is going to shoot him dead in a gunfight."

"Dax is not a villain. He's just a misunderstood hired gunslinger doing his job."

"He shot Rory and almost killed him!"

"But he wasn't happy about it."

They continued to bicker as they walked down Main Street. Dirk walked behind with Emery.

"Are they always like this?" he asked.

Emery looked at her friends and smiled. "Ever since I've known them, and especially concerning the Tender Heart stories."

"I'm not much of a reader, but after listening to y'all, I think I might have to read the series. Of course, I think I'll wait until the final book is out. I hate to wait for my endings." His gaze wandered across the street to the motor lodge. "Which could be sooner rather than later. It looks like Gracie came to you."

Emery followed his gaze and saw a dark-haired young woman and a blonde in a wheelchair talking to Mrs. Crawley in front of the motor lodge office. When Mrs. Crawley noticed them, she pointed. The girl in the wheelchair wheeled around to face them.

"Is that Gracie?" Carly asked. "She's not much younger than this snot-nosed kid." She elbowed Dirk, but he didn't respond. He seemed to be as focused on Gracie as Emery was.

Fear settled in her stomach. What if her gut was wrong?

What if the letter was a fake and someone had just used this poor girl as a cover? The news would crush Emery's dreams of giving her beloved characters a happily-ever-after and of becoming a successful editor. Of course, she couldn't achieve her dreams if she was too chicken to find out the truth.

Taking a deep breath, she headed across the street. Her friends followed her, but once they got to the motor lodge parking lot, Carly grabbed Dirk and Savannah's arms.

"I think Gracie will be more willing to talk if she's not surrounded. We'll see you later, Em."

As soon as the three of them were headed to Carly's rental car, Emery walked to the women in front of the office.

"There you are," Mrs. Crawley said. "I knocked on your door earlier, but I guess you and your friends were up bright and early. I see they got in okay." Her mouth puckered. "I also see that Dirk has latched onto you. If he gives you girls any kind of trouble, you just let me know. I'm planning on kicking him out anyway."

"I hope you're not doing that on our account. Dirk hasn't given us any trouble."

Mrs. Crawley snorted. "Just give him time." She waved a hand at Gracie and the dark-haired girl. "This here is Rebecca and Gracie Arrington. They stopped by to chat and I was just telling them about you girls and your Tender Heart trip. This is Emery Wakefield, girls."

Both young women were pretty, but Gracie was breathtakingly beautiful. Her long hair was thick and a rich golden blond, and her features were model perfect from her sapphire blue eyes to the full lips she bit nervously.

"Nice to meet you." The dark-haired girl held out a hand. "Just call me Becky." She gave Emery's hand a firm shake. "So a girl's trip, huh? Now that sounds like fun." She glanced at Gracie. "What do you think? Maybe we should hit the road for my twenty-fifth birthday? We could head down to South Padre, get drunk on margaritas, and get us some tattoos."

Mrs. Crawley's eyes widened, and Emery figured she'd be spreading the news around town as soon as Becky and Gracie left—something that Emery wondered if Becky hadn't planned all along. There was a mischievous glint in her blue eyes that said she liked causing turmoil. Gracie's look was just the opposite, and she quickly tried to correct the situation.

"You know as well as I do, Beck, that Cole and Zane would throw a fit if we got tattoos . . . or even talked about going on a road trip."

"We're over eighteen, Gracie. We can do whatever we want." Becky smiled at Mrs. Crawley. "I believe Winnie got a tattoo just last year. Didn't she, Mrs. Crawley? The big ol' state of Texas tattooed right over her—"

Mrs. Crawley cleared her throat. "Yes, well, I don't have time to chat with you girls all day. I need to go home and fix Sunday supper." She looked at Emery. "I was in such a hurry to get to church this morning that I forgot the diary, but I'll bring it with me tomorrow."

"No hurry," Emery said.

Mrs. Crawley looked back and forth between them as if waiting for them to disperse. When they didn't, she shook her head and hurried to her car, parked right in front of the office. "Be careful crossing the parking lot, Gracie," she called back over her shoulder.

"Yes, ma'am." Gracie rolled her eyes, then waited for Mrs. Crawley to pull away before she turned to Becky. "Can you give us a minute, Beck?"

Becky didn't look surprised by the request. "Sure. I need to head over to the pharmacy and pick up some tampons anyway. If I ever get a chance to talk to Eve, I'm going to give that woman hell for giving into a little craving. Chocolate I could understand, but an apple?" She shook her head as she walked to a pickup truck parked in the handicapped space.

As soon as she had pulled away, Gracie turned to Emery. "So you got my letter?"

"Etta had a secret. And the funny thing about secrets is they always get out."

CHAPTER EIGHT

S OME OF THE TENSION LEFT Emery's shoulders. So Gracie had sent the letter. Now all she could hope for was that she still had the manuscript and hadn't sold it to another publishing house.

"Yes," she said. "Did you get my letters?"

Instead of answering, Gracie glanced around, then gripped the wheels of her chair and rolled to the side of the office. Emery followed, wondering if she should take the handles and help push. She hadn't been around anyone with a disability and didn't know the protocol. But just when she was about to offer, Gracie stopped at a picnic table in the shade. It was obviously a smoking spot for either the motor lodge customers or employees. Cigarette butts littered the ground around the table.

Emery was too nervous to sit. But since Gracie was already sitting, she felt it would be rude not to. Once she was seated, she clasped her hands in front of her to still their shaking. Gracie seemed to be nervous too. She fiddled with the end of her braid and refused to look Emery in the eye.

"So I guess you came all the way out here because you're interested in the book," she said.

Interested didn't quite cover it, but Emery held back her excitement and nodded. "I was hoping you would send me more . . . or at least answer my letters."

Gracie's cheeks turned pink. "I haven't had a chance."

Since it had been a month, it was an obvious lie. And Emery couldn't help but wonder about the real reason she hadn't replied. She could only hope that it didn't have to do with another publishing house. The thought terrified her, and she wanted to end the torture and just come out and ask. But since Gracie already looked like she was ready to bolt, Emery knew she needed to proceed with caution.

"So I'm assuming you've read the series. Who's your favorite character?"

Gracie visibly relaxed and finally looked at Emery. "Daisy McNeil. I love that she's the youngest mail-order bride, and also the feistiest. She reminds me of my cousin Becky. Becky could so stare down a dangerous outlaw and make him fall in love with her."

"And you don't think you could?"

Gracie looked down at her lap. "Maybe once, but after the accident . . ." Her voice drifted off.

Emery wanted to ask about the accident, but instead changed the subject. "Well, I love all the characters, but my favorite is Etta Jenkins who came to Bliss as an under-cover newspaper reporter hunting for a story. I loved how appalled she was at the idea of women being ordered like dessert at a restaurant. And Rory had no intention of choosing one of the brides until he set eyes on Etta—not that she made a good first impression when she stepped off the stage and fell in the mud."

Gracie laughed. "It wouldn't have been so bad if Rory hadn't laughed. Poor Etta."

"I don't know about that. What's a little mud when you

end up with the cutest Earhart?"

"You think Rory is the cutest?" A big smile creased Gracie's face. "No wonder you kissed my brother."

Emery couldn't help being surprised . . . and embarrassed. "Cole told you?"

"No. Cole never shares things like that with me. He thinks I'm still ten years old. My cousin Becky told me. She was driving past and texted me. Cole only confessed when I teased him about it."

"So what did he say?" Emery tried to act casual, but it was hard to be casual when she was dying to know what Cole had told his sister.

"Just that you were a school teacher looking for the last of the Tender Heart books. Why didn't you tell him why you were here?"

"Because he's not exactly what you would call a Tender Heart fan."

Gracie nodded. "Sometimes I think he hates the series."

"Is that why you didn't tell him about the book?"

Gracie blushed again, something she obviously had in common with her brother. Cole blushed so easily. Emery couldn't help but find it endearing, especially when coupled with such a tough cowboy demeanor. "No," Gracie said. "I just didn't want him to take over. He can be pretty controlling."

"I know how that works. I have two older brothers who love to stick their noses into everything I do. It can be very annoying. Or more like aggravating. Exasperating. Hair-pullingly frustrating. Especially when they view me as being their baby sister who constantly needs their guidance."

Gracie leaned closer. "I know, right? Since Daddy died, Cole thinks he is the only one who knows what's good for me." She thumped a fist on the wheel of her chair. "He's so dang stubborn, he doesn't even listen to me anymore. So I decided to keep the book from him until I have all the details ironed out." Her gaze grew intent. "Which is why I'd just as soon you didn't mention anything about the book or why you're here until I talk to him."

"Of course." After the kiss, Emery had no desire to see Cole again. So it was a promise she could keep. "But you'll have to tell him some time.

"I know," Gracie said. "And I will . . . soon."

Emery paused before she asked the next question, terrified of the answer. "Have you contacted any other publishing houses?"

"No. You're the only person I contacted."

She wanted to kiss Gracie, and then jump up on the table and start dancing. This was exactly what she'd hoped for—exclusive rights to the book. If she could get her to sign a contract, Emery would have job security. Not to mention she'd get to edit the last book in her favorite series of all time. This was her destiny. She just knew it. The chance to prove that she wasn't just taking up room on this planet, but that she was here for a reason. That reason was to give Tender Heart a happily-ever-after.

But if she wanted Gracie's signature, she needed to keep her cool.

"Thank you," she said. "I'm glad you chose me."

Gracie shrugged. "After reading your research paper online, I knew you loved Tender Heart as much as I do. It just seemed like fate."

Emery smiled. "I think so too. All my life I've wanted an ending for my beloved characters. I'd love to be the one who edits the story and helps to get it out to the millions of Tender Heart fans."

There was a long stretch of silence before Gracie spoke. "So how much would I get for the book? Like are we talking six figures?"

"At least that. If not more."

Gracie's eyes widened. They weren't the deep blue of Cole's. They were lighter, but just as beautiful. Obviously, the young woman didn't realize the jackpot she'd hit. Emery didn't want to increase the price her publishing house paid for the book, but she also didn't want to lose the chance to another house that was willing to offer more.

"And what if it's horrible?" Gracie asked. "What if everyone hates it?"

"It doesn't matter. If Lucy Arrington's name is on the cover, it will sell. Besides, I won't let it be horrible. I love the Tender Heart series and know every character and plot line inside and out. If you choose me as your editor, I'll make it the best book it can possibly be."

"Promise?"

She drew a cross on her chest. "Cross my heart."

Gracie hesitated for only a second before she reached for the tote bag that hung on the handle of the wheel-chair. Emery's heart rate accelerated. Could it be? She had barely finished the thought when Gracie handed her the tote. And as soon as she felt the weight, she had her answer.

She reverently set the bag on the table, then reached in and pulled out the stack of aged paper. Tears formed in her eyes as she stared down at the title page. *Riding Off into the Sunset: The Final Book in the Tender Heart Series* by Lucy Arrington.

"It makes sense, doesn't it?" Gracie voiced Emery's exact thoughts. "After she wrote it, Lucy did ride off into the sunset."

Emery touched the page. "Yes, she did. But she left us this." She turned the page and read the dedication.

To Bonnie Blue.

She was surprised. All of Lucy's other books had the same dedication: *To the mail-order brides who tamed Texas with their strength, determination, and tender hearts.* And now this one was dedicated to a single person. While this would make most people nervous, it made the book more authentic to Emery. If a plagiarist were trying to pass off a fake as the final book, they would've used the same dedication as Lucy had used in all the other novels.

"Bonnie Blue?" she said.

Gracie rolled closer. "I was hoping you'd know who that was."

Emery stared at the name. "I don't have a clue. I don't remember the name at all from when I was researching Lucy, but it could've been a close friend . . . or even a favorite pet. Lucy loved animals and had numerous pets over the years." She turned to the next page.

She immediately recognized the first chapter, but now it was on aged paper instead of copy paper. The paper coupled with the funky tail on the lowercase *t* and the faded *p* only added to its authenticity. She had read this chapter dozens of times and could almost quote it verbatim. It was the other chapters she needed to look at.

"It will take me a while to read," she said. "So why don't I take this to my room and I'll get it back to you tomorrow." She knew it was a mistake when Gracie tensed.

"I would rather not have it out of my sight." She glanced at the watch on her wrist. "And I don't have a lot of time today."

Since the book was worth so much, Emery could understand Gracie not wanting it out of her sight. Still, she couldn't help the strong desire to scoop up the manuscript and race off with it. All she needed was about six hours to find out what happened to her favorite characters. But the determined look on Gracie's face said she wasn't going to get that.

"Very well." She pinned on a smile. "But if you don't mind, I'll just take a quick look. Then I'll read it more carefully later."

"Okay," Gracie said, but it was obvious by her fidgeting that she didn't even like that. So Emery was extremely careful as she turned each page and scanned it for the funky *t* and *p*. They were there, making it obvious that the book had been written on Lucy's typewriter. When she came to the last page, tears filled her eyes once again. For decades, the Tender Heart characters had been waiting for *The End*, and now, like ghosts released into the ever after, they had it.

"So?" Gracie said. "What do you think?"

Emery lifted her tear-filled eyes and smiled. "I think your life is about to change dramatically."

"Rory didn't know what the heck he was doing at the board-inghouse all slicked up in his Sunday-go-to-meetin' clothes with cologne still stinging his just-shaved jaw. Especially when Etta came down the stairs looking like she'd just swallowed a bushel of lemons. 'What do you want?'"

CHAPTER NINE

W HILE HE WAITED FOR ZANE, Cole worked on Gracie's car. He changed the oil, charged the battery, and got it in running condition so he could put it on craigslist. The entire time he worked, his mind kept going back to Emery and the kiss they'd shared. Not that *kiss* was a good enough definition. A kiss made you think of a soft brush of lips. It didn't make you think of tangled tongues and wet heat that made a man's knees weak and his cock so hard it could hold up a circus tent. Of course, now every time he heard the word *kiss*, he'd think of Emery.

Which wasn't good. It wasn't good at all.

The woman was just passing through. She could be gone already for all he knew. And even if she wasn't gone, he didn't want to get involved with a dreamer who believed in fairytales and happy endings.

The sound of a truck coming up the road had him peeking around the open hood of the car. Zane pulled in between Gracie's car and Cole's truck. The slick black

Ram might be newer than Cole's old Chevy, but in his opinion, Chevrolet beat out Dodge hands down.

Zane got out and whistled through his teeth. "Damn, it's a hot one. If spring is like this, there's no telling how hot summer will be." He took off his cowboy hat and brushed an arm over his forehead before putting it back on. He finally noticed the car Cole was working on. "This is Gracie's car, isn't it? Becky didn't say anything about her being ready to drive again. Of course, Beck hasn't been talking to me after I chased off her last boyfriend. I'm thinking peppering his tailgate with buckshot might've been overkill." He swatted at a fly. "I swear that girl is more trouble than she's worth."

"She might be giving you hell, but I appreciate all the time she spends with Gracie. She came and got her today and took her into town."

"Well, that's good news." He nodded at the engine. "Is that why you're working on it? Are you thinking she'll be able to drive again soon?"

Cole swallowed down the pain that seemed to rise to his throat. "No. I don't think she'll be able to drive ever. I'm getting it ready to sell."

Zane looked down at his boots. "Damn, I'm sorry, man. I thought the doctors said she had a good chance of recovering the use of her legs."

"They did, but the physical therapist isn't as optimistic. I guess Gracie isn't making much progress. She just won't make the effort, and I don't know what to do about it."

"There isn't anything you can do. Little sisters have minds of their own." Zane placed his hands on his hips and studied him. "Everything else okay?"

Cole knew why he asked. He was wondering why Cole had invited him out to the ranch on a Sunday. It wasn't to talk about Gracie. It was to tell Zane about his plans to sell the ranch. But for some reason, he couldn't seem to get the words out. He had always been competitive with his cousins and selling the ranch would be like admitting that he'd failed. He *had* failed, but he wanted to put off admitting it for as long as he could.

"You want a beer?" he asked.

Zane shrugged. "Sure. Why not?"

They drank their beers on the porch in the hickory rockers that had been used by six generations of Arringtons. But they didn't talk about the past. Nor did they talk about the future. They talked about the Dallas Cowboys' last season and the Rangers' chances of getting into the World Series. When they had exhausted sports conversation, they sat and rocked until Zane finally asked.

"So why did you want to meet today, Cole? We could've talked about sports on Saturday when we play pool."

Cole downed the last of his beer and set the empty bottle on the railing, the chipped and peeling railing that could use a good sanding and two coats of paint. The sight gave him the strength to say what needed to say. "I'm selling the ranch."

Zane choked on the sip of beer he'd just taken. When he caught his breath, he turned and stared at Colt. "What? But why? I thought you were going to breed horses. I thought that's what you were going to do with the money you made working on that horse ranch in Kentucky."

That had been Cole's plan. Between the job and what his father had saved, he would've had plenty of money to start the type of horse ranch he dreamed of. And it hadn't been Gracie's accident that had drained most of the money. It had been his father's weakness for one woman.

Refusing to think about the past, Cole shrugged. "Plans change."

"But it wasn't just your plan, Cole. It was your dream.

You've talked about breeding the best horses in Texas since we were kids. And don't tell me Gracie wants to move. That girl loves this land as much as Becky does."

Cole rolled to his feet. "It's not Gracie. It's me. I want to sell the land. And I thought you'd want it. But if you don't, I can always sell it to someone else."

Zane released his breath. "Like hell you will. If that's what you want, I'll buy you out."

"You don't sound that excited about it. This is your chance to make the Arrington Ranch even bigger. Your dad will be thrilled."

Zane stared off in the distance before he nodded. "Yeah, old Daddy will be overjoyed." He glanced at Cole. "So what are you going to do?"

"The ranch in Kentucky offered me my job back. And Lexington has a good physical therapy program for Gracie. I'm hoping it will motivate her to at least try to walk again."

"She's probably still mourning, Cole. She loved your dad. He was the only parent she had—the only parent you both had."

It was hard to keep the bitterness from consuming him. His father had been a good man with only one weakness. It was too bad that weakness had destroyed everything Cole had worked for.

"I know that Gracie is still mourning," he said. "That's why I think a change of scenery will do us both good."

"And will Gracie go along with selling the ranch?" Zane asked.

"You saw my dad's will. You know he never got around to changing it after Gracie showed up. He left the ranch to me. So she doesn't have any choice."

Zane rested his elbows on his knees and stared down at the warped porch boards. "I never pictured things this way when you, Raff, and I were kids swimming naked at Whispering Falls. I never thought that Raff would spend time in jail, or your sister would end up in a wheelchair, or you would end up leaving Texas. I thought we would be the ones who ended the feud between our families and brought the ranches back together. I thought our wives would gossip about us being arrogant cowboys and our kids would swim naked together." He dug his hands through his hair. "Damn, I hate it when things don't turn out the way you plan."

At one time, Cole had wanted that too. But life had a way of taking dreams and turning them into nightmares. All you could do was force yourself to wake up and face the truth. He leaned back in the rocker and stared out at the land. Arrington land. Cole's land.

At least for a little while longer.

"Yeah," he said. "Me too."

Zane rocked for a while before he asked. "You still have your arrowhead?"

Cole fished in his pocket and pulled out his keys. He held up the Indian arrowhead he had found as a kid. "It took me so long to find it, you think I'd throw it away?"

"It did take you a lot longer than it took me and Raff." Zane reached inside the collar of his shirt and pulled out a chain with an arrowhead dangling from it. "As always, Raff was the first to find his."

Cole studied his arrowhead. "So have you heard anything from him?"

"No. Last time I talked with him was the same time you did—at the courthouse when the judge dropped the charges." Zane shook his head. "He was always the wild mustang of the bunch. But I figure he'll head home soon enough." He lifted his arrowhead. "If he still has his arrowhead, it will point him back to Texas . . . just like yours will."

Cole stared at his arrowhead. Maybe he'd leave it behind with everything else.

After Zane left, he went back to working on Gracie's car. He felt depressed as hell. Which probably explained why he drank the last two beers. They didn't make him feel any better. In fact, the alcohol only loosened his mind and had him thinking about things best forgotten.

Like Gracie as a kid, and how she used to tag around the ranch behind him and want to do whatever he was doing. If she had been closer to his age, it might've annoyed him. But she was a good seven years younger than he was and it was hard to be annoyed with a cute little blond-headed munchkin who looked at him with adoring eyes. So he'd taught her what his father had taught him. He put her on her first horse and led it around while she giggled with glee. He took her fishing and taught her how to bait a hook. He took her to auctions and taught her how to determine a thoroughbred from a nag.

As a kid, he'd never questioned why he was the one to teach Gracie these things and not his father. He just figured it was his job as a big brother. It wasn't until later that he realized that wasn't the case.

Hef Arrington had never out-and-out resented Gracie for not being his. He adopted her and gave her as many gifts on birthdays and holidays as he gave Cole. But he didn't give her the praise and attention he gave Cole. Which probably explained why Cole loved Gracie so much. He wanted to compensate for his father . . . and their mother. And maybe that was why he felt so damned depressed. Gracie had had so little love in her life and now he was going to take her away from the only place she'd ever called home.

Needing a distraction from his thoughts, Cole packed

up his tools and headed into town to check on Gracie. But he had no more than reached the turnoff for the highway when he spotted Becky's truck barreling toward him. It was just as new as her brother's, but fire engine red and with a lot more dings. Watching as she turned off and barely missed hitting his front bumper, Cole could understand why, and he had to wonder if letting Gracie go with her had been such a good idea.

"Hey, Cole," Becky greeted him as she rolled down her window. "You going somewhere?"

Since he didn't want Gracie to know he was checking up on her, he stretched the truth. "I was just headed into town to get some motor oil for Gracie's car. Did you two have fun?"

The girls exchanged a look that pretty much said they'd been up to no good before Gracie answered. "We did. Becky got the prettiest lipstick at the pharmacy, and we ran into Ms. Marble and she had us over for ham salad and chocolate cake."

"I thought Ms. Marble just discovered she was diabetic."

"She did," Gracie said. "She can't eat the sweet desserts she makes anymore, but she says she can't stop baking them. She sent the rest home with us, and I'll put it in the kitchen in case you want it when you get back."

Now that he'd told the fib, he had to go with it. "Okay then. I'll be back in a while."

To ease his guilt about lying to his sister, he did go to Emmett's gas station. It closed at six on Sundays, but he had a key and grabbed a few cans of oil before he headed back home. When he passed the motor lodge, he couldn't help glancing over. Emery's rental car sat in the carport of room number seven. Of course, that didn't mean she was there. She could be with her two friends searching for clues to the last Tender Heart book. Or having dinner with Dirk Hadley at the Watering Hole. That thought didn't sit well, and before he knew it he was pulling in to the motor lodge and parking. He sat there a few minutes trying to talk himself out of being stupid. When he couldn't, he got out and walked to the door.

The woman who answered didn't look like an uppity English teacher in business clothes or the sassy woman who showed up at the Watering Hole in a sexy dress. This woman wore baggy pajama bottoms and a t-shirt that would've fit Cole. Her hair was pulled up on top of her head in a messy nest with a red pencil sticking out of it. When she saw him, her green eyes widened behind the lens of her red-framed glasses. The kind of glasses a sexy librarian would wear.

He pushed down the thought and rolled his hat brim through his hands. "So you're still here, I see." *Real smooth, Cole.* He cleared his throat. "I mean, I thought you and your friends would be long gone once you figured out that there's nothing much of Tender Heart left."

"Oh." She looked surprised. "I thought . . ." She shook her head. "Never mind. If you came to apologize for the kiss, you don't need to. It was just a kiss."

Damn, the woman was too blunt for her own good. Well, if she could be blunt, so could he. "Nope, I didn't come to apologize. I never apologize for things I enjoy."

She blinked, and her mouth opened as if she wanted to say something. When she didn't, he brought an end to the torture. "Look, I just stopped by to say 'hey', but I can see that you're busy. So . . ." He started to leave, but she stopped him.

"Would you like to come in?"

He shouldn't. He damn well shouldn't. But he did. He stepped right over the threshold, making sure to keep his gaze anywhere but on the beds. "So where are your friends? Did they get bored with Bliss and leave?"

She moved the stack of paper that sat on the closest bed over to the nightstand, then climbed up on the mattress and folded her legs in front of her. So much for keeping his eyes off the beds. "They went to Austin for the afternoon and haven't gotten back yet."

"Why didn't you go?" He sat down in the only chair. "The bluebonnets are in bloom. It's a pretty drive."

She hesitated before nodding at the stack of paper. "I had some work to catch up on."

"Work? Do you always grade papers on your vacations?"

She fidgeted as if uncomfortable talking about it. "I never seem to catch up on my workload. So what did you do today?"

"Just worked."

"At the gas station? I didn't see you when I walked past this morning."

The thought that she'd looked for him made him feel a little less stupid about being there. "I don't work on Sundays. Just Monday through Saturday when there's a car that needs fixing—which in this town is always."

She tipped her head, and her messy nest of hair shifted. "It must be hard to keep up with a ranch while being the town mechanic."

"It's not too bad. Especially since I don't exactly have a working ranch."

She studied him, her eyes looking like two deep lagoon pools behind the lenses. "Why is that? I mean, I would think that with your heritage, herding cattle would be in your blood."

He squinted. "You know a lot about my heritage, do you? Or are we talking Tender Heart?"

She smiled. She had a nice smile. Not too toothy. Just soft and . . . sexy as hell. "You're right. I seem to get the two confused." She took off her glasses, then reached for the pencil in her hair and pulled it out. A waterfall of chestnut brown fell around her face in silky waves, and it was a good thing that Cole was sitting down because he felt a little dizzy from all the blood that rushed to his crotch. He didn't realize that he'd closed his eyes until Emery questioned him.

"Are you all right?"

He opened them and forced a smile. "I'm fine. Just resting my eyes." *Resting my eyes?* Good Lord, he sounded like his Granny Fay before she passed away. "Well, I probably should get going. I just stopped by to . . ." He let the sentence drift off because the only thing in his head was "kiss the daylights out of you" and he couldn't very well say that. He started to get up, but she stopped him.

"Have you eaten?" When he shook his head, she continued. "Me either. And I know where we can get an amazing dinner."

"I hope you're not talking about the Watering Hole. Because everyone in town knows you can't get an amazing dinner there."

Her eyes twinkled with excitement. Cole was pretty excited too, but not about food. It was about this soft woman who was much too close for comfort. She leaned in and whispered as if someone else was in the room. "Before I take you there, you have to promise that you won't tell anyone. You also have to promise that you won't have me thrown in jail."

Suddenly he wasn't as excited as he was curious. "Do you just need my word or should I pull out my pocket knife?"

"Blood oath won't be necessary. You look like a man of your word."

The compliment made him smile. "Then you have my

word I won't tell anyone or have you tossed into jail—although, just to clarify, I don't do drugs."

She laughed as she sprang to her feet. "No drugs." She grabbed a pair of shorts from the open suitcase and hurried into the bathroom. Within seconds, she was back. She slipped into flip-flops on her way to the door. "Come on, I'm starving."

Cole pulled on his hat and followed. Since there was no place in town that had good food, he expected her to head for her car. Instead, she headed for the street. He caught up with her on the sidewalk. "Just where are we going?"

She smiled. "It's a surprise."

He should've pushed her to give him a little more information. But lust won out over curiosity. Or maybe it wasn't lust. When he was with her, he didn't think about the ranch, Gracie, or the past. He didn't feel worried, guilty, or sad. He just thought about the way her hair blew in the breeze, the way her long-legged strides matched his, and the way her smile warmed his insides.

At that moment, he would have followed her anywhere.

"When the newspaper had given her the job, it hadn't included having dinner with a handsome cowboy. But there she was . . . trying her best to keep from losing all thoughts of her assignment in Rory's eyes."

CHAPTER TEN

W HEN EMERY OPENED THE DOOR and saw Cole standing there, she thought Gracie had told him about the book and he was there to talk business. Or yell at her for not being honest about why she was in Bliss. But within seconds, it became clear that Gracie hadn't told her brother. It also became clear that Cole was there because he wanted to see Emery again.

While that made one part of her feel all giddy, the other part knew that it wasn't a good idea to mix business with pleasure. And after her talk with Gracie that afternoon, Cole was now her business. He was Gracie's big brother. Which meant that he would have a say in the sale of the book. If he was as controlling as Emery's brothers, he might be able to sway Gracie's decision to sell her book.

Emery couldn't let that happen.

That was why she had stopped him from leaving and was taking him to the diner and plying him with Carly's cooking. She needed to make him forget the kiss and start thinking of her as more of a friend than a conquest.

Of course, that might be hard to do. Especially when she was having trouble forgetting the kiss. Every time he looked at her mouth, her stomach fluttered like a thousand butterflies just released from their cocoons. And he looked at her mouth a lot. Like right now as he took her elbow and guided her around a pothole in the street.

"So how illegal?"

She tried to net the butterflies and keep her eyes on the prize. "Not too." She led him around the diner to the back alley. "We're just going to cook—or not cook, so much as eat. Carly already made the braised beef."

"Is that anything like roast beef?" The spark of interest in his eyes made her smile.

"Yep, with roasted baby carrots and red potatoes." She opened the back door of the diner and sent him a questioning look. "Are you in?"

He smiled as he held open the door. "For roast beef and baby carrots? Hell yeah."

Once inside, Emery searched for the switch on the wall, but Cole caught her hand. The heat of his skin and strength of his fingers brought the butterflies back in a rush of fluttery wings.

He leaned closer, his breath falling like steam against her lips. "We can't turn on the lights," he said in a low, sexy voice. "We don't want the sheriff showing up. There are steep penalties for breaking and entering here in Texas. My cousin Raff could tell you all about that."

She tried to control her breathing, but with him so close, it wasn't easy. "Your cousin is a criminal?"

The brim of his cowboy hat brushed her forehead right before his lips brushed her ear. "There are numerous outlaws in the Arrington family. I guess you could say that naughty runs in our blood."

It was surprising how one word could make all kinds

of *naughty* thoughts sizzle through Emery's brain. But he didn't try a one. He left her standing there feeling thoroughly disappointed as he headed back to the kitchen. She heard a drawer open, and only a moment later, he returned holding a lit candle.

"Surprisingly, the emergency candles were still in the same drawer they were in when I worked here." He took off his hat and hooked it on the corner of a metal shelf before he took her hand and pulled her into the kitchen.

She liked the feel of his hand wrapped around hers a little too much and realized that she needed to get control of the situation and quickly. "You worked here?" she asked as she pulled her hand free.

"I bused here in high school." He lit another candle with the candle he held and placed both on the prep counter before he rubbed his hands together. "So what do I need to do to get that roast beef in my stomach?"

While Emery's brothers had never done anything to help with meals, Cole didn't seem to have a problem helping in the kitchen. He pulled the big roasting pan out of the oven and found a platter for the beef and vegetables. As she filled the platter, he set the counter with plates and utensils, then went to the pantry and returned with a dusty bottle of red wine.

"Not the best, but perfect for two partners in crime." He winked at her, then pulled out a barstool for her. She couldn't remember the last time a man had pulled out her chair. But not wanting him to think this was a date, she pulled out the one next to it and sat down. He cocked his head, but didn't say a word as he sat.

The braised beef was delicious, but Emery had trouble keeping her attention on the food. Her gaze kept wandering to Cole and the way the candlelight danced over his handsome features and the inky waves of his hair.

He glanced over and caught her staring. "Don't tell me you're one of those girls who doesn't eat."

"No, I love to eat. Cheeseburgers are my weakness—although the Watering Hole almost ruined cheeseburgers for me forever."

He laughed. "They are pretty bad. I'm assuming that's why you and your friends broke into the diner." He glanced around the kitchen. "How long did it take you to clean this place up? It had to be filthy since it's been years since the diner was open."

Not wanting to throw Dirk under the bus, she hedged. "Umm . . . not very long." She took a sip of wine. "So tell me about your family."

His gaze locked with hers. "Are you still trying to find similarities to Rory Earhart?"

"Actually, I want to know about Cole." It was the truth. She tried to convince herself that it had to do with business. It was always good to know who she'd be working with. But deep down she knew that was a lie. There was something about Cole that drew her like a moth to a porch light. Something that had nothing to do with Tender Heart.

She expected him to hedge. She'd figured out quickly that he wasn't a man who liked talking about himself. But he surprised her. After taking one last bite, he pushed away his plate and wiped his mouth with a napkin.

"There's not much to tell. My mother left when I was a kid. My father died just this past year from a heart attack. And my sister . . ." He paused. "My sister lives with me."

The words were spoken with no emotion whatsoever. Which made them all the more heartbreaking. Gracie had mentioned their father dying, but Emery hadn't realized it had happened so recently. And she knew nothing about their mother leaving. What kind of a woman left her son and disabled daughter?

As much as Emery wanted to keep her distance from Cole, she couldn't help reaching out and covering his hand that rested on the counter. "I'm so sorry."

"So am I." Cole turned his hand and linked their fingers. "And what about you? I bet you're an only child with doting parents."

She should've pulled her hand away, but she couldn't. "Not hardly. I have two pain-in-the-butt big brothers—of course, my parents are still doting."

"Two older brothers? That had to be tough."

She had thought it was tough, but after hearing about Cole's life, it now seemed like a walk in the park. "It wasn't that bad. Just typical big brother stuff. No guy I've dated is good enough and they still razz me for flunking out of med school."

"You wanted to be a doctor?"

"Not really. My entire family is in the medical field—Dad's a psychiatrist, Mom's a gynecologist, Jeff's a plastic surgeon, and Ryan's a pharmaceutical scientist. So I felt like it was expected. But I much prefer to have my nose in a novel than a medical journal." She paused. "Still, it's hard to disappoint your family."

"I know what you mean," he said. "My family thought I was the one who would bring back the Arrington dynasty. Instead, I'm the one who's selling out." Before she could ask what he meant, he swiveled on the stool and took her other hand. "And just for the record, I think that shaping the minds of our future is a pretty honorable profession and something to be proud of."

She had promised Gracie that she wouldn't tell Cole why she was here until Gracie had told him about the book. But after hearing about the tragedies of his life and sharing confidences, she couldn't continue to lie to him.

"There's something I need to tell you," she said.

His thumbs stroked back and forth over her knuckles, sending heat skittering through her body. "There's something I need to tell you too." He smiled. "My cousin Zane owns this building. So there was never any danger of us getting arrested."

Her eyes widened. "Then why didn't you let me turn the lights on?"

"Because I thought candlelight would make you more receptive to this." He leaned in and kissed her.

Unlike the other kiss, this kiss wasn't rushed or devouring. It was slow and thorough. His hands moved up to cradle her face as he gave her deep, drugging pulls from his lips and subtle, soft sweeps of his tongue. He hooked his boots in the rungs of her barstool on either side of her legs and scooted her closer. So close, her bare knees pressed against the center seam of his blue jeans and the hard ridge beneath. And yet his hands never wandered. His lips never strayed. The single-minded focus with which he kissed was more intimate than anything she'd ever experienced. And suddenly, she felt scared. Scared that Cole Arrington was taking much more than she was willing to give.

She pulled away. "I'm sorry. I can't do this."

His forehead wrinkled in confusion for only a second before it smoothed out. "You're married."

"No, I'm not married."

"Serious boyfriend?"

"No." She stood and picked up the plates. Her plan to become Cole's friend had backfired. Now she needed to regroup. She also needed Gracie to be honest with her brother. Something she was going to insist upon tomorrow. Until then, she needed to keep her distance from Cole. "I better get back to the motor lodge. My friends are probably there by now and worried about me."

He studied her for a moment before he nodded and got to his feet. "I'll help you clean up."

"There's no need to help. Doing the dishes was always my job when I lived at home. I'm an expert at it." She took the dishes to the sink and turned on the water, hoping he would take the hint and leave. Instead, he moved next to her and rolled up his sleeves.

"You might be an expert, but I don't leave messes for other people to clean up. Especially when they shared their dinner."

The dishes would've gotten done faster if Cole had just left. Distracted by his proximity, she became anything but an expert at washing dishes. She dropped a glass in the sink and broke it, then scalded her hand when she turned on the hot water instead of the cold. By the time they left the diner, Emery felt like the clumsiest klutz ever. Especially when he looked over at her with a slight smile.

"Do you want to tell me why you're acting like a startled doe who thinks she just stepped into the sights of a thirty-thirty rifle?" While she struggled to find an answer to his accurate analogy, he stopped on the street corner and pulled her around to face him. "I just wanted to kiss you, Emery. I didn't expect anything else."

She didn't know why tears welled in her eyes. Maybe because she felt like everyone expected something from her. Her parents expected her to become a doctor. Her brothers expected her to remain their sweet little virginal sister. Her boss expected her to find the next bestseller. And now here was someone who didn't expect anything but a kiss.

"I'm sorry," she said. "I just felt like things were moving too fast. Especially when I'll be leaving in a few days."

He studied her for a moment before he nodded. "Fair

enough." He released her, and they walked the rest of the way without touching. When they reached the motor lodge, he nodded at Carly's car, now parked behind Emery's. "It looks like your friends got back. You better go in and ease their minds." He turned and headed for his truck.

She pulled the room key from her back pocket, but before she placed it in the door, she couldn't help glancing back at Cole. He had his truck door open, but instead of getting in, he was looking at her. She should've turned away. That would've been the smart thing to do. But she didn't. She stared at him like he was staring at her. And finally, he slammed the door and came striding over.

"Damn it, Emery, I don't know what you expect. How can a man take it slow when he's only got a few days?" He took off his cowboy hat and slapped it against his leg, then walked a few feet away and stared up at the sky. His shoulders slumped, and he released his breath. "Fine. If a slow week is all you're offering, I'm willing to take it." He glanced at her. "Do you like barbecue?"

Emery was confused. Not just about the barbecue question, but also about all the conflicting emotions this man made her feel. All the stupid things he made her do. She shouldn't have kissed him. She shouldn't have lied to him. And she certainly shouldn't eat barbecue.

"Kansas City or Southern?" she asked.

He rolled his eyes skyward. "We're in Texas, woman. That means spicy rub, slow cooked, and sauce optional."

She couldn't help but smile. "Yes. I like barbecue."

"Good, I'll pick you up tomorrow at six." He headed for his truck, calling over his shoulder. "And if your friends peeking out the window want to come, they're invited too."

Emery glanced back just in time to see Carly and Savannah duck down and the cowboy curtains flutter closed.

"Etta had the sassiest mouth this side of the Pecos, which didn't explain why Rory wanted to kiss it so darn bad."

CHAPTER ELEVEN

❦

WHAT THE HELL HAD COLE been thinking when he invited Emery and her friends to dinner? *Do you like barbecue?* Hell, he didn't even know how to make barbecue. Although he had watched his dad do it. His dad had made the best barbecued ribs in Texas. Of course, it took him all day to make those tasty ribs.

Which explained why Cole hadn't gone to work at Emmett's garage that morning, even though there was an old Buick that needed a new carburetor sitting in one bay. Instead, he'd run into town for baby back ribs. When he got back, he fired up his dad's old smoker. Then he'd pulled out every spice he could find in the cupboards, rubbed them on the ribs, tossed them in the smoker, and crossed his fingers.

After that, he'd cleaned the house, mowed the weeds, and was now sanding the porch railing before he slapped on a fresh coat of paint. He tried to tell himself that he was just killing time while he kept an eye on the ribs. But deep down he knew there was another reason he was busting his butt.

He didn't want Emery too disappointed.

In her mind, his ranch would resemble the Earhart

Ranch. It would have a big red barn filled with thorough-bred horses and a white-fenced corral. It would have a cookhouse and a bunkhouse. And a sprawling ranch-style home with a wraparound porch that didn't need a fresh coat of paint.

Of course, no amount of painting, cleaning, or mow-ing was going to lessen the blow when Emery saw his ranch. It didn't come close to being the beautiful spread in Tender Heart—that was Zane's ranch. Cole's was just a simple one-story house with a porch that needed more than just paint. A small barn with only one horse. And a falling-down chicken coop with no chickens.

If Cole were smart, he'd leave the railing as is and head into town to Emmett's garage. At least he'd get paid for his time. Zane wasn't going to pay him more for the property just because he'd painted the porch railing. But spruc-ing up the ranch wasn't about money. It was about pride. When he drove Emery up the gravel drive, he knew she'd be disappointed. He just didn't want her to feel embar-rassed for him. Or maybe he didn't want to be the one who felt embarrassed.

The screen door slammed, and he glanced up to see Gracie maneuvering out the door. He hadn't told Emery about his sister, and he probably should have. Some peo-ple were uncomfortable around the physically challenged and it was unfair to spring it on Emery at the last minute. But it was too late to worry about it now. Just like it was too late to worry about what she thought of the ranch. He went back to sanding as he greeted Gracie.

"Good mornin'." He glanced at the sun. "Or should I say good afternoon?" He wanted to get after her. She didn't need to be sleeping in so late. She needed to be getting up and doing the exercises the therapist wanted her to do. But his guilt kept him from saying more.

Gracie rolled closer. "So why are you still here? You're usually at Emmett's by now."

"I took the morning off. I thought I'd catch up on some things that need to be done around here." He concentrated on sanding for a few moments before he tossed out his next words as nonchalantly as possible. "Oh, and I invited some people over for dinner tonight."

There was complete silence, and when he glanced over, Gracie looked stunned. He couldn't blame her. He'd never invited anyone for dinner before. He'd done most of his dating in college and Kentucky. Once he'd gotten back to Texas, he hadn't had time to date. Which was probably why he was so damned keyed up and nervous about tonight.

He cleared his throat and continued to sand. "I thought after I take you to your therapy, we could swing by and pick up Emery and her two friends."

"You invited Emery Wakefield for dinner?"

"Yeah, I know. It's probably stupid as hell to waste my time on a woman who's just passing through. But it's too late now. I already have the smoker going with ribs and I thought you could help me with some sides." He glanced at her. "Unless you don't want to."

She studied him for a long moment before a smile lit her face. "I don't think it's stupid at all. And of course, I'll help you make some sides. We'll have plenty of time because I cancelled my physical therapy today."

It wasn't the first time Gracie had canceled her physical therapy appointment. Lately, she'd been canceling more and more. She used every excuse under the sun: She was too tired. She had a headache. Her therapist was mean. But Cole knew the real reason. She'd given up hope of ever walking again. And like Zane said, there was nothing he could do about it.

"So I guess you like this Emery Wakefield a lot." Gracie leaned down and picked up a piece of sandpaper, then started working on the other end of the railing.

"I wouldn't say a lot. She's nice."

There was laughter in her voice. "Nice enough to smoke some ribs for and sand the porch railing. I'd say that's liking someone a lot."

His face heated. His sister had a point. He'd never gone to this much effort for a woman before in his life. Probably because no woman had made him feel the way Emery did. It wasn't just physical. There was something in her eyes that drew him. A sparkle of innocence that he'd long forgotten even existed.

"Okay," he said. "I like her a lot, but don't get any ideas, Brat. Emery's leaving town in a few days." Which explained why he felt comfortable chasing after her. She was a distraction for a few days. Nothing more. Even if she stayed longer, it wouldn't matter. He was leaving soon.

He glanced at his sister. He should tell her about selling the ranch to Zane, but he couldn't seem to find the words. So instead, he went back to sanding. He would have to tell her eventually. But not today. Not when Emery was coming. He could only deal with one disappointed female at a time.

"Hey, y'all!"

Cole looked up to see Dirk Hadley striding down the gravel drive. His straw cowboy hat was tipped back on his head, and his perpetual smile beamed as bright as the late morning sun. Cole might've been perturbed by the smile if he hadn't been confused by what Dirk carried.

"Chickens!" Gracie gushed. "Oh my gosh, just look at those little sweethearts." She rolled down the ramp to greet Dirk and the two fat red hens he was carrying, one tucked under each arm.

Dirk set the hens down in the yard and beamed with pride. "These little ladies are Gingernut Rangers, a mix between a Rhode Island Red and a Light Sussex. The guy who gave them to me for removing his dead poplar tree said they were some egg-producing mamas." He reached in his bulging shirt pocket and pulled out a handful of dried corn that he sprinkled on the ground. The chickens immediately went to pecking around his scuffed boots. He laughed. "Now don't be hogs. There's plenty for all."

Gracie rolled closer. "I love chickens. I used to enter my pullets in the county fair every year."

"I bet you took first place."

She smiled a sassy smile that Cole hadn't seen for months. "Of course. Everyone knows that's the only place that counts. I never settled for second with my chickens or my barrel racing." Her words caused guilt to spear through Cole. She wouldn't be taking first place ever again in barrel racing.

He got to his feet. "I'm not interested in buying chickens."

Dirk squinted at Cole. "Do you have something against chickens?" Before Cole could answer, he glanced at the railing and whistled through his teeth. "It looks like you got your work cut out for you. You planning on sanding that entire railing by hand? Don't you have a power sander?"

The guy grated on Cole's last nerve. "I have a sander, but it's broken. And I'm not doing the entire porch. I'm just doing the top rail."

Dirk tipped his head. "Now I'm not one to tell a man how to do a job, but my daddy always said that a job half-done is a job not done."

"And my daddy always said to never wear your teeth on the outside. It's a sure way to get them knocked out. Now just what part of 'I don't want or need your help' don't you understand?"

"Cole!" Gracie said. "There's no need to be rude."

He pointed at Dirk. "I told him I'm not hiring, and the man can't seem to get the message."

Dirk flipped some more corn to the chickens. "I got the message loud and clear that you don't have money to pay a handyman. But I've been thinking about that car you got sitting there. And while I don't have the money to buy it, I am willing to work for it. I can start by helping you with that railing. Then I can fix the chicken coop and get these ladies settled in. They aren't for sale." He smiled at Gracie. "They're a gift."

Cole headed down the ramp. "We don't need chickens. I have enough to take care of as it is."

Gracie blocked his way. "Then let me take care of them. It's not like you let me do anything else."

Her words took him back . . . and ticked him off. "What do you mean? I let you do whatever you want. Including sleeping in until almost noon and canceling your physical therapy."

Her cheeks turned pink. "That's not what I'm talking about, Cole." She glanced at Dirk, who had his hands on his hips and was looking out at the north pasture like he wasn't listening. "But now isn't the time to talk about it."

Damn, he hated it when his little sister was right. They had no business airing their dirty laundry in front of a stranger. "Fine," he said. "But we're not keeping the chickens or hiring him to help out." He thought that would be it, but his sister surprised him by rolling up the ramp after him and speaking low enough so Dirk couldn't hear.

"Daddy willed you the ranch, Cole. I have no say about you selling it or the animals you want to keep on it. But Daddy gave me that car. And we both know that I'm never going to drive it again. So if I want to sell it or trade it or set it on fire, that's my right."

That took all the starch right out of him. Not only because she was right, but also because it had been a long time since he'd seen so much fire in Gracie's eyes. It gave him hope that the accident hadn't taken all the spunk from his baby sister.

"Fine," he said. "Do what you want with your car. And you can keep the chickens. But don't be getting too attached to those hens. We're giving them right back to Dirk when we go."

A smile spread over her face. "If we go."

He shook his head and went back to sanding while Gracie rolled down the ramp to Dirk. With the scrape of the sandpaper, he couldn't hear what they were talking about, but they must've struck a deal because only moments later, Gracie and Dirk joined him on the porch.

Cole wouldn't admit it under torture, but Dirk Hadley was a damned good worker. With his and Gracie's help, they sanded the entire railing in just a couple hours. An hour after that, they had it painted a fresh white.

After he cleaned the paintbrushes, Cole went to check on the smoker. But wouldn't you know it, as soon as he lifted the lid, Dirk was right there offering his two cents' worth.

"What kind of wood did you use? Hickory gives a nice flavor, but it's a little too strong for me. I prefer cherrywood, myself."

Cole didn't have a clue what kind of wood he'd used. He'd just tossed in the chips he used for kindling. But he was getting sick and tired of a man who was younger than him knowing more than he did about almost everything. So he lied through his teeth. "I used a special wood that we Arringtons have used for years. I'd tell you, but then I'd have to kill you." He smiled. "Family secret."

Dirk flashed his big, annoying smile. "Well, I wouldn't want to die before I get to taste those ribs."

"Oh no. You're not invited to dinner. Get that out of your head right now. In fact, you've done enough for today. You can come back tomorrow."

Dirk shrugged. "I hate to point this out, but you're not my boss. Miss Gracie is. And speaking of Miss Gracie, what exactly happened to put her in that wheelchair?"

"That's none of your business."

"Just curious. If she's still going to therapy, it must've happened fairly recently." He paused. "Although it sounds like she's not going to therapy. Which can't be good. I worked with a physical therapist once—"

Cole turned and headed for the house before Dirk could impart any more of his limitless knowledge. He needed to make the sides that would go with the ribs. He'd started a crockpot of beans that morning, so he only needed to flavor them with some salt and bacon. He was pretty proud of the result. But the potato salad was a different story. Even with Gracie's help, it hadn't turned out well. He overcooked the potatoes so they were too mushy and undercooked the eggs so the yolks were too gooey, then he tried to camouflage both by adding extra mayo and mustard.

Gracie gagged after taking a taste. "That's disgusting. You can't serve that to Emery. She'll never go out with you again."

"It's not that bad," Cole said as he took another taste. "And this is not a date."

He had to question that statement when it took him twice as long as usual to shower and get dressed. He couldn't get his hair right, couldn't decide on what shirt to wear, and couldn't get his boots polished to the perfect shine. When he finally noticed the time, he had to give up on perfection and accept the reflection in the mirror. What he couldn't accept was Dirk Hadley leaning on his truck when he stepped out the front door.

"What are still doing here?" Cole asked as he walked down the ramp.

"I worked on the chicken coop."

Cole glanced over to the coop to discover that it had been almost entirely rebuilt with the scrap lumber he kept on the side of the barn. The two hens were behind the chicken wire pecking happily at the corn Dirk must've had in every one of his pockets. It was hard to swallow his pride and thank the man. Hard, but something that needed to be done.

"It looks good," he said. "Thank you."

Dirk grinned. "You're welcome."

"I guess I'll see you tomorrow." He reached for the door handle of his truck, but his hand froze when Dirk spoke.

"Actually, you'll see me sooner than that." When Cole looked at him, Dirk shrugged. "Gracie invited me to dinner. And since you're headed that way, I was wondering if I could catch a ride so I can clean up a little."

"Having grown up in an orphanage, Etta couldn't help the deep longing for family and home that tightened her chest when she first laid eyes on the Earhart Ranch."

CHAPTER TWELVE

IT WASN'T THE EARHART RANCH that Lucy had described in Tender Heart, but there was something about Cole's ranch that struck a chord with Emery. Maybe it was the quaint front porch with the rocking chairs. Or the chicken coop with the two fat hens. Or the land that seemed to stretch on forever. No buildings blocking the horizon. No hordes of people hurrying to get somewhere. Just miles and miles of rolling hills, pretty wild flowers, and budding trees below a deep blue sky that matched Cole's eyes.

Those eyes turned to her as he parked in front of the porch. "I know it's not what you expected the Earhart Ranch to look like."

"No, it's not," she said. "But then this isn't the Earhart Ranch." She smiled at him. "It's the Arrington Ranch. And I think it's beautiful. So are all three ranches called Arrington?"

"No." Cole turned off the engine. "My dad wasn't what you would call lucky, but he won the card game the brothers played to determine who would keep the name. My uncles had to come up with different ones."

"What are their ranches called?"

A smirk tipped Cole's mouth. "What else? The Earhart Ranch and the Tender Heart Ranch."

She laughed. "That's perfect."

"Of course, you would think so." He climbed out of the truck and came around to hold her door as she got out. "So what did you and your friends do today? Did you find any new clues to the whereabouts of the final Tender Heart book?"

Emery had hoped Gracie would've told Cole about the book by now. But it was obvious that she still hadn't mentioned a word. Before she could hedge around the question, Carly, Savannah, and Dirk pulled up in Carly's rental car.

"Do you always drive like you're in a grand prix, Cole?" Carly asked as she climbed out. "If not for Dirk, we would've lost you at the first stoplight in town and never found this place." She sent him a knowing look. "One would think that you were trying to lose us on purpose."

"Not at all, ma'am," Cole said as he took off his hat. "I guess we Texans are just a little heavy footed. I'm happy that you and Savannah could join us for dinner." It was quite obvious that Dirk had been left out of Cole's happiness. It was also quite obvious that Cole had done it on purpose. He made no bones about not liking Dirk. Dirk, on the other hand, seemed to take it in stride.

He smiled widely as he came around the front of the car. "Well, it was certainly nice of you to offer your hospitality." He sniffed the air. "But I'm thinking if you don't pull those ribs off shortly, there might not be any meat left on the bones."

Cole's eyes widened, and he started backing toward the barn. "If you'll excuse me, ladies. I'll be right back." He waved his hat at the front door. "Just make yourselves at home." He turned and sprinted around the barn to where a trail of smoke rose in the air.

"I think I'll go with him," Carly said. "I want to get a look at his smoker." She tossed Dirk her keys. "Get the salad I made out of the trunk."

Dirk saluted. "Yes, ma'am."

While Dirk got the walnut, pear, and gorgonzola salad, Savannah and Emery climbed the ramp that led to the front door.

"It doesn't look anything like the Earhart Ranch," Savannah said. "I wonder where Lucy got her inspiration?"

"A lot can change in sixty years. And this is just a piece of the ranch." Emery reached out and set a rocker to rocking. "Besides, I kind of like it. It's rustic country."

Savannah glanced at her as if she'd lost her mind. "I would not call this rustic country. It's more like rundown farmhouse."

"What happened to the woman who sees potential in everything?"

"There are some things that are just too dilapidated to save." She looked around, and her eyes narrowed. "But you're right, with an expert designer, this place could actually be kind of cute. Industrial farm design is big at the moment."

Before Emery could ask what that was, the door creaked. Gracie sat behind the screen door wearing a shy smile.

"Hi." She nudged the door open with her wheelchair, and Emery quickly grabbed it and held it.

"Hi, Gracie. Cole is checking on the ribs and told us to come on in."

Gracie smiled. "He's been worried sick that they won't turn out right." She held out a hand to Savannah. "I'm Gracie."

"Nice to meet you," Savannah said. "I'm Emery's friend, Savannah. It was so sweet of you and Cole to invite me to dinner."

"Hey there, Miss Gracie." Dirk came up the ramp with the bowl of salad. "You look like cool limeade in that pretty green dress."

Emery knew that Dirk was just being Dirk, and compared to the more suggestive compliments he'd given Carly, Savannah, and Emery, this was mild. But it was obvious from Gracie's flushed cheeks and muttered "thank you" that she was taking the compliment to heart. Why that would worry Emery, she didn't know. It wasn't like Gracie was her sister, or even her friend. Still, she couldn't help sending Dirk a warning look. He must've gotten the message, because he quickly redirected the conversation.

"I better get this salad into the refrigerator and see if Cole needs some help with those ribs." Dirk held the door for Emery and Savannah, then followed them inside.

The inside of the house wasn't as quaint as the outside. In fact, closed in and dismal came to mind. The rooms were small and sparsely furnished and the windows had heavy valances and curtains that blocked most of the sunlight.

Emery hid her thoughts, but Savannah's face registered dismay. Before Gracie could read it, Emery rammed her friend in the ribs and spoke over Savannah's soft grunt of pain.

"Very nice home."

"Thank you," Gracie said. "We had a lot more furniture and knickknacks, but Cole cleared most of it out after the accident. He didn't want me running into anything." Emery wondered again what kind of accident had left the beautiful young woman unable to walk.

"Is the kitchen this way?" Dirk asked as he nodded at

the doorway to his left.

"Yes," Grace said. "Let me show you." She motioned at the antique love seat "Please make yourselves at home, Emery and Savannah. I'll just be a second. I need to get the beans out of the crockpot and set the table."

Savannah's southern manners finally kicked in. "Why don't you let me help you with that, honey. I'm the worst cook this side of the Mississippi, but no one sets a table better than I do." She followed Dirk to the kitchen. Gracie started to go after them, but Emery stopped her.

"Could I talk to you, Gracie?" When Gracie wheeled around, Emery asked, "Why haven't you told Cole about the book yet?"

Gracie looked contrite. "I was going to, but then he was so excited about tonight that I didn't have the heart to ruin it. Cole doesn't like secrets. And he's going to be upset when he finds out that I've kept the book from him."

"But he needs to know. And he won't be able to stay angry once he finds out how much money will be involved." Emery had talked to her editor-in-chief that morning and told her where she had gone on her vacation. Her boss was still leery that the book might be a hoax, but she had given Emery the green light to stay in Bliss as long as it took to determine that.

"Cole isn't really caught up in money," Gracie said. "And I would die from embarrassment if he yelled at me in front of Dirk."

The thought of Cole yelling at Gracie—and at her—made Emery concede. "Fine, but you need to tell him after we leave. Otherwise, I'm going to tell him in the morning."

Gracie brightened. "Tonight. I promise."

Savannah came into the room. "Where will I find some

festive placemats for the kitchen table?"

By the time Cole and Carly came in with the ribs, the kitchen table was set with bright-colored placemats and Fiestaware dishes. In the center, Savannah had placed a large pitcher of bluebonnets she'd had Dirk pick and surrounded it with bowls of salad, baked pinto beans, cubed watermelon, a basket of store-bought sliced bread, and a bear of honey.

Once the platter of ribs was placed on the table, Dirk and Cole pulled out chairs for all the women. When everyone was seated, Cole sat down and immediately bowed his head. Why that simple act would cause the butterflies to return, Emery didn't know. As she lowered her head and listened to his deep voice ask for God's blessing, she reminded herself once again why she was there. It wasn't for Cole. It was for Tender Heart.

After grace, neither man wasted any time filling their plates—as did Carly, who was always in a big hurry to taste something she hadn't cooked. Once she took a big bite of ribs, she slowly chewed and described every ingredient she tasted.

"Brown sugar. Garlic. Cumin. Black pepper. Cayenne pepper." She paused and looked at Cole. "Coriander?"

Cole swallowed and wiped his mouth with a napkin. "I don't have a clue. I just threw in whatever spices were in the cupboard."

"Well, these are amazing." She pointed the rib at him. "Although it probably has more to do with your smoker than the rub. You wouldn't be interested in selling it, would you?"

Cole glanced at Gracie, who was watching Dirk eat his ribs like he was a contestant on *America's Got Talent,* before he looked back at Carly. "Maybe."

"And just how are you going to get a smoker to California?" Savannah stared at the ribs on her plate, her fork and knife posed in mid-air.

"I can get it there. The right smoker is hard to find." Carly rolled her eyes. "Are you kidding me, Savannah? Just eat the damn rib with your hands like the rest of us."

"If my Aunt Fanny was here, you would be dismissed from the table for such language." Savannah daintily worked at getting a piece of pork off the bone. "And just because our meal is on a bone doesn't mean we have to eat it like a pack of wolves."

"Go right ahead, Miss Manners," Carly said. "But you're missing out." She took another big bite of the rib and closed her eyes in ecstasy.

Savannah went back to cutting, but after only a few minutes, she set down her fork and knife and picked up the rib. When all eyes turned to her, she shrugged. "When in Rome." She took a big bite of rib and everyone laughed.

The incident seemed to put people at ease. Conversation flowed as rib platters and bowls were passed around the table. Emery didn't do much talking. She had always been more of a listener. She enjoyed listening to Dirk's stories about the different jobs he'd had, Carly's stories about the mishaps that took place in a restaurant kitchen, and Savannah's stories about the elderly woman who was mad at her for not hiring the Property Brothers to help decorate her house. Cole didn't talk much either, and whenever Emery glanced over, he was watching her. She tried to look away, but it wasn't easy pulling her gaze from those intense blue eyes.

"So you mean this was Lucy Arrington's house?" Carly asked, pulling Emery's attention back to the conversation.

Gracie nodded. "Her brothers built it for her so she'd have a place to write where she wouldn't be interrupted. Cole sleeps in her room."

Emery looked at him. "You sleep in Lucy's room?"

"Yes. I'll be happy to give you a tour when we're finished eating."

At the prospect of seeing Lucy's room, Emery couldn't wait for dinner to be over. And if sensing her impatience, Cole wasted no time finishing his meal and pushing back from the table. She quickly set down her napkin and got up, but Carly and Savannah didn't seem that interested in a tour of Lucy's room.

"Aunt Fanny always taught me to let my food digest before I leave the table," Savannah said.

"And I want to try the chocolate cake that Gracie was telling us about." Carly reached for the covered cake plate. "This Ms. Marble sounds like a woman right up my alley."

Dirk nodded. "I'd like to try that cake myself. Wouldn't you, Miss Gracie?"

When Gracie agreed, Cole smiled at Emery. "I guess that just leaves you and me."

She should've stayed and had cake. Being alone with Cole in a bedroom wasn't a good idea. But her desire to see the place where Lucy had created Tender Heart dissolved any misgivings. Except he didn't lead her to his bedroom, instead he led her outside to the porch.

"I thought you were going to show me your room," she said.

"I plan to. But there's something I thought you'd want to see before it gets too dark." He took her hand as they headed down the ramp.

The sun hung just over the horizon, a fiery ball of orange in the dusky blue of the sky. She had only a moment to admire it before Cole opened the driver's side door and helped her in. She would've scooted across to the window, but he hopped in and reclaimed her hand, keeping her right next to him.

"It can get a little chilly in the evening," he said. "We might want to share our heat."

It wasn't chilly. In fact, Emery was too warm. And she got even hotter when, after Cole backed up, he rested his hand on her knee. She wished she'd worn jeans instead of a skirt. The feel of his calloused thumb stroking back and forth on her bare skin sent tingling waves of desire straight up the inside of her thigh to the spot beneath her panties.

By the time he pulled up to a copse of trees, the only thing Emery wanted was for Cole to never stop touching her. She no longer cared about keeping their relationship friendly. She only cared about the warm, sexual glow the stroke of his thumb had built deep inside her. The glow continued as he helped her out of the truck and reclaimed her hand.

"Where are we going?" she asked as they moved through the trees.

"It's a surprise." He used the words she'd used the night before. "But I promise that it's not illegal."

"I don't really like surprises. Two older brothers can do that to you."

He laughed as he ducked beneath some low-hanging branches. "You're going to like this one."

Emery bent to avoid the branches and followed him into a clearing filled with Texas bluebonnets. But it wasn't the gorgeous flowers that made her breath catch. It was what sat in the midst of the purplish-blue sea.

The little white chapel.

"'What I'm saying, Mr. Earhart, is that women don't want to be married in a courthouse,' Etta said. 'They want to be married in a church. And since you're the one who invited us here, you're the one who needs to build that church.'"

CHAPTER THIRTEEN

WHILE THE TOWN OF BLISS and Cole's ranch had looked nothing like the descriptions in the books, the chapel looked exactly like Tender Heart. From the tall spire that split the dusky sky to the stained-glass windows that gleamed in the setting sun. And Emery couldn't explain the feeling that welled up inside her. It was like going to Universal Studios and hanging out at *The Wizarding World of Harry Potter*. Or going to Disneyland and walking through Cinderella's castle. But instead of feeling like a tourist, she felt like she was right where she belonged.

Which was crazy. She belonged back in New York City in her small apartment with a view of the next-door building's fire escape and the alley dumpsters. She did not belong in Texas in a small chapel. Yet, she couldn't shake the feeling that she had finally found the one place where she would fit.

"You aren't going to cry on me, are you?" Cole asked.

"No," she whispered in a choked voice that made her answer a complete contradiction.

"Glad to hear it." His hand rested on the small of her back and rubbed up and down as she continued to take in every detail of the church.

"I didn't think it would look like this," she whispered. "Not after all these years."

The gray shingles on the pitched bell tower and roof looked new, as did the pristine white siding. A cobbled pathway wound through the brilliant bluebonnets like a river of gray leading the way to the wooden steps and the double arched doors. The same doors that eleven pretty brides had been carried out of amid a shower of rice and well-wishes.

"Yeah, well," Cole said, "it's not exactly the church that was built over a hundred years ago. It's been renovated numerous times—including just last year. Zane had some of his ranch hands fix the roof, check the supports, and redo the siding."

Emery turned to Cole. "Zane? Is the church his?"

"No. It sits on the only land still owned by all three of us. Not one of our fathers was willing to part with the chapel so they split it three ways." He looked at the church, and she felt his fingers tighten on her waist. "Of course, in a few weeks, it won't belong to all three of us." Before she could question him, he took her hand. "Come on. I know you want to get a peek inside."

As she followed him down the pathway, her stomach tightened with anticipation and... something else. Something that didn't have anything to do with seeing the inside and everything to do with walking toward the chapel with her hand tucked in Cole's. She felt like Etta Jenkins on her wedding day, like Rory Earhart was leading her to a happily-ever-after. It was silly. Emery wasn't a mail-order bride eager to be wed. She had things to prove to herself and to her family. But no matter how

hard she tried, Emery couldn't stop the fantasy from playing through her mind as Cole pushed the doors open.

"You don't lock it?" she asked. "Aren't you worried
someone might take something?"

"There's nothing to take."

She stepped inside and realized he was right. Besides
a few pews, there was nothing in the church but dust
and cobwebs. Yet that didn't make it any less beautiful.
The setting sun hit the stained glass with its last brilliant
rays, turning the windows into glowing works of art. They
weren't of religious symbols or biblical characters. Each
of the six windows depicted a different Texas flower. And
standing in their midst was like standing in a field of God's
vibrant beauty.

She turned to each window and recited the names of
the flowers that she knew by heart. "Bluebonnet. Texas
Sagebrush. Indian Blanket. Greenthread. Winecup—"

Cole came to stand next to her and said the last one
with her. "Primrose."

She looked at him and smiled. "They're so beautiful and
look exactly like I thought they would."

He lifted a hand as if he was going to touch her, but
then let it drop and turned to the windows. "Did you
know that they were created by a mail-order bride? Not
a fictional one, but a real one?"

"Was she related to you and Lucy?"

He shook his head. "She was Hank's ancestor. He's the
bartender and owner of the Watering Hole. He claims she
was related to the stained-glass artist William Jay Bolton
who made the windows for the Holy Trinity Church in
New York."

The more Emery heard about the real mail-order brides,
the more intrigued she became. She couldn't wait to read
Mrs. Crawley's diary. The woman had yet to drop it by her

room, although they had been out of the room for most of the day looking for the chapel. Carly and Savannah would be so envious when they found out where Cole had taken her.

Emery turned to him. "Thank you. It's everything I thought it would be and then some. It's a shame more people don't get to see it."

"After Zane renovated the outside, we talked about finishing the inside and opening it up to the public, but his sister Becky threw a hissy fit. She's as big a Tender Heart fan as you are and refuses to let some clumsy ranch hands destroy anything in the church. She claims she wants to do the inside renovations herself." He pointed to a gaping hole in the floor. "Although it doesn't look like that's going so well."

Emery smiled. "She is quite a firecracker." She didn't realize her slip until Cole called her on it.

"You met Becky? When?"

Trying to hide her flaming cheeks, she walked over to one of the windows and studied the cobweb that hung in the corner of the intricately designed glass. "I met her in town yesterday. She was talking with Mrs. Crawley." She tried to change the subject. "So we'd probably better get back. I'm sure you'd like to get some of Ms. Marble's chocolate cake before it's all gone."

There was the soft sound of boot heels on worn wooden floors as Cole walked up behind her and closed his hands around her waist. His breath ruffled the hair at her ear. "I'm not interested in chocolate cake." His lips brushed over the sensitive spot behind her ear. "I want to taste you." He flicked his tongue against her skin, and desire skittered through her like tiny hot electrical currents. His hands tightened on her waist as he nibbled his way down her neck. "In fact, I want to gobble up every last morsel."

Suddenly, the plan to never mix business with pleasure didn't matter anymore. The only things that mattered were the strength of Cole's hands on her waist and the heat of his mouth on her neck.

"Let me taste you," he whispered between nibbles. "I promise I won't do anything you don't want me to."

At the moment, she couldn't think of one thing she didn't want him to do. But she made one last effort to stop what was certain to be a mistake.

"I'm leaving soon." She spoke so softly she was surprised he heard.

"I know. But you're here now." He wrapped his arms around her and pulled her close as he buried his face in her neck. "Do you know what you do to me, Emery? Do you have any idea?" He flexed his hips, and she got a pretty good idea. While she felt like melted butter, he felt like solid steel. The hardness of his body and the contrasting gentleness of his touch dissolved the last of her resistance.

"Cole," she moaned.

"Hmm?" He hummed on the sensitive spot behind her ear. "What do you want, Sweet Em?" When she didn't answer, he continued. "I know what I want." He paused for two heartbeats. "I want to know what you have on under that cute little skirt."

He didn't wait for a reply. Not that she could've replied. There were no words in her head. Her brain was completely focused on her body and what he was doing to it.

He loosened his hold and one hand slipped to the waistband of her skirt. His fingers lightly traced the band in a back and forth motion that was dizzyingly sensual before they slowly slipped down the gauzy material. He stopped at the dip between her legs for one heart-stopping second, and the material shifted in a way that made her breath catch. It hung in her lungs until he released her and moved to the hem of her skirt. He gathered it into his hand, then slowly traced his hot fingers up her thigh, inch by breathless inch.

"I love the way your skin feels," he breathed. "I love the warmth . . . and the softness . . . and the tiny little goose bumps that spring up where I touch. Do I give you goose bumps, Em?"

He gave her more than goose bumps. The calloused fingers skating up her inner thigh made her feel like a lit fuse that was about to ignite a stick of dynamite. When he finally reached his destination, she felt ignited. She dug her head back into his shoulder and released a groan as his hand cupped her through the skinny strip of her panties.

"So you are wearing panties." His fingers stroked along the slick satin. "Tiny little panties that would be so easy to slip off." His breathing was rapid and fell in rolling waves of heat against her neck, her shoulder, then back up to her ear. "Let me take them off, Emery. Let me touch you like I want to touch you."

She wanted him to touch her. She wanted him to touch her more than she had ever wanted anything in her life. Unfortunately, she couldn't seem to say yes. Her brain might not be working, but her moral compass certainly was. Through the haze of desire, her heart knew that having sex with Cole when he didn't know who she truly was or why she was there would be wrong.

Emery savored one more brush of his fingers and lips before she pulled away and walked over to the window. She stood there and stared at the stained-glass pink primrose, trying to catch her breath. Behind her, she could hear Cole's breathing. It was just as harsh as hers, but when he spoke there was a teasing note in his voice.

"I guess going slow isn't one of my strong suits."

The words lightened the mood, and she turned to find him smiling. It wasn't the type of smile that took up his entire face. It was more reserved, yet sincere and contagious.

She smiled back. "I guess it's not one of mine either. Especially with you." She glanced around. "My family isn't exactly religious, but my mother would have a heart attack if she ever found out what I almost did in a church."

"Not my smartest move. That just goes to show what you do to me." He held out his hand. "Come on, let's go get some of that chocolate cake."

Once they were outside the chapel, Emery turned for one more look. The sun had sunk below the horizon, leaving only a tint of heavenly pink amid the twilight blue of the sky. "So you never have church services here?"

"Not in the sense of Sunday mornings with a preacher and congregation. At least not while I've been alive." He led her along the path. "After my mother left, my daddy used to bring me out here every once in a while. We'd sit in a hard pew for a good hour. For an energetic five year old, that hour was pure torture. I couldn't understand what we were doing just sitting."

The image of a young boy sitting next to a heartbroken dad made Emery's own heart break. "Where was Gracie?"

"She wasn't born yet." They reached his truck, and he opened the door and helped her up. She scooted across the seat. "My mother didn't get pregnant with her until after she left." He got in and squinted at her. "Is there a reason you're sitting so far away?"

There was a reason. A good reason. When he touched her, she couldn't think clearly. And she needed to think clearly. Especially when she needed to piece together his words.

"So I don't understand," she said. "Are you saying that

your father wasn't Gracie's father?"

He started the engine. "My father was the only father she ever knew. He didn't hesitate to become her father after my mother left her. Gracie was the best present my mom ever gave me." He patted the seat next to him. "Now if you're done with the interrogation, would you mind scooting your butt over here? I'm not going to bite." He flashed a smile. "At least, not too hard."

But Emery didn't scoot. Her mind was too consumed with what she'd just learned. Gracie wasn't an Arrington. And if she wasn't an Arrington, then she had no rights to the final book in the Tender Heart series. She'd had no right to contact Emery. And no right to sell it. The only person with that right sat in the seat next to her. Which meant one thing.

Emery was in big trouble.

"Why couldn't women be more like horses? Rory wondered. Keep your horses well fed and offer them the occasional apple, and they were more than willing to let you saddle up."

CHAPTER FOURTEEN

"I CAN'T BELIEVE I TOOK A woman to a church and expected to get laid." Cole unwrapped the peppermint and held it out to Brandy. "Obviously, I've lost my mind. I didn't even think about where we were. All I could think about was how pretty Emery looked framed by the stained-glass window. She looked like an angel. An angel I just couldn't keep from touching."

Brandy munched on the hard candy and studied him with her big, soulful eyes. That was the nice thing about horses. They didn't condemn you . . . especially when you were feeding them sweets. Of course, Cole was doing enough condemning on his own.

"I just couldn't take it slow," he continued. "I just couldn't be satisfied with a few kisses. I just had to know what she had on under that skirt." He kicked at the dirt. "Damned horny fool!"

His loud voice and the flying dirt startled Brandy and she whinnied and skittered back. He instantly felt contrite. He needed to get a grip. Emery wasn't his girlfriend. She was just a woman passing through. And what happened that evening would make no difference in the long run.

Her life was in New York and his was . . . in turmoil. And he certainly didn't need to add a woman to his problems.

He clicked his tongue, and Brandy hesitantly walked back over. "I'm sorry, girl," he said. "I seem to have lost my touch with women and horses."

"Now that's a sad state of affairs."

This time, Cole was startled. And since he recognized the voice, he quickly jumped up from the hay bale he'd been sitting on and strode straight over to the stall where the voice had come from. Dirk was sprawled out on a blanket spread over a fresh pile of hay with his hands behind his head and the usual stupid smile on his face.

"Good evening," he said. "Or would that be good morning, seeing as it's well past midnight?"

"What the hell do you think you're doing?" Cole asked. Not only was he ticked that the man was sleeping in his barn, he was also ticked that Dirk had been privy to his private conversation with Brandy.

"I was planning on sleeping until some yahoo decided to flip the light on and have conversation with his horse." Dirk sat up and scratched his bare chest. "You do realize that sweets aren't exactly good for horses."

The gall of the man was so unbelievable that Cole had a hard time finding words. While he was searching, Dirk kept on talking, proving he'd heard every word of Cole's stupid yammering.

"So it sounds like you made more than one female a little skittish tonight. Which explains why you're prowling around like a hunting dog that's lost the scent."

The young pain in the butt had accurately hit the nail on the head. Cole had made Emery skittish. When they got in the truck she'd refused to sit next to him, and when he'd offered to give her a ride back to the motor lodge, she'd flat out refused and left with her friends. Which *was* exactly why he was prowling around like a dog that had lost the scent. But he'd be damned if he'd share that information with Dirk.

"You really are asking for a butt-kicking," Cole said. "First you conned my sister out of her car by bringing her chickens that I don't want or need, then you weaseled a dinner invitation from her so you could spend the entire night monopolizing the conversation, and now you think you can live in my barn. Well, you've got another think coming, kid." He jerked open the stall door.

Dirk took his sweet time getting to his feet. "I think you're stretching the truth a little. You need help around here and a car that you're not even using seems like a fair trade. And I didn't weasel an invitation from Gracie. She just happens to be friendlier than her brother. As for monopolizing the dinner conversation, I only did so because you sat there mooning over Emery and I figured you needed some help. And I don't plan on living in your barn." He scratched his chest. "Especially on an itchy wool blanket and poking hay."

Cole crossed his arms. "Then what are you doing here? You left with Emery, Carly, and Savannah."

Dirk shrugged. "Even the best laid plans can go awry." He grinned. "When I got back to my room at the motor lodge, the locks had been changed. I guess Mrs. Crawley got tired of waiting for me to pay my bill. So since I planned on painting the chicken coop first thing tomorrow anyway, I figured you wouldn't mind if I stayed the night—just until I get things worked out with Mrs. Crawley." He studied Cole for a minute. "But if that's too much to ask, I guess I could hitch a ride back to town and sleep with the girls. I'm sure Emery wouldn't mind sharing her tiny little bed."

Cole had never wanted to hit anything as badly as he

wanted to hit Dirk's face. The man had a way of turning every situation in his favor. Cole wasn't about to let him hitch a ride back into town and worm his way into Emery's bed. Not that Cole thought he could. He just wasn't willing to take the chance.

"Fine. Stay the night." He pointed a finger. "But once you paint that chicken coop, I want you out of here."

The annoying grin returned. "Sure thing. I wouldn't want to overstay my welcome."

Cole rolled his eyes. "You succeeded in doing that the moment you set foot on my property." He turned to leave, but Dirk stopped him.

"I think it's only fair to tell you that if you tried anything ungentlemanly with Emery, I'll be the one doing a little ass kicking. I've gotten kinda close to those sweet gals and I don't like the thought of Emery being taken advantage of."

He turned and cocked an eyebrow. "This coming from a man who takes advantage of every situation life hands him."

"I don't take advantage of women."

"Neither do I."

Dirk studied him, this time without the dopey smile. "Fair enough." Cole nodded and started for the door, when Dirk added. "She likes you. And it's obvious that you like her. So what's the problem, dude?"

It was pathetic how quickly three words made a difference in Cole's bad mood. He turned to Dirk. "She likes me? She told you that?"

The grin reappeared. "Man, you've got it bad. Yes, she likes you. And if you write a note asking her to go steady, I'll pass it to her during recess tomorrow."

"Don't be a wiseass," Cole said, but there was no anger in the words. Emery liked him. He moved closer. "So what did she say exactly?"

Dirk rolled his eyes. "She didn't say anything. She proved it the very first night she got into town by choosing a plow horse over a thoroughbred. She had the chance to get ice cream with me and chose to stay at the Watering Hole with you."

Cole should've been mad at the plow horse metaphor, but he ignored it and voiced his biggest concern. "That was just because she found out I own the ranch where Tender Heart was written. In fact, her infatuation with the story is the only reason she's been hanging out with me." Deep down, he hoped that Dirk would deny it and was disappointed when he didn't.

"You could be right. She does love that Tender Heart story. All of those women do. The other two were plenty pissed when they found out you took Emery to that church without them. You would've thought it was the Taj Mahal that they'd missed out on seeing, instead of a tiny white chapel with three dusty pews and a bunch of cobwebs."

Cole started to ask if Emery had said anything about what happened in the church when a thought struck him. "How do you know how many pews there are?"

Only a second passed before Dirk grinned. "Why, Emery told us. Carly and Savannah demanded all the details right down to the cobwebs." He placed a hand on his chest. "The last place this sinner wants to be is in church."

It made sense. And yet, he couldn't shake the feeling that Dirk was lying. Of course, what difference did it make if the drifter had been in the chapel? There was nothing to steal. But the uneasy feeling reminded him that he shouldn't trust the kid and had no business talking to him about Emery.

"One night," he said as he shut the stall door. "That's

all you get." He waited for some smart-assed remark, but Dirk remained silent while Cole put Brandy in her stall for the night. But after closing the door, he turned to see the annoying guy standing in the doorway of the opposite stall.

"What happened to Brandy to make her so skittish?" Dirk paused for just a moment before he went on. "It was the same accident that put Gracie in that wheelchair, wasn't it? That's why she doesn't like being around Brandy. She associates the horse with what happened."

"Give the man a star." Cole's voice dripped with sarcasm. "Now I'm going to bed." He walked to the light switches and turned off the lights. In the darkness, he followed the flood of moonlight to the open barn doors. He had almost reached them when Dirk spoke.

"You know that Gracie needs as much tending as Brandy does. The scars might be healed on the outside. But from what I can tell, there's still plenty on the inside."

Instead of replying, Cole stepped outside and pulled the barn doors closed. He hated Dirk for the feelings that clawed at his gut. But if he was truthful, he hated himself even more. All Dirk had done was point out the truth. Gracie did have scars. More scars than Cole was willing to acknowledge.

Knowing that there was no way he could go to sleep with his insides roiling, he walked down the same road he'd taken with Emery only hours earlier. But then he hadn't stopped at the bend in the road or the clearing on the left. In fact, he hadn't even looked at it. He'd kept his eyes straight ahead and his mind on Emery. But now he walked through the weeds and wild flowers to a huge hole in the ground. As he stared down at it, he allowed his mind to wander back to the events of that night.

Cole had just gotten home from Kentucky. With everything he'd learned on the thoroughbred horse ranch, he had big plans of how he and his father could implement the same business techniques here in Texas and turn the Arrington Ranch around. All they needed was a little capital. And they had that. Since Cole had started working, he and his father had been saving every spare penny in a joint account. They'd referred to it as the Arrington Dream Account. Even Gracie had contributed to the account with her barrel racing winnings.

That was why Cole had been so pissed off when his father told him the money was gone. If his father had spent it on more cattle or a chunk of land, Cole might've been able to forgive him. But he couldn't forgive him handing it over to the one woman Cole despised. Especially when Ava Arrington had made a fool of his father twice already. And his father never learned. Even at the expense of his son's dream. He just damned well never learned.

When he broke the news to Cole, he actually believed that Ava was going to pay him the money back with interest. His unfailing faith in a woman who had done nothing but disappoint was so ludicrous that Cole had exploded. He'd called his father all kinds of a fool. And when his father just stood there looking confused, Cole had wanted to hit him. He'd wanted to hit him until he woke the hell up.

Instead, Cole had gotten in his truck and torn out of the drive. He headed for the chapel, the one place where he hoped to find some solace for the hell his life had become. But he never reached the chapel. And he hadn't known what hell was until he saw Brandy, too late.

The scream, half human and half horse, still haunted his dreams, as did the sight of his sister flying through the air. She had landed in the same spot that Cole now stared at.

But back then a boulder had occupied the hole.

After the accident, his father had worked for days to dislodge the rock that Gracie had landed on. He wanted the reminder gone. It was much easier to blame a piece of stone than to blame his only son. But removing the boulder had been too much for his father's heart. Or maybe his father just couldn't live with what had happened. Either way, he had died in this clearing while Cole was at the hospital with Gracie. And now Cole wasn't just getting rid of a boulder. He was getting rid of the entire ranch.

Dirk was right. The internal scars took the longest to heal.

He stood staring down at the hole for only a moment more before he headed back to the house. The narrow line of light that framed Gracie's door didn't surprise him. Especially when she slept in most mornings. He tapped on the door before he turned the knob and peeked in. He expected her to be in bed reading or writing in her diary. Instead, she was sitting at her desk typing.

When she saw him, she started. "Cole!"

"Sorry," he said. "I didn't mean to startle you. Can I come in?"

She hesitated for so long he wondered if she'd heard him. But then she nodded. "Of course." She quickly gathered up the stack of papers on the desk and placed them in the top drawer. "So why are you still up? You're usually in bed long before me."

He grabbed the desk chair that had been shoved into one corner and brought it over to the desk. Once he was seated, he searched for the best way to start the conversation. When he couldn't find it, he settled for the straightforward truth.

"I'm selling the ranch to Zane, Gracie. I've already talked to him and he's willing to buy us out." Her face lost all color, but he refused to stop. "I know you don't want to leave, but you need to. You need to move on, and so do I."

"I don't want to move on, Cole. This is my home—your home."

He thumped his fist on the desk. "Damn it, Gracie, would you stop being so stubborn and see things for what they are? You're just like Daddy. If you love something, you refuse to see the truth. Daddy loved steak and refused to see it was bad for his heart. He loved this land and refused to see that he wasn't a good rancher. And he loved Mama and refused to see that she was never going to stay. He just stuck his head in the sand and ignored the truth. But I refuse to let you do that, Gracie Lynn. This place holds nothing but bad memories."

Tears shimmered in her eyes. "You're wrong, Cole. There were good memories. Lots of good memories, but all you seem to do is fixate on the bad. Maybe Daddy wasn't as good at ranching as his brothers. Maybe we didn't get new trucks and fancy jeans. But he was a good man who took me in when he didn't have to. And I know he wouldn't want you to sell this ranch. He wanted you to save it."

Cole jumped up from the chair. "Well, maybe I don't want to save it! Maybe I want to let it and all the bad memories die like Daddy!"

"No." She shook her head. "You can't mean that. You're just still grieving over Daddy's death and what happened to me. I get that you feel guilty for causing the accident, but I don't blame you, Cole. I never blamed you. You are my brother and I love you. But I swear if you make me leave, I'll blame you forever. This ranch is all I have left, and I'm not leaving it. Especially when I've found a way to save it."

He released his breath in a long sigh. "By fixing up old trucks?"

Her eyes sparkled. "No. By selling the final book in the Tender Heart series to Emery Wakefield."

"Etta didn't know what grabbed her attention more—the pretty chapel that was almost complete or the bare-chested man who had built it."

CHAPTER FIFTEEN

("

"HOLY CRAP! IT LOOKS JUST like the chapel in Tender Heart." Carly spoke so loudly that the birds in the trees took flight. Emery was about to tell her to keep it down, but of course Savannah took care of that for her.

"Would you lower your voice, Carly Sue?" Savannah glanced around. "Sweet Baby Jesus. First, I allow you to talk me into breaking and entering. And now I let you talk me into trespassing. If word of our nefarious activities on this trip ever gets back to Miles's mother, she'll have a stroke and I'll have a broken engagement." Her gaze returned to the chapel, and the look of awe on her face said it all. "But this does make the trip all worth it." She gave Emery a quick hug. "You did it, honey. You found a piece of Tender Heart."

Emery hooked her arms through Carly and Savannah's, and all three of them stared at the little white church with its stained-glass windows and tall spire. She had little doubt that they were all thinking of Tender Heart and the brides who had found their happily-ever-afters. This was proven when Carly spoke.

"It's seems like fate, doesn't it? I mean we became friends because of Tender Heart and now here we stand in front of the little white chapel where it all started."

"Why, Carly Sue Hanover, are you getting sentimental?" Savannah teased. "But you're right. It does seem like it was meant to be." She took their hands and made a circle. "Let's all make a wish that we end up as happy as the Tender Heart brides."

"I have no desire to get married," Carly said.

"Of course you do. Now stop being a party pooper and close your eyes."

Carly huffed but did as Savannah instructed. And Emery did as well. As soon as her eyes were closed, an image of Cole popped into her head. An image of him carrying her out the doors of the chapel amid a shower of rice. She quickly opened her eyes as Carly pulled them toward the chapel.

"Come on. Let's go inside."

Emery held back. "Maybe Savannah is right. Maybe we should wait until Cole invites us." It didn't feel wrong bringing her friends to the chapel, but it did feel wrong to step inside without permission. Unfortunately, Carly was too stubborn to pay attention.

"Are you kidding? I traveled hundreds of miles to see some remnant of Tender Heart, and now that I've finally found it, I'm not leaving until I've seen the entire attraction." She released their hands and climbed the steps. "Besides, if they wanted to keep people out, they'd lock the door." She pushed it open.

Savannah glanced at Emery and shrugged. "Maybe I'll just take a quick peek." She hurried in after Carly.

Emery stood at the bottom of the steps and finally admitted to herself that it wasn't the thought of trespassing that bothered her as much as the thought of stepping into the building where she had done something really stupid. And she couldn't decide if the stupid thing was letting Cole touch her, or stopping him before she'd been thoroughly touched.

Savannah and Carly's bickering voices drifted out the door. If she didn't want bloodshed, Emery needed to intervene. She walked in to find Savannah chastising Carly.

"You most certainly did say a cuss word in the house of the Lord. I'm surprised God hasn't struck you down with a bolt of lightning by now."

Carly snorted. "*Damn* is not a cuss word. It's an expression of surprise. And I'm sure it's in the Bible. God damned a lot of people."

"Don't you dare take the Lord's name in vain, Carly Sue. Especially in His own house."

"Let's talk about taking the Lord's name in vain, shall we . . . Sweet Baby Jesus?"

"That is not taking the Lord's name in vain," Savannah said. "I learned that from my mama." She lifted a hand. "God rest her soul. Mama was the most devout Christian woman you'd ever want to meet. We are not blaspheming when we say that. We are merely asking Jesus to help with whatever shocking situation made us say it."

Carly squeezed her eyes shut for a second before she looked at Emery. "It's hopeless, you know? There's just no reasoning with that kind of logic."

Emery laughed. "Which is exactly why we love her."

"You, maybe." When Savannah's face registered hurt, Carly quickly recanted. "I'm kidding. I love you, crazy thinking and all." She glanced around. "So this isn't exactly what I expected after seeing the outside. This place needs an entire team of mini-maids." She looked up and froze. "Are those spider webs?"

Despite being so tough, Carly had a major fear of spiders. The sight of one tiny spider could turn her into a squealing girlie girl in a hurry. Which is why Emery quickly tried to alleviate her fears.

"I'm sure they're old webs and the spiders that made them are long gone."

Savannah ran a hand along the back of a pew. "Would you look at the craftsmanship of this? Antique pews make the most gorgeous benches for dining tables or large foyers." She leaned down to examine the maker's stamp on the back of the pew. "In fact, I would love to get my hands on these for the shop. I wonder if Cole would sell them."

"No!" Emery spoke a little too loudly and emphatically. She blushed when both Carly and Savannah looked at her. "I mean they belong here. They're part of the chapel. It's a shame that all the other ones have been taken."

"Emery's right," Carly said. "The pews should stay. And someone should put a lock on the door so these don't disappear too. This chapel isn't just a fictional icon, it's a piece of history that needs to be preserved."

"I guess you're right." Savannah stopped coveting the pew and walked up to the altar. "Remember how Reverend Flanders stood here for all the weddings?" She motioned with her left hand. "And the grooms stood here? All the heroes had stars in their eyes when they watched their brides come down the aisle." She got a dreamy look on her face. "And this summer it will be me walking down the aisle."

Emery was close enough to hear Carly talking under her breath. "And making the biggest mistake of your life."

"What was that?" Savannah asked.

Emery shot Carly a warning look and quickly amended. "Nothing. Carly just said that she hopes she doesn't make a mistake when she walks down the aisle as your bridesmaid."

Savannah immediately looked worried. "You don't know how to walk down an aisle, Carly? Why didn't you say something before?" She flapped her hands. "Let's practice now so I can see how much work we have to do."

Carly shook her head. "I'll practice at your rehearsal."

"Oh, come on," Emery said. "It will be fun." She moved up the aisle and stood next to Savannah. "You can pretend you're a Tender Heart bride, and I'll be the groom with the stars in my eyes."

Carly exhaled. "Fine. But I'm not kissing you. I kissed a girl once, and I didn't like it."

"You did?" Savannah asked. "And you never once shared that information with us?"

"Unlike you, Savannah, I don't share everything." Carly moved to the end of the aisle and held her hands in front of her like she was carrying a bouquet. "Okay, let's get this foolishness over with."

Savannah started to hum the "Wedding March," and Emery couldn't help but laugh when Carly just walked straight down the aisle toward them. Savannah stopped humming.

"No. No. No. You're supposed to pause between steps. Now go back and start over." When Carly just glared at her, she clapped her hands. "I mean it. I don't want you embarrassing me in front of Miles's family. Now try again. It's step, pause, step, pause."

Grudgingly, Carly returned to the end of the aisle. She took a step and paused just like Savannah had instructed, then she took another step and paused. Except this pause was much longer than the last. When Emery noticed the moving black dot on Carly's arm, she understood why. The high-pitched scream and wild dance that followed verified what the dot was.

Carly swatted and slapped at her hair, then she jerked

off her shirt and slapped and swatted some more. She was such a tornado of motion that it took Emery a moment to react. Before she could, the door to the chapel burst open and Zane Arrington strode in. In her panicked state, Carly ran right into him.

"Get it off!" she screamed as she continued to slap. "Get the spider off!"

Zane looked confused for only a second before he reacted. Like he was wrangling a steer, he pulled Carly to him and pinned down her flailing arms with one arm while he quickly and thoroughly ran his hand over her body.

At that point, Emery should've hurried over to help her friend. But she was too stunned by the scene that played out before her eyes. With the chapel as the backdrop and Zane looking so much like Duke Earhart, it was like watching a scene from Tender Heart where the hero rescued the heroine.

Savannah must've felt the same way because she sighed. "Oh my."

Finally, Zane plucked something from Carly's hair and then stomped his foot on the floor. But when he lifted his boot, there was no squashed spider.

"I killed it, sweetheart," he said. "It's dead and there's not any more."

Carly stopped in mid-squeak and spoke into Zane's chest. "You promise there aren't any more?"

"On my grandma's grave."

Carly finally stepped back. When she looked at Zane, her face turned bright red and she quickly crossed her arms over her bra. "Thanks." Her gaze swept over to Emery and Savannah. "Especially since my two best friends were no help."

Zane took off his cowboy hat and smiled. "No problem.

I never mind saving a damsel in distress. Even if it's only from a tiny ol' spider."

Carly's expression darkened, and Emery had little doubt that she was about to set Zane straight about her being a damsel in distress. But before she could, Savannah jumped in.

"Yes, Carly is just our little damsel," she said with a smirk in her voice. "Why, she can't even tie her shoes without help."

While Carly glared at Savannah, Zane reached down and picked up her shirt and handed it to her. "Nothing wrong with making a man feel needed." He winked at her, completely unaware of the viperous look she sent him before she jerked her shirt on. He turned to Emery. "So what are you girls doing here in this dusty old chapel?"

"We were just looking around." Emery stepped down from the altar. "I hope you don't mind."

"I don't have a problem with it. Just don't let my sister catch you. She's been very attached to the chapel lately. I was going to send some hands to clean it up, and she flat out refused." He glanced around and shook his head. "I guess she wants it to look like her room. Which was a bone of contention between her and Rachel before Rachel—" He paused as if he'd said more than he should've. "Anyway, you can look around all you want." He glanced back at Carly. "Just stay away from those itsy-bitsy spiders. That scream almost knocked me off Indigo."

He tipped his hat, then strode out the door as quickly as he had walked in. When he was gone, Carly turned to Emery.

"Who is that?"

"That's Zane Arrington's, Cole's cousin," Emery said. "I'm sorry I didn't introduce you. Your spider dance distracted me."

"I did not dance. I never dance."

"You were dancing then." Savannah hurried to the door and peeked out. "Sweet Baby Jesus," she breathed. "It is Indigo." Emery and Carly joined her in the doorway.

Zane was leaving on a beautiful black stallion that restlessly snorted as Zane wheeled him around and guided him through the trees. Not only did the horse look like Duke's horse in Tender Heart and have the same name, but the brand on the calf that was roped to the saddle horn was an E inside a heart.

"Holy shit," Carly said, and this time Savannah didn't correct her. She only sighed.

"I wish I had been the one the spider dropped on. I wouldn't have minded being pressed against Duke's bulging muscles." She waited until Zane had disappeared from sight before she turned to Carly. "What did it feel like having his hands run all over you? Were they strong and calloused like Duke's?"

Carly shrugged. "To be honest, I was too scared to notice." But the pink in her cheeks said otherwise, and Savannah wasn't about to let it go.

"You tell that to someone else." She smiled slyly. "I saw the sexual awareness on your face. And I don't blame you. If I weren't a promised woman, I'd be a little flustered myself by such virility."

"I was not flustered by the man," Carly said. "I was flustered by the damned spider."

"Which is a good thing," Emery said. "Because Zane is married."

Carly looked at her. "He is?"

Savannah laughed. "See, you were flustered. As flustered as Emery gets every time she looks at Cole."

Emery didn't argue. Cole did fluster her. But it was time to put her infatuation behind her and move on to the real reason she'd come to Bliss.

"Come on," she said. "I need to stop by Cole's ranch."

When they reached Arrington Ranch, Emery wasn't surprised to find Cole's truck gone. On their way out of town, she'd noticed it parked at Emmett's garage. Which was the reason she wanted to stop by and talk with Gracie. She wanted to make sure that she had talked to her brother. If she hadn't, Emery planned on talking to him herself. It was time to drop the pretenses.

"What's Dirk doing here?" Carly asked as Emery parked in front.

"He appears to be painting the chicken coop," Savannah answered. "I swear that boy has more hats than the Kentucky Derby. I don't think there's anything he can't do."

"Including seducing women," Carly said. "It looks like he has Gracie's heart all tied in a bow."

Emery finally noticed Gracie sitting in her wheelchair by the chicken coop. Even from that distance, the girl looked totally infatuated. Her gaze didn't stray from Dirk as he put his paintbrush down and stepped out of the coop.

"Perfect timing," he said as soon as they got out of the car. "I was just finishing up and need a ride back into town."

"I told you that you can take my car, Dirk," Gracie said. "You've certainly earned it."

Dirk sent her a stern look. "Now don't you let me off that easy, Miss Gracie. I've got a fair amount of work left to do before I earn that car. I'll be back tomorrow." He turned to Emery. "Let me just clean my paintbrush and I'll be right with you."

"No hurry," Emery said. "I need to talk with Gracie, anyway."

"And I want to get another look at that smoker." Carly

headed toward the barn.

Dirk winked at Savannah. "Which means that it's just you and me, Miss Georgia. Do you like chickens?"

Savannah lifted a perfectly shaped eyebrow. "Only with dumplings and gravy. I'll be content sitting right there on the porch."

Dirk laughed as he walked back to the coop to get his paintbrush.

Emery glanced at Gracie. "Could we talk inside?"

"Sure." Gracie wheeled up the ramp.

Once they were sitting in the sparsely furnished living room, Emery wasted no time getting to the point of her visit. "Why didn't you tell me that you and Cole are half siblings?"

Gracie's eyes widened, and she quickly looked down at her lap. "Because I didn't think it made a difference."

"It makes a lot of difference, Gracie. If you're not an Arrington, you have no right to sell the book. Only Cole has that right."

Her gaze lifted. "But I was the one who found it, and when I showed him the book, he didn't even look at it before he tossed it in the trash."

Emery's heart sank. "He tossed it in the trash? Didn't you tell him how much it's worth?"

"He didn't give me time to tell him. And I'm starting to wonder if it even matters. He doesn't want anything to get in the way of him selling the ranch and leaving Bliss."

Emery was shocked. But then she realized she shouldn't be. He'd given her numerous hints. She'd just been too wrapped up in getting her hands on the book to pay close attention. And maybe it wasn't just that. Maybe, deep down, she didn't want to believe that Cole would live anywhere else. It would be like Rory selling the Earhart Ranch and leaving Tender Heart. It was wrong. All wrong.

"But Cole can't sell the ranch. This is his home. His heritage." She paused. "This is his Tender Heart."

Tears glistened in Gracie's eyes. "That's exactly what I told him, but he doesn't believe anymore, Emery. He doesn't believe in Tender Heart. And he doesn't believe in himself." She rolled closer and took Emery's hands. "I contacted you to help me sell the book so I could save Lucy's home, but now I'm asking you to help me save my brother. Save him, Emery. Save him from himself."

"It had been a mistake to put the ad in the newspaper and invite ten women into Rory's Garden of Eden . . . ten women and a tempting, lying snake who went by the name of Etta Jenkins."

CHAPTER SIXTEEN

T HE WRENCH SLIPPED FROM COLE'S fingers and hit the cement floor with a loud clang. But it was no louder than the string of cuss words that followed. He had thought he was alone, but Emmett's laughter indicated otherwise.

"Well, it sounds like someone didn't get their cup of coffee today."

Cole duck out from underneath the hood of the Pontiac and glowered at his boss. "I had my coffee—if that's what you call the thick sludge you make every morning."

Emmett tapped his chest. "It puts hair on your chest. Although it hasn't really worked for you, has it?" He grinned and limped over. "So if it's not lack of caffeine that has your tail feathers up, what does? Is it that good-looking woman who lost her wallet? Rumor has it that you've been sniffin' after her like she's a dog in heat. And I figure that's why you took yesterday off."

Since his foul mood did have to do with Emery, Cole didn't reply as he got down to retrieve his wrench from beneath the car. Of course, that didn't stop Emmett from continuing.

"I guess it's hard on the young men in this town that there's such slim pickings. And even harder on you Arrington boys, since most of the good-looking females are related to you." He chuckled. "Your cousin Becky was in yesterday with her dirt bike. I guess she broke an axle trying to jump the ditch out on Woodpecker Lane."

Cole got to his feet and continued to work. "That girl is going to kill herself if she's not careful."

"She is a bit of a daredevil . . . and one helluva mechanic. I told her to leave the motorcycle and I'd have you look at it today, but she just asked to borrow some tools and went about fixing it herself." He paused, then shook his head. "It's a shame Gracie can't go dirt bike riding with her anymore. How's she doing?"

"Fine." It was a lie. Gracie wasn't fine. She was no doubt devastated because Cole had refused to go along with her new harebrained scheme. But she'd had no business sending a letter to a publishing house. Especially when there was little doubt that the book was a fake. His relatives had scoured the house after Lucy had passed away looking for the final manuscript and had found nothing. Whatever Gracie had found was probably just the first draft of one of Lucy's other novels.

Still, he shouldn't have yelled at her and tossed the stack of paper in the trash without even looking at it. But he had been pissed. Pissed that his sister wouldn't give up on her quest to save the ranch. And pissed that she had come up with a bizarre plan centered around a series Cole was starting to hate. But most of all, he was pissed at himself for having the same susceptibility as his father to deceitful women.

Emery wasn't an English teacher who came to town looking for clues to the final Tender Heart book. She was a crafty editor who thought she'd already found it. An editor who was willing to use her feminine wiles on a hick cowboy who caved at the first bat of her eyelashes. Which explained why she suddenly became so friendly when she found out who he was. It also explained why she wanted to take things slow. She was willing to share a few kisses to get the book for her publishing house, but she wasn't willing to have sex for it.

He bit back a cuss word as Emmett continued to ramble.

"I don't know if fine is an accurate description for Gracie," Emmett said. "That girl hasn't been fine since the accident. It's obvious she needs more time to heal. And I'm not talking about her body. The physical healing doesn't take long, but the mental part sure as hell does. After I got back from Vietnam, it didn't take more than a year for my body to accept the loss of my leg and heal. But my mind took a lot longer. Joanna's love and patience was the only thing that got me through it."

Cole had a lot of love for his sister, but his patience had run out. He was tired of her schemes. It was time for her to accept the fact that he was selling the ranch and they were moving. Once they were in Kentucky, her mind could start healing . . . and hopefully his too.

"Love and patience," Emmett continued. "That's what Gracie needs right now—that and the occasional kick in the butt."

Cole shot a glance over at him. "Excuse me?"

Emmett laughed. "I don't mean literally. But sometimes when something tragic has happened to you, you get to feeling sorry for yourself. That's when you need a swift kick from a hard ass to get you moving again. And you're not much of a hard ass with Gracie. Otherwise, she'd be going to her physical therapist, and at least making the effort to walk again."

"She's been through enough. She doesn't need me bullying her."

"I'm not talking about bullying, Cole. I'm talking about pushing her just enough to get her motivated." A click of heels on cement had Emmett's head turning. "Well, hello. Emery, isn't it? Just like the board Joanna uses to file her nails."

Cole froze, and his hand tightened on the wrench. He wasn't ready to see her again. He was still too ticked off. Unfortunately, he didn't have much choice. He wasn't about to hide and act like what she'd done made any difference to him. He had given her enough. He refused to give her any more. He set down the wrench and moved from beneath the hood.

Emery stood in the open bay door, the late afternoon sun casting her features in shadow and her chestnut hair in burnished red. She wore faded jeans today and a loose top that fluttered in the breeze.

"I hope I'm not interrupting," she said, never taking her eyes off of Cole.

"Not at all." Emmett hobbled toward the office door. "Cole was just going to take a break, and I was just going to go over some receipts." He stepped inside the office and closed the door.

When he was gone, Emery moved out of the sunlight. Her expression was solemn, her eyes unsure. "If you're busy, I could come back."

Cole pulled a rag from his back pocket and wiped his hands, but didn't answer. She shuffled her feet, then glanced at the radio sitting on the worktable.

"Do you like country music? I didn't used to like it, but Savannah got me hooked on it. She adores all the old country singers and used to play Hank Williams, Johnny

Cash, Loretta Lynn, and Patsy Cline so loudly in our college dorm that people were repeatedly calling the campus police."

"Would that be the same college where you got your teaching degree?" he asked snidely.

Her gaze lowered to the floor. "I didn't say I was a teacher."

"You didn't deny it." He flung down the rag, no longer caring about holding his temper. "Just like you didn't deny being a tourist."

Her chin came up. "I am a tourist. I've been wanting to come to Bliss ever since I read the series."

"But that's not the reason you're here now. You're here because my sister sent you a letter about the final book in the series and you think you're going to make millions."

She laughed. "Obviously, you don't know very much about publishing. I'm not going to make anything on the book. I'll be lucky to get a bonus. I'm here because I think your sister has found the final book in a series that millions of people love. And yes, I want to be involved in getting that book on the bookshelves. But not for money. I want to do it because I'm one of the millions of people who love the series. And I want Tender Heart to have an ending."

"So you're telling me that it's all about your love of the story. Is that what you want me to believe?" He didn't wait for an answer. "Then you're lying to yourself. You might love the series, but you didn't travel hundreds of miles just for the love of a story. If you're not here for money, then you're here for fame. Once word gets out that the last book in the series has been found, the entire town of Bliss will be flooded with camera crews and reporters, along with every rabid Tender Heart fan in the world. And you'll be right in the center of it." He leaned closer.

"If that happens, I'm going to sue the hell out of you and your publishing house. I won't have my sister scrutinized by a bunch of media hounds looking for a story. Especially since the book is a fake."

"And just what makes you think that?"

"Because after Lucy died, the search was on for the last book. I was raised on stories about all the crazy places my grandfathers, grandmothers, great-aunts, great-uncles, and cousins searched for the book. And I'm not just talking about the buildings. I'm talking about digging holes all over the property. And not one page was found." He tipped his head. "And yet you believe that, over fifty years later, a young woman in a wheelchair stumbled upon it. Where did she say she found it? The attic? The hayloft?"

"Gracie didn't tell me where she found it. But just because something doesn't seem likely doesn't mean it can't happen. Maybe Lucy hid the book in a place that no one thought to look. Houses have lots of nooks and crannies, especially old ones."

"As a kid, I played in those nooks and crannies, and I never found anything that looked like a manuscript."

Emery shrugged. "Then maybe Gracie didn't find it in the house. Maybe she found it in the barn . . . or the chapel. I don't know. But what I do know is that it's not a fake."

Cole laughed. "Because Gracie told you? Did you ever think she might be lying?"

"Why would she do that?"

"Because I'm selling the ranch, and she would do anything to keep me from selling it. Including coming up with a fake manuscript. Now if you'll excuse me, I have work to do." He ducked under the hood and acted like he was working, but when Emery was around there was no concentrating on anything but her.

Especially when she came and stood right next to him. The heat of her body seemed to wrap around him like a warm fire on a chilly evening and the citrusy scent of her shampoo filled his head with each breath. She stood there so long, he actually started to sweat from the tight reins he held on himself. Then she finally spoke, her voice low and filled with conviction.

"I've spent my life reading and rereading the Tender Heart series. I studied it in college and did my senior thesis paper on it. I know Lucy Arrington's writing inside and out. And she wrote the first chapter I read. I'd stake my reputation on it. But if you'd like to get a second opinion, that's fine with me."

He came out from beneath the hood. "I don't want a second opinion. I want you to get the hell out of town and forget the book."

Her eyes widened. "But why? Don't you understand what this could mean to you? To your entire family? The advance alone could help you keep the ranch. You wouldn't have to move. You and Gracie could live in Bliss forever."

"I don't want to live in Bliss forever!" He moved toward her. "I can barely stand to live here for one more second. You don't understand what it was like to have to grow up with the entire world holding you to a standard that can only be achieved by a fictional character." He tapped his chest. "I'm not Rory Earhart. I'm not some hero who can rope a steer at full gallop, shoot a gun out of a rustler's hand, or turn a few cows into the biggest cattle ranch in Texas. I'm Cole Arrington. My mom left me when I was five, my dad didn't know shit about raising cattle, and I put my sister in a wheelchair because I was pissed that my dad could never get over loving my deadbeat mother." He cocked his head. "Now does that sound like a hero to you?"

He expected her to run out of the garage and never look back. He did not expect her to stand there with tears shimmering in her beautiful green eyes. Nor did he expect her to absolve him.

"Heroes aren't perfect, Cole. They're just ordinary men who do the best that they can. If you'd read the entire series, you'd know that Rory made his share of mistakes."

"I don't believe he paralyzed his only sister."

"And I don't believe that you did either."

He should've left it at that, but he couldn't seem to do it. "You would if you'd seen her twisted body after Brandy threw her when my truck almost ran into them."

Once the truth was out, the world seemed to stop for a heartbeat. The radio continued to play, but all Cole heard was Emery's heavy silence. A tear slid down her cheek. Sympathy was the last thing he wanted. He didn't need sympathy from a liar. And yet, when she walked over and wrapped her arms around him, he didn't move a muscle to stop her.

"Oh, Cole." Her cheek pressed against his thumping heart. "I didn't realize . . . I didn't know. But it was an accident. You can't blame yourself."

He held his body rigid, fighting the need to hold her close and never let go. "No it wasn't. I was going too fast. If I had been going slower, I wouldn't have spooked Brandy. And the funny thing about it is that Gracie never once blamed me. She never once hated me for ruining her life that night. She might not be my dad's blood, but she's more like him than I am. When she loves you, she can forgive anything."

Emery pulled back. Tears had made wet tracks down her cheeks. The sight caused his heart to tighten with a need he had no business feeling. A need for the happily-ever-after that seemed to elude his family. "If she can forgive you, why can't you forgive yourself?" Her hands came up and cradled his face. "Just forgive yourself, Cole." She kissed him. It was just a soft brush, but the comfort and caring in her warm lips almost sent him to his knees.

"Don't," he said, but he didn't mean it, not when at the same time he was pulling her in for a deeper kiss.

She tasted like redemption. And once he started kissing her, he couldn't seem to stop. In her arms, he felt like he could lasso a steer at a full gallop. Or shoot a gun from an outlaw's hand. Or make his ranch something to be proud of. Was this how his father had felt with his mother? Was this how he had ended up such a broken man, he had fallen for all the lies? Emery wasn't interested in him. She was interested in Tender Heart. And Cole needed to remember that.

He pushed her away. "Go home, Emery. Go back to New York where you belong and leave us Arringtons to our own sad endings."

She stood there staring at him for what felt like forever before she turned and walked away. He watched as she climbed into her rental car and backed out. Before she pulled away, she gave him one last look that punched him in the gut and made a lump form in his throat. At that moment, he had two choices. He could accept the truth and move on, or he could give into his desires and make a fool of himself.

He turned away from Emery and pulled the cellphone from his pocket. As soon as his cousin answered, he didn't waste any time getting to the point. "Hey, Zane. It's Cole. Is there any way we can get the sale contract written up today?"

"Etta didn't say a word when Rory confronted her with the lie. She just stared back at him with tears brimming in her beautiful eyes. And darned if he didn't cave faster than a weak roof in a rainstorm."

CHAPTER SEVENTEEN

OF ALL THE ARRINGTON RANCHES, Zane's Earhart Ranch was the most similar to its fictional counterpart. The sprawling ranch-style house with the wraparound porch had been built in the early 1900s and had been the epicenter of the Arrington ranches since then. With a deal of the cards, Zane's father had ended up with it. But Cole viewed it more as fate. While Raff's and Cole's dads had clung to the "cowboy way of life" their forefathers had believed in, Zane's dad had changed with the times. From livestock head gates to cattle feed trucks, everything on the Earhart Ranch was the newest, most innovative equipment. And Cole would've given his right arm for the horses in the large stables. Becky rode up on one of those horses as soon as Cole climbed out of his truck.

"Hey, Cole!" She swung down from the huge white stallion before the animal had even come to a dust-spitting halt. "What are you doing here?"

Since Cole wanted to be the first one to break the news to Gracie that the sale was final, he kept his answer brief and vague. "I have some business with Zane." Unfortunately, Becky was a little too smart for her wranglers.

"You're talking to Zane about selling your ranch, aren't you? Gracie texted me this morning." She patted the horse's neck. "I wish we could figure out a way to keep you here. First Raff leaves, and now you and Gracie. Not only am I losing all my cousins, but my kids aren't going to have any cousins to play with either."

"I'm sure Zane will have plenty of kids to play with your kids."

She glanced at the house and spoke under her breath. "Are you kidding? Miss Priss wouldn't mess up her body with a kid—something my brother has yet to figure out."

Since Cole wasn't about to get into that can of worms, he moved on to another subject. "New horse?"

"I got him from a ranch outside of Austin. What do you think?"

Cole tried to get a closer look, but the animal was having none of it. He jerked the reins from Becky and would've bolted if Cole hadn't grabbed the reins and held firm. "Easy, boy. No one's going to hurt you." He waited for the horse to stop fidgeting before he stepped closer and gently stroked his withers until he calmed down. "That's it. Just relax." The horse released a heavy breath and settled.

"Okay, so he's a little high-strung," Becky said. "But you can't deny that he's a beauty. You could borrow him, you know? I wouldn't even charge you a stud fee. His offspring could be the start of your thoroughbred horse ranch."

He grinned. "Thanks, cuz, but it's not going to work. I'm still leaving."

"Even if it will break Gracie's heart?"

"Even then. But I want to thank you for watching out for Gracie. You've been a good friend to her."

She shrugged. "She's been a good friend to me too. I don't know what I'll do when I don't have her to bitch to about Cruella Deville." She glanced at the house, and her eyes narrowed. "With Gracie gone, another Arrington could end up in jail. Unless I can figure out a way to plan the perfect crime."

Before Cole had to answer, Zane pulled up in his truck and spooked the horse. Cole pushed Becky out of the way of flying hooves just in time and reined in the horse. Zane hopped out and immediately started in on his sister.

"Damn it, Becky! I thought I told you not to ride that horse until we get him broke in."

"Ghost Rider is broken in. He's just high-spirited." She took the reins from Cole and hopped up in the saddle. The horse immediately started to fidget and prance, but Becky kept a good seat as she wheeled him toward the corral.

Zane shook his head. "I swear she is going to be the death of me—or herself." He motioned for Cole. "Come on inside. I haven't gotten a chance to work on the bill of sale, but it shouldn't take me long to write something up. I'll have the money transferred into your account by the end of the week."

Cole wasn't worried about the money. He was more worried about how Gracie was going to take it once she found out. She was going to fight the reins as much as Becky's horse. But in the end, she would have to give in. There was no other choice. He followed Zane up the front steps.

The inside of Zane's house was a far cry from the rustic outside. Rachel had just recently redecorated the entire house. Now it looked like it should be in a women's magazine. It was so perfect with its designer furniture, expensive knickknacks, and gleaming wood floors that

Cole was afraid to move or touch anything.

"Should I take off my boots?" he asked.

Zane tossed his hat onto a hook. "No. Rachel tried putting one of those stupid signs by the door that asked folks to remove their shoes, but she took it down when Becky completely ignored it and I kept forgetting to do it. I can understand it if you live by the beach and wear flip-flops, but cowboy boots are too damned hard to get off and on."

Cole still hesitated. "Where is Rachel?"

"She's in Austin again. If it's not one charity board meeting, it's another."

It was no secret that Rachel spent a lot of time out of town serving on her charity boards, while Zane stayed in Bliss and worked the ranch. It seemed like a strange marital situation to Cole. Of course, what did he know about the perfect marriage? All he had to go on was his father's bad one.

"Did you want something to eat?" Zane headed for the kitchen. "I'm starving." He was always starving. In high school, he could put away an entire large five-topping pizza all by himself. Cole followed, but he wasn't hungry. Ever since Emery had walked away, his stomach hurt like hell. Or maybe it was his heart that hurt.

The kitchen was one of those high-tech chef's kitchens with a multi-burner stove, double ovens, and a refrigerator the size of a small shed. Surprisingly, the huge refrigerator had very little in it.

"Well, damn," Zane said as he stared at the empty shelves. "Our housekeeper and cook quit last week and Rachel must've forgotten to go to the store before she left."

"Loretta quit? But she's worked for your family for years."

"I know. She was like a second mom to me and Becky." He grabbed the last two bottles of water out of the refrigerator and handed one to Cole. "She was getting up there in age, but I think she would've stayed if not for Becky and Rachel's constant squabbling. I swear those two can fight over anything."

Cole didn't have any doubts who started the fights. Rachel had always been soft-spoken and rather shy, while Becky was as high-strung as her stallion. But he knew underneath all that sass was a heart of gold, which made him wonder why she had never warmed up to Rachel. Was there something about Zane's wife that Cole hadn't caught? Or was Becky just jealous about having to share her brother? The latter seemed likely. Everyone knew how much she idolized Zane. Sort of like Gracie used to idolize Cole.

"Well, it looks like Becky and I will be eating at the Watering Hole tonight." Zane unscrewed the cap of his water and drank half of it before continuing. "Which means I'll have a choice of a burned burger or an under-cooked Brat."

"Or greasy Buffalo wings," Cole said. "Remember it's Twofer Tuesday Drink and Wing night."

"Great." Zane headed through the kitchen and back to his office.

While the rest of the house was newly decorated, Zane's office looked much the way it had when Cole's uncle had lived in the house. A huge stone fireplace covered one wall, bookshelves another, and comfortable leather chairs sat in front of a large desk. The only new additions were a flat screen television over the fireplace and John Wayne movie posters on the walls. Zane was a diehard Wayne fan. Unlike Cole, Zane had read the entire Tender Heart series and loved Duke Earhart—the character his aunt had patterned after her favorite western movie star.

"Looks like you added to your collection since I was

last here." Cole took one of the chairs in front of the desk and unscrewed the cap of his water. "What possessed you to get *The Quiet Man*? I mean, Wayne was great in it, but I thought you preferred his westerns."

Zane glanced at the framed poster. "Rachel got it for me for my birthday. It's the only John Wayne movie she likes—something about a rain-drenched kiss." He looked back at Cole and rolled his eyes. "Women. I will never understand them. That's why I gave up trying years ago." He took the chair behind the desk, then finished off his water and tossed the bottle into the trashcan. He leaned back and looked at Cole. "So why are you in such a hurry to finalize the sale? I thought you didn't need to be in Kentucky until June."

"I don't. But I thought it would be best to get the paperwork done. That way Gracie won't be coming up with any more harebrained ideas to save the ranch."

"She just wants to do whatever she can to stay, Cole." When Cole didn't say anything, Zane nodded. "Okay, I get it. No one can talk you out of leaving. So what idea has Gracie come up with now? I kind of liked the idea of restoring the old trucks. I wouldn't mind buying one of our granddad's old trucks for Becky's birthday—anything to keep her away from skittish stallions and motorcycles."

"I wouldn't mind restoring a truck for Becky if I were staying. But this scheme doesn't have to do with restoring old trucks." Cole took a drink of his water before he dropped the bomb. "Gracie claims she's found the final book in the Tender Heart series."

Zane's eyebrows lifted. "You're kidding?"

Cole shook his head. "Nope. She even went so far as to contact an editor at a publishing house—Emery." It was a struggle to even say her name, especially when he had spent the last few hours trying to forget it.

His office chair squeaked as Zane sat up. "Emery's an editor? But I thought she was a Tender Heart fan. I found her and her friends in the chapel the other day."

The fact that Emery and her friends had trespassed only added to Cole's anger. "That's what she claimed, but it turns out she's a New York editor who wants to make a name for herself by exploiting my little sister."

It had always annoyed Cole just how levelheaded Zane was. Especially when Cole was still so pissed off. Instead of backing him up, he sat there for a few minutes, as if digesting the information, before he spoke. "It sounds to me like Gracie was doing her own exploiting." When Cole shot him an annoyed look, he shrugged. "You did say that Gracie was the one who contacted Emery, not the other way around."

"But it was Emery who wasn't truthful about why she was here."

"Maybe she was just trying to get the lay of the land. You know as well as I do that there have been plenty of people over the years claiming that they've found the last book in the series. Maybe Emery just wanted to make sure it wasn't another hoax."

He jumped up from the chair, sloshing water on his shirt. "She wasn't being careful. She was being deceitful. She spent an entire evening at my house, ate my food, and enjoyed my hospitality. Hell, I even took her to the chapel. And she never said a word about the real reason she had come to Bliss."

Zane studied him before he squinted his eyes. "So are you pissed because she's an editor or because you like her and she lied to you?"

"I don't like her!"

Zane tipped back his head and laughed. "Right. Just like you didn't like Sara Caudwell in high school, and yet you couldn't seem to keep your hands off her. When she moved away, you moped around for an entire week."

"I had strep throat."

"You had lovesickness."

"Ha! That's just plain crazy." He paced in front of the fireplace. "And even if I did love Sara, I certainly don't love Emery."

"Maybe not, but you do like her. I figured that out at the Watering Hole the first night I saw you two together. And I get that you're upset about her not being truthful with you. But that's business, Cole. My daddy always taught me that in business deals, it's always best to keep your cards close to the vest. It seems to me that's all Emery was doing."

Cole really wanted to argue, but damned if he could. Zane was right. Emery had just been doing her job. Which was why he was so pissed off. He didn't want to be part of her job. He'd thought that she liked him as much as he liked her. The truth was that she'd just been using him to get to Gracie . . . and the book. But that wasn't Emery's fault. It was Cole's. He should've never let his heart be in charge of his head.

He stopped pacing and glanced up at the poster of John Wayne as Big Jake. "I wish you were more like Raff. I could always count on him to agree with me whenever I was ticked off about something. In fact, he always had a good plan for revenge."

"Because he's a hothead—which is exactly how he landed in jail. He just doesn't think before he reacts." Zane paused. "So I guess Emery was pretty upset when she discovered that there was no final book."

"That's the thing." He turned back to him. "There is a book."

Zane's eyes widened. "What?"

Cole moved back over to the desk and sat down. "Gracie did find a book, and Emery is convinced that it was written by our great-aunt."

"But you don't think so?"

"It's doubtful. You and I both know that every inch of Arrington land has been searched for that book. It makes no sense that Gracie could have stumbled upon it. And even if by some twist of fate she did find the final book, it's not going to make a difference to us. All the royalties from Lucy's books go to the state libraries."

Zane swiveled his chair around to the set of filing cabinets behind him and opened the top drawer. "That might be true for the books that are already published, but it's not true for the unpublished ones."

"What do you mean?"

He turned back around with a hefty stack of legal papers. "This is Lucy Arrington's will. After I graduated from law school, I went over it extensively. It specifies that all proceeds of published books go to the Texas state library system. It says nothing about unpublished books. And since the house was willed to you, I would think that everything in it is yours as well."

While Cole tried to process this, Zane got up from his chair and came around the desk to thump him on the back. "Which means that if the book is legit, you just won the lottery, cuz." He grinned. "Which in turn means that we're not signing any papers today."

"All Etta had wanted was a story. She hadn't wanted to get attached to the women who had sacrificed so much to be here. Nor had she wanted to get attached to the kind-hearted cowboy who had invited them."

CHAPTER EIGHTEEN

❦

"MAYBE COLE'S RIGHT, EM. MAYBE you should just leave well enough alone." Carly banged on the vibrating mechanism attached to the side of the bed. "Why won't this thing work when you want it to?"

Savannah pulled another shirt from the closet and carefully folded it on the bed next to Emery. "And leave the book unpublished? Are you crazy, Carly Sue?"

"Would you quit calling me that? My name is Carly Renee, not Carly Sue. And why are you packing now when we're not leaving until tomorrow?"

Savannah shrugged. "I like being prepared. Just like I like Carly Sue better than Carly Renee."

If Emery hadn't felt so sad, she might've laughed. But after talking with Cole that afternoon, she didn't feel much like laughing. She felt like a gigantic fist was squeezing her heart. The pain had nothing to do with the book and everything to do with what Cole had told her. No wonder he wanted to sell his ranch. Who would want to live where such a tragic accident had taken place? She couldn't blame him for wanting to run from such a horrific past. Just like she couldn't blame him for hating her for lying.

"Carly Sue does have a nice ring to it." Dirk, who was lying on the other side of Carly, leaned over her shoulder and watched her thump the metal box. "You know, you don't really need a vibrating bed. I'd be more than happy to—"

A knock sounded on the door, and Emery jumped up from the bed as if she had springs in her butt. But it wasn't Cole standing on the other side of the door. It was Mrs. Crawley.

She held out a cookie tin. "Here's that diary I've been promising you. I would've gotten it to you sooner, but I had to evict that no good Dirk Hadley."

Emery stepped further into the doorway to block her view of the room. "I'm sorry to hear that." She looked at the old dented cookie tin. As much as she had wanted to read the diary, it no longer held any interest for her. Even publishing the last book in the Tender Heart series didn't matter any more. All that matter was how much she'd hurt Cole. "Thank you for bringing the diary, but I'm afraid I won't get time to read it. I'm leaving with my friends tomorrow."

Mrs. Crawley's eyebrows lowered. "But you booked the room until Friday."

"There's been a change of plans. But I'll be happy to pay for Wednesday and Thursday nights. Especially since I didn't give you seventy-two hours' notice."

"You'll do nothing of the kind. I'm not some big chain that cheats folks out of their hard-earned money. You pay if you stay. If you don't, that's just the way it goes." She pushed the cookie tin at her. "And you might not have time to read it all, but you can read a little before you head out in the morning. Unless you plan on heading over to the Watering Hole for Twofer Tuesday."

Emery took the tin. "Twofer Tuesday?"

"Two beers and two buffalo chicken wings for the price of one. It's the only night the entire town shows up to party."

Since the last thing Emery felt like doing was partying, she declined. "Thank you, but it's the last night I have with my friends. So I think I'll pass."

Mrs. Crawley nodded. "I don't blame you. I only go from five to six, after that it becomes a circus of drunken fools." She turned to leave. "Be careful not to rip the pages."

After Emery closed the door, she carried the cookie tin over to the bed and carefully opened it.

"What's that?" Carly asked.

"It's an actual diary from one of the mail-order brides. Mrs. Crawley's a direct descendant." She reverently took the leather-bound book out of the tin. The worn cover and tattered pages brought tears to her eyes.

"That settles it." Savannah placed her hands on her hips. "You are not going anywhere, Emery Wakefield. While Carly and I love the Tender Heart series, you have some mystical connection to it. Which is one of the reasons I agreed to come here instead of Mexico. And I'll be darned if I've wasted the last few days for nothing." She pointed a finger. "You are going to get the final book published. And you're not going to let anything stand in your way."

Carly continued to thump on the vibrating machine. "Damn, I hate it when Savannah is right. But she's right this time. You can't leave with us tomorrow, Em. You came all this way to follow your dream and you can't give up so easily."

Emery placed the book back in the tin and sat down on the bed. "But Cole doesn't even believe that the book was written by Lucy."

"Then convince him," Savannah said.

"That's easier said than done. Cole is pretty stubborn."

Dirk raised his hand. "I can attest to that."

"Then use some of your womanly wiles on him," Savannah said. "Miles can be stubborn too, but he doesn't stand a chance when I set my mind to something. While Carly and I have to get back tomorrow, your boss told you to take as much time as you need. And since it only took God six to create the Earth, I figure you can sway one stubborn cowboy in much less."

Emery wished it was that easy. "But you don't know the full story, Savannah. Cole has a good reason for wanting to sell the ranch and leave Texas."

"So let him sell the ranch if he wants to," Carly said. "What we can't let him do is keep the last Tender Heart book from getting published. People need that ending—I need that ending. And it sounds to me like Cole needs the money. Did you tell him how much he'd be raking in?"

"No. I didn't get a chance to tell him." It was hard to talk when your heart was in your throat and you were about ready to burst into sobbing tears. Even now, she felt like crying. Not just about Gracie's sad accident, but also about leaving Bliss.

After living in big cities all her life, she thought she could never be happy anywhere else. But the last few days, she'd felt happier than she had in a long time. She liked being able to walk down a street without crowds of people and lines of beeping, honking traffic. She liked seeing the sun rise in its morning softness on one side of the horizon and set in all its fiery glory on the other. She liked the smell of all things green and growing and the fields of breathtaking wild flowers. But most of all, she liked Gracie and Cole—Cole much more than she was willing to admit.

"Then that's your problem," Carly said. "You need to tell Cole about the money. People try to act like money doesn't matter. But once a fistful of cash is held out to them, there are few who can resist taking it."

Emery wondered if maybe Carly was right. Maybe she should let Cole know exactly how much he'd make if he published the book. With that kind of money, he could live anywhere he wanted and pay for the best physicians and therapists for Gracie.

Giving up on making the bed vibrate, Carly sat up. "For now, I think we should get dressed up and head on over to the Watering Hole. I want to check out these wings. And while we're there, we can celebrate Savannah tying the knot."

"Don't be hypocritical," Savannah said as she went back to packing. "Everyone knows you don't want me to get married."

"It's not that I don't want you getting married. It's just that I think you're marrying the wrong guy." Before Savannah could open her mouth, Carly held up a hand. "I know. Miles is the most wonderful man in the world. And I've finally come to terms with the fact that you are going to marry him—whether it's a mistake or not. That being the case, you need a proper send off. And I'm not talking about the frou-frou tea party your southern friends are throwing for you a few days before the wedding. I'm talking about a down-and-dirty, alcohol-soaked last hurrah with your best buds." She glanced back at Dirk. "And maybe a hot cowboy we can bribe to strip off some of his clothes."

Dirk grinned. "No bribery necessary." He winked at Savannah. "I don't mind being part of your last hurrah. And it just so happens I have a little experience at stripping. In fact, I would probably still be working at the male strip club in Houston if that Texas Ranger hadn't gotten so pissed about his wife putting most of their retirement fund in my banana hammock."

Savannah laughed. "Is there any job you haven't had?"

Dirk thought for only a second. "Husband and father. I haven't had those jobs, and I have no desire to apply." He leaned over Carly's shoulder. "Are you ready to let me take a look?"

"Go right ahead, Mr. Fix-it." Carly moved out of the way. "If you can make it work, your beer and wings are on me."

Dirk examined the metal box attached to the bed frame for only a second before he pulled out a pocketknife. Within minutes, the bed started vibrating. He flashed a grin at Carly. "I like my beer frothy and my wings hot."

☾

IT TURNED OUT THAT MRS. Crawley was right. While most nights were dead at the Watering Hole, Twofer Tuesdays were a circus. It was a good thing they walked, because the parking lot was completely full and more cars and trucks spilled out along the streets. Inside, people stood shoulder-to-shoulder at the bar, or crammed into booths, or bounced off of one another on the dance floor that had been made by pushing the center tables against the walls.

Mrs. Crawly sat at one of those tables with a balding older man. When she saw Emery, she waved and toasted her with her brimming-over beer glass. But her smile faded when she saw Dirk.

"I get the feeling that Mrs. Crawley doesn't like you too much," Carly teased.

"Some women don't," Dirk replied as he herded them over to an empty table on the opposite side of the dance floor. "You ladies stay here and I'll get us some beers." He headed for the bar.

"I think we should pay," Savannah said once he was gone. "When we were walking over, he mentioned that he had to sleep in Cole's barn last night."

Emery was surprised since Cole made no bones about his dislike for Dirk. "He slept in Cole's barn? Did Cole know about it?"

Savannah shrugged. "I guess they called a truce."

Emery desperately wanted to call a truce with Cole. She hated the way they had left things. She knew he had every right to hate her, but she didn't want him to. She wanted them to end things, if not on a happy note, at least on a semi-friendly one. Which meant that she needed to stay in Bliss long enough to apologize. And long enough to make him understand exactly what he was passing up if he didn't publish the book. He didn't have to publish it with her. He just needed to publish it.

But she wasn't going to worry about it tonight. Savannah and Carly were leaving in the morning, and this was the last time they would be together before they met up for the wedding in August. Since Emery had messed up their spring vacation, the least she could do was make sure Savannah had a good bachelorette party.

It turned out to be a great bachelorette party. Mainly because of the beer Dirk kept bringing them.

"You're drunk." Carly leaned on Savannah's shoulder. "That's the only way you can continue to eat those disgusting wings."

"I am not drunk." Savannah polished off another wing. "These aren't that bad."

"No, you're drunk." Emery took another sip of beer and

giggled. "Or maybe I'm drunk."

"I think you're all drunk." Dirk flashed his adorable grin. "Now about that foursome? I promise to only touch when asked."

Carly leaned over the table, and Emery thought she was going to punch Dirk in the arm. Instead, she cradled his jaw and gave him a big smacking kiss right on the mouth. "If you weren't such a young 'un, I'd take you to bed and blow your mind. Instead, I'm going to take you out on the dance floor and give you a workout."

"Yes, ma'am," Dirk jumped to his feet. "Dancing is almost as good as lovemaking . . . almost."

Once they were gone, Savannah laughed. "Well, that just proves that Carly is the drunkest. She hates to dance. And she's never so nice. We'll just have to make sure she gets plenty of champagne at the wedding."

"I don't mind being in charge of that." Emery lifted her glass. "To you and Miles. I hope you're as happy as a Tender Heart couple." She waited for Savannah to lift her glass. Instead, her friend stared down into her beer.

"I'm scared, Em."

The fear in her voice sobered Emery instantly, and she lowered her glass. "Of course you are. Pledging to live with someone for the rest of your life is scary business. Especially when you're an independent woman who's used to taking care of yourself."

Savannah blotted at the condensation ring on the table with a cocktail napkin. "I'm not really an independent woman. Miles's hefty loan is the only thing that's kept my business from going bankrupt."

"But I thought you were doing so well."

Savannah sighed. "I sorta fudged a little on that. It's just that Carly's a big executive chef and you're a big New York editor. I just didn't want to be the only one who was a failure in our little group."

Emery placed a hand on her back. "You're not a failure. You're the only one of us who had enough guts to start your own business. Okay, so maybe you've run into a few bumps. That's just part of being a business owner. It's not easy. And so what if you had to get a loan from your fiancé? I'm sure Miles was more than willing to help you out."

Savannah tore the napkin in two. "Overjoyed is more like it."

That didn't sound good, but Emery tried to remain upbeat. "See. He's a generous man."

"Or a controlling one." The words were barely audible, and once they were out, Savannah shook her head. "Of course, you're right. Miles is generous. And I shouldn't be having any second thoughts about sharing my life with him. I guess I've just been listening to Carly too much."

"You can't listen to Carly. If you love Miles and he loves you, that's all that matters." She hesitated. "You love him, right?" It took a little longer than it should have for Savannah to answer.

"Of course. He's everything I've ever wanted."

"Then you have nothing to worry about. Just like in Tender Heart, love conquers all."

Savannah smiled and lifted her glass. "You're right. To my wedding and a happily-ever-after for Tender Heart." They toasted and took a sip before her gaze drifted over Emery's shoulder. "So when you said that Cole was mad at you, just how mad is he? Like making-a-huge-scene-in-a-public-place mad?"

"I don't think Cole is the type to make a huge scene. He's more a private scene kind of guy."

Savannah's shoulders relaxed. "That's good to know. I hate big scenes—especially in crowded bars."

Her meaning finally sank in, and Emery turned and looked over the crowd. It didn't take her long to spot Cole on the dance floor. He wore his usual plaid western shirt, faded jeans, and boots. His cowboy hat was pulled low and his hair curled at his collar . . . only inches from the woman's fingers that were curved around his neck.

Jealousy wasn't something Emery was familiar with. At least, not regarding men. She was jealous of skinny women who pigged out on chocolate desserts at restaurants, or people who had time to lounge on a park bench in Central Park and read, or editors who got to edit a book she wanted. But she'd never felt any jealousy over the men she dated. So she was surprised by the intensity of the anger that hit her.

As if reading her mind, Savannah reached across the table and squeezed her hand. "It's probably just one of his many cousins. The man is related to half the town."

"Guys don't usually slow dance with their cousins." Emery took a big swig of beer in hopes that it would stifle the sudden urge to waltz out on the dance floor and scratch the girl's eyes out.

"That's not slow dancing," Savannah clarified. "That's called the two-step."

It didn't make Emery feel better. The two-step still involved Cole's hand riding the woman's waist and her arm around his neck. And when she stroked her fingers through Cole's curls, Emery felt blood rush into her face.

"You look as hot as I am, Em." Carly flopped down next to her and fanned her face. "It was hotter than a pizza oven out there. I have to give it to Dirk. He can flat out dance." When Dirk sat down and opened his mouth, she held up a hand. "Please. I don't want to hear how you worked for a week at Arthur Murray. Just take the compliment and shut up."

Dirk laughed. "Thank you, Carly Sue. Too bad I couldn't talk you into dancing to this song. I'm much better at a waltz than I am at a two-step."

Emery jumped up. "I'll waltz with you." Before he could say a word, she grabbed his arm and pulled him out to the floor, weaving through the people until she got as close to Cole and the skank he danced with as she could get.

"Slow down, darlin'," Dirk said. "If you want to be in my arms so badly, we can skip the dancing and head right on back to the motor lodge where you can be in my arms all night long. And when your friends show up, I'm sure you won't mind sharing."

"Be nice or I'll swat you." She had never been the type of girl who used jealousy to get a man's attention. And yet, there she was wrapping her arms around Dirk's neck and looking at Cole from the corner of her eyes.

He was looking right back.

Her heart gave a little leap. When she'd left the garage that morning, she'd thought she would never see him again. Just the sight of his familiar blue eyes made her feel like she had found something she'd lost. He took up her entire field of vision, consumed every space in her mind . . . and in her heart. Suddenly, she realized she liked Cole much more than she'd thought. If the jealousy wasn't enough of an indicator, the wild thumping of her heart was.

"Ahh," Dirk said, "so it has nothing to do with my arms and everything to do with Cole's."

Emery didn't even try to deny it. "Who is she?"

Dirk expertly guided her around a couple, blocking Cole from view. "That's Winnie, Mrs. Crawley's daughter."

"I thought she was after you."

"Winnie is one of those girls who believes in loving the one she's with." He pulled her closer and executed a perfect one-two-three turn. "Sorta like me." Emery was about to scold him for holding her so close, but he stopped her. "Calm down. I'm just helping you out. If you want to make him jealous, then we need to have less than five inches between us. We need to be snuggled together like two peas in a pod." His fingers tightened on her waist. "Two peaches on a branch." He buried his nose in her hair. "Two grapes on a vine."

It turned out that Dirk knew as much about making men jealous as he knew about everything else. Only a second later, he was being jerked away from Emery and a very angry looking Cole was taking her hand and pulling her off the dance floor.

And Emery didn't resist. She was through resisting.

"Rory had reached the end of his patience with the woman. She either needed a good spanking or a good kissing. And since he didn't want to bruise his hand . . ."

CHAPTER NINETEEN

𝕮

AFTER GRACIE'S ACCIDENT, COLE HAD sworn that he would never let his emotions get the best of him again. But since a certain chestnut-haired filly had entered his life, he felt like he was on an emotional roller coaster. One second, he was at an all-time high, and the next second, he'd hit rock bottom. And all Cole wanted to do was get off the ride and get on with his life. But it was too late. There was no way to do that now.

As it turned out, Emery wasn't some fortune hunter looking to exploit his sister. Thanks to Zane's Internet research, Cole now knew that she was an experienced editor with a reputable publishing house who had a degree in literature and had written a hundred-page thesis on Tender Heart. If anyone could authenticate the book Gracie had found, it would be Emery.

Which meant that if Cole was smart, he would stop looking at her as a woman who'd lied to him and start viewing her as the person who might just change his string of bad luck. If the manuscript turned out to be real, all his dreams were about to come true. He could buy his own horse ranch in Kentucky, and he and Gracie could live happily ever after. It all hinged on him keeping a clear head.

Unfortunately, his head fogged up as soon as his gaze connected with hers on the dance floor. And he stopped thinking about books and horse ranches and keeping his cool. All he could think about was getting her away from Dirk.

Cole's hand tightened on hers as he weaved around the tables to the side door that led to the alley. Once in the alley, he turned her to face him. The light over the door was out, but the moon was full enough to reflect off the rich reds and browns of her hair and the startling green of her eyes. She stared back at him for only moment before she spoke.

"Cole."

The one word was like a punch in the gut. And as much as he wanted to vent some of the hurt and anger he felt, he didn't. Instead, he pulled her into his arms and kissed her. For a moment, he gave in to the heat of her mouth as she kissed him back. The feel of her arms as they curled around his neck. And the fit of her body as it snuggled into his. But then he remembered that her reaction to his kiss wasn't real. She didn't want him. She wanted Tender Heart.

He pulled away and stepped back. "You don't have to pretend anymore, Emery."

She looked thoroughly confused. "Pretend? What are you talking about?"

He pointed between them. "This. I'm talking about this. You don't have to pretend like you're attracted to me any-more. I realize it's all just an act to get your hands on the final Tender Heart book."

She actually looked hurt. "Is that what you think?"

"It's what I know. Why else would a big-shot editor

from New York City waste her time on a dirt-poor cow-boy from Bliss, Texas? You came here for one thing and one thing only. You're obsessed with Tender Heart and the final book."

Her wounded look turned to anger. "You're right. I did come here for the final book. And some people might consider my love of Tender Heart to be an obsession. When I was growing up, Lucy Arrington's stories were more than just stories to me. They were a way to escape the fact that I've never felt like I fit in. When I read them, I'm not an awkward baby sister who isn't as smart as her brothers, or a scared editor scrambling to be a success. In Tender Heart, I'm a strong, determined Etta Jenkins. A shy, hard-working Melanie Davenport. A sexy, vivacious Valentine Clemons. A sassy, blunt-talking Daisy McNeil. And a loyal, kindhearted Laura Thatcher. Reading Lucy's stories, I become a heroine. And I'll admit my love for the series. But I didn't use you to get to Tender Heart, Cole."

It was the first time he'd gotten a true glimpse of Emery's past. It took some of the starch out of his anger and made him realize why she loved the series so much. But rather than support her argument, it gave credit to his.

"Of course you did. We all are willing to do whatever it takes for the things and people we love. Even lie and manipulate. As my cousin Zane pointed out, business deals are filled with lies and manipulation. And that's all I ever was to you, Emery—a business deal. So now that we have that figured out, let's not play any more games. If the book actually is the last book in the Tender Heart series, then it's yours. So now you don't have to waste your time flirting with a dumb cowboy."

He turned to walk back into the bar, but she grabbed his arm. When she pulled him around there was fire in those pretty green eyes.

"You're right. You are a dumb cowboy. You're dumb if you think for one second that whatever this is—" she waved a hand between them, "has anything to do with Tender Heart. I'm not an idiot, Cole. I know that mixing business with pleasure is a sure way to screw up a deal. And if I'd been thinking of Tender Heart, I would've stayed completely away from you as soon as I found out who you were. Instead, I let my heart rule my brain and fell for a pigheaded cowboy who doesn't know something good when he sees it."

While he was playing catch up, she swept right past him and disappeared inside the bar. He stood there dazed as he tried to process her words. Two phrases stuck out like a pair of diamonds in a coal bucket: *I let my heart rule my brain. Fell for a pigheaded cowboy.* Hope got his emotions back on the roller coaster track and hovering at the very top of the highest peak. He wanted to believe her, but she'd lied to him about her reasons for being here. She could be lying now. There was only one way to find out.

He found her at the table with her friends and Dirk. But he didn't even acknowledge them as he took her arm.

"You fell for me?"

Her voice was as vicious as a rattlesnake, and the truth of her words took a bite right out of his heart. "Hook, line, and sinker, dumbass."

Cole might be as stupid as his father, but damned if he didn't believe her. The relief and happiness that flooded him washed away all his anger and resentment, and he felt like a kid who had just been passed a note in school from his girlfriend. Emery liked him. Which meant he had some major kissing up to do. He figured he had two ways of doing things. He could spend the rest of the night trying to win her forgiveness with smiles and drinks, or he could cut through all the B.S. and get straight to the point. Being a no-bullshit kinda guy, he chose the latter.

Bending his knees, he lifted her up over his shoulder. This time, she didn't go along with him so easily.

"Put me down!" She kicked and squirmed, knocking his hat to the floor.

Cole tightened his hold on her legs and dipped to pick up his hat, but Dirk beat him to it.

"Now I realize that sometimes a man has to take the upper hand in order to make his girl see reason," Dirk said. "But I think it's only fair to let you know that if you hurt Emery, I'm going to have to hurt you."

"Only after I kick his ass," Carly said.

"Bottom," Savannah corrected. "And if he hurts Em, I get him first. I have a white belt with green tips in karate."

"I have no intention of hurting her," Cole grabbed his hat and sidestepped Dirk before heading for the door. People looked on with interest, but no one else tried to stop him. In fact, Zane held the door open.

"Have a good night, cuz," he said with a wink. Cole didn't answer. He had his hands full trying to keep Emery from kicking him in the family jewels. She almost succeeded when he released her legs to open his truck door. He tossed her inside a little more roughly than he'd intended.

"Are you okay?" He asked as he slid in.

She scrambled across the seat and glared at him. "No, I am not okay. I'm being abducted against my will."

He held up his hands. "Fine. You want to go back into the Watering Hole and discuss what we need to discuss in front of the entire town?"

"We don't need to discuss anything. I think we've said everything that needs to be said." She crossed her arms, and damned if his gaze didn't go down to her breasts that pushed up so nicely in the vee of her shirt. "Don't you dare gawk at me now, Cole Arrington. You lost that right after being such a jerk."

It was hard not to smile. Emery's sassiness was more than a little cute. Although it would be a whole lot cuter if she was sitting closer. But it didn't look like that was going to happen any time soon.

"I aim to get back that right. Which is exactly why we need to talk. And I'd rather not do it in the parking lot of a bar." He nodded his head at the door where Dirk, Carly, and Savannah were now standing. "Especially with all your friends watching. So could you just wave at them to let them know you're all right and I'll take you for a drive so we can talk . . . please."

Emery shot him a mean look before she nodded. "Okay, but only a short drive. Savannah and Carly are leaving in the morning, and I want to spent time with them before they go."

He waited for her to wave to her friends before he started the truck and pulled out of the parking lot. When they were on the road, he glanced at her and smiled. "I'm glad you're not leaving in the morning."

Her chin came up. "I thought that's what you wanted. I believe your exact words were 'go home and leave the Arringtons to their own sad endings.'"

He cringed. "Yeah, well, I might've been a little ticked at the time." He shot her another glance. "I want you to stay, Emery." He hoped the words would soften her up. Instead, they made her stubborn chin hike even more.

"I plan to. I have some *business* to attend to." She fastened her seatbelt with a decisive click, a sure sign that she had no plans of getting any closer. "So what made you change your mind about the book? I thought you were convinced it was a fake."

He returned his attention to the road. "You did. I looked

you up on the Internet and read your paper on Tender Heart." He glanced over and grinned. "So what happened to your hair in college?"

"My hair? What was wrong with my hair?"

"Nothing. I just like it better long." He reached over and lifted the strand that curled on her shoulder. "It's pretty."

"Don't try to ingratiate yourself with me. I'm still mad at you."

"I figured as much. You're sitting over there in the corner like a badger in his hole ready to strike."

She uncrossed her arms and released a sigh. "I just can't believe you thought I used you to get the last book. I wasn't exactly honest, but Gracie didn't want me—" She stopped in mid-sentence. "It doesn't matter. I can see where you would've thought the worst."

So it had been Gracie who asked Emery to keep the secret. Cole wasn't surprised. Especially when she had kept the book from him. He couldn't help but wonder what else his sister was keeping a secret. But he would worry about that later. Right now, he didn't want to think about anyone but the woman next to him.

"So if you're not angry at me anymore, do you think you could scoot a little closer?"

"I didn't say I wasn't angry at you. I just said I could see how you would think the worst." She turned away to look out the side window. "If you had any feelings for me at all, you wouldn't have thought it."

He should've told her right then that he had feelings for her, but for some reason, he struggled to find the right words. He waited until he pulled off the highway and was deep into Arrington land before he parked the truck under an old oak tree and turned to her.

"I'm a little screwed up where relationships are concerned. I guess you could say that I have trust issues. I don't trust my own feelings, let alone anyone else's." He unhooked his seatbelt and scooted closer. "And you cuddling up next to Dirk on the dance floor didn't exactly help matters. I'm going to assume you were trying to make me jealous."

She refused to look at him, and a knot formed on her brow. "Is that why you were dancing with Winnie?"

It wasn't. He hadn't even known Emery was there until he'd seen her with Dirk. He was drowning his sorrows in beer when Winnie had refused to take no for an answer and pulled him out on the dance floor. Now he figured he owed the woman. If she hadn't forced herself on him, he wouldn't be sitting here right now.

He slid closer and lifted the strand of hair before bringing it to his lips. "Were you jealous?"

"Not at all. I always want to scratch girls' eyes out."

He smiled as he smoothed the strand of hair behind her ear. "Okay, then. No more dancing with other women."

The tension in her neck visibly released. He took that as a good sign, and moved even closer as he traced a finger around her ear and along the stubborn curve of her jaw. He gently turned her face until he could see the moonlight reflected in those pretty green eyes.

"So am I forgiven?" He lowered his head and brushed her lips with his. He pulled back, but only a fraction of an inch. "Please?"

She spoke so softly that he felt rather than heard her words. "For now." She wrapped her arms around his neck and kissed him. Not a simple brush, but a deep, wet slide that took his breath and his sanity.

Without pulling back from the kiss, he unhooked her seatbelt and pulled her onto his lap. One kiss followed another until the windows of his truck steamed and the tightness of his fly grew more than little uncomfortable.

He pulled back from her lips and sipped his way down her neck. "I want you, Emery. I've wanted you from the moment I laid eyes on you."

She tipped her head back and gave him full access to her neck as she wiggled her sweet ass against his hard fly. "And I want you, Cole . . . from the moment I noticed you looking at my breasts."

He smiled. "I want to do more than look."

He slipped a hand beneath her shirt and over the soft skin of her stomach to the silky cup of her bra. He should've shown a little patience and taken his time, but he had lost all patience where Emery was concerned. He didn't want to go slow anymore. He wanted to dive right in. She filled his hand perfectly, and he gently squeezed. Beneath his palm, he felt her nipple harden. He groaned in her neck, then brushed his thumb back and forth over the hard peak until she released a guttural sound deep in her throat and pushed hard against his fly.

He had always prided himself on control. But he had no control now. He was locked and loaded and seconds from release. He quickly pulled her shirt off and tossed it to the floor, then with a twist opened the hooks on the back of her bra. But before he could dip his head and taste what he'd been touching. She pulled back, holding her bra in place.

Even in the darkness, he could read the concern in her eyes.

"Whatever happens tonight has nothing to do with the book, Cole. This is us. The book is business. You have to promise me that you won't confuse the two. That whatever happens with the book, it won't affect us."

He kissed her softly before making a pledge he wasn't sure he could keep. "I promise." He slipped off the bra.

"Rory kissed like he did everything else—with a focused thoroughness that took her breath away."

CHAPTER TWENTY

❡

EMERY HAD NEVER BEEN AN exhibitionist. So it was a little embarrassing to be sitting on Cole's lap half naked while he looked down at her breasts with eyes that seemed to burn right through his lowered lids. He stared for so long that she might've been worried he found her lacking if his breathing hadn't been harsh and uneven and if she hadn't felt the hard length of his desire pressing against her bottom.

Both things confirmed that he liked what he saw. But besides his breathing and his hand tightening on her thigh, he didn't move. And every nerve ending in her body seemed to be on high alert waiting for his touch. Finally, when she didn't think she could stand it a second longer, he lowered his head and placed a soft kiss on her nipple.

"Pretty," he whispered, right before he pulled it into his warm mouth.

The sweet tug of lips and the rough sweep of tongue sent hot sparks of desire skittering to the spot between her legs. The sparks were fanned into a raging fire when Cole gently cupped her breast and sucked even harder. She undulated her bottom against the hardness of his fly and ran her fingers through his hair as he gave her other breast the same delicious attention. When she thought she couldn't take a second more, he laid her back on the seat.

Her legs were draped over his lap, and his gaze roved over her naked breasts as his hand skated up her thigh to the waistband of her jeans. With just a twist and a slide, the button was open and the zipper down. His finger brushed along the lacy top edge of her panties.

"Bikini or thong?" he asked in a soft, rough voice.

She had to clear the lust from her throat to answer. "Thong."

"I'd like to see the backside. Not now . . . but soon." His fingers dipped into her panties, and Emery's breath whooshed out. He lifted his gaze and watched her face with intense moonlit eyes as he tested her slick heat.

She bit down on her bottom lip to keep from moaning, but it was a lost cause. The moan came out anyway as he flicked his thumb over her most sensitive spot. He flicked again. And again. And again. With each flick, the fire inside Emery burned hotter and higher. When two of his fingers thrust deep, the flames finally burned out of control, unfurling into a white-hot orgasm. When the last of the cinders floated down and flickered out, she cracked open her eyes to find Cole grinning.

"So you're a moaner."

"I am not a moaner," she said.

"I don't know what you'd call it when you scared that flock of pheasants from those trees." When her mouth dropped, he laughed. "Okay, maybe not that loud, but loud enough to make me feel pretty darned proud."

It was arrogant, but cute. "I'm glad I could stroke your ego."

"You're not finished yet." He peeled open her jeans and pushed them down her hips. They got stuck on her thighs, and he had to get on one knee and tug. The action caused him to bump his head on the roof. She giggled as he smiled sheepishly. "Obviously, truck lovin' isn't as easy as I thought it would be."

She couldn't help feeling a little giddy that this was his first time in a truck.

He gave one final tug and tossed her jeans to the floor before he pulled open the snaps of his shirt and stripped it off. The sight of all that hard muscle left her a little lightheaded and a lot speechless. Cole had working man muscles, broad shoulders, ripped abs, and knotted biceps that made her tremble.

Unable to help herself, she sat up and placed her hand over one hard pec. The muscle jerked and his heart thumped against her hand as rapidly as hers thumped against her ribs. She absorbed the rhythm as she looked into his eyes. Eyes that, in just a few days, had become as familiar to her as the Texas sky.

"Well, I never did like things easy," she whispered.

His eyelids lower. "No?"

"I much prefer things to be *hard*." She slid her hand down his body, over the ripped muscles of his abdomen to the waistband of his jeans. She thumbed open the button, then carefully worked the zipper down the bulge beneath. When she had his fly wide open, she traced the cotton seam of his underwear.

"Boxers or briefs?"

The answer came out on a groan. "Boxers."

She stroked the hard length beneath the cotton as she searched for the opening. "Mmm, I'd like to see the backside of these—but not now . . . later." She dipped her hand inside and released him from his boxers. She fisted him tightly before stroking from tip to base then back again.

He tipped his head toward the roof and released a hiss between his teeth. "Oh, honey, you're going to get something hard." He removed her hand and pulled the wallet from his jeans.

She watched as he unwrapped the condom and rolled it over his hard length. He lifted his gaze and their eyes locked. For a second, she was scared. Scared of the intensity of the feelings that flooded her. Scared that when she left, she would never get over these feelings. But when he pulled her onto his lap and kissed her, all fear dissipated. Being here in his arms felt right. More right than anything she had ever felt in her life. She wanted to remain skin-to-skin forever—to absorb him and never let him go. This desire grew when he adjusted her legs around him and slid deep inside.

When she was firmly seated, he touched his forehead to hers. "Emery." Her name came out of his mouth like a prayer.

"Cole." She answered with a sigh.

His hands tightened on her waist and he lifted her, then guided her back down as he thrust his hips. They both groaned at the deep penetration. He started to lift her again, but she took over. As she made love to him, it was like all her senses came alive. She became intensely aware of everything. Not just the meeting of their bodies and the brush of hot skin against skin, but also the squeak and groan of the seat springs, the condensation gliding down the windows, and the moon inching further down in the sky and reflecting in the desire in Cole's eyes.

"Em!" he hissed through his teeth.

Emery had never had an orgasm during intercourse before, but her passion-filled name and the beautiful sight of his release was enough to send her over the edge. She pulled him deep one last time, before moaning out her release and slumping against him.

"And you're not a moaner?" he whispered into her hair.

She lifted her head expecting to see his smile. Instead, his lips were serious. His eyes intense. "Come home with me."

Emery shouldn't. She was already in way over her head. But she couldn't bring herself to say no to those Tender Heart eyes.

"Okay," she said. "But only for a little while."

He kissed her. "Only for a little while."

☾

EMERY WOKE TO A FLOOD of bright sunshine and the incessant ringing of her cellphone. She tried to roll onto her back so she could reach for the phone, but a hard body blocked her. As the phone stopped ringing, she blinked and looked down at the hair-sprinkled arm resting on her waist.

Cole.

She smiled and would've gone back to sleep if the phone hadn't started ringing again. Who would be calling her this early in the morning? The answer to the question made her throw off Cole's arm and jump out of bed.

"Crap!"

Cole sat up in alarm. "W-what? What happened?"

"It's morning!" She searched around for her phone. It stopped before she could find it.

Cole flopped back in the bed and yawned widely. "That's real good, Sweetness. I bet you were top of your class in high school."

She continued to search. "Don't be a smart butt. I was only supposed to stay a little while. I wasn't going to spend the night." Her phone started ringing again, and she found it in her purse under Cole's jeans. She bent over to get it, and he released a low whistle.

"Now that's what I call a great morning view."

She whirled around and glared at him as she answered. "Hello."

"So I guess Cole hasn't dismembered you and gotten rid of the evidence in his smoker," Carly said with a whole lot of sarcasm.

Guilt ate at Emery. "I'm so sorry I didn't call you, Carly. I went back to Cole's house and we . . . sort of lost track of the time."

Carly laughed. "I bet you did. And to be honest, I wasn't really worried about you. Cole and his cousin Zane are more like boy scouts than bad boys."

Emery glanced back at Cole. He was propped up on pillows with his hands tucked behind his head, obviously thoroughly enjoying the view of her standing naked in front of him. His eyes were hot, and the sheet over his lap tented.

Since she couldn't find her clothes, she grabbed his shirt off the floor and slipped it on. "Listen, I can't talk right now, but I'll be at the motor lodge in under fifteen minutes."

"Too late," Carly said. "If we don't leave now, we'll miss our flights."

"But you can't leave before we say goodbye?"

"There's no need to say goodbye, Em. We text or talk to each other almost every day. And this summer, we'll be in Atlanta for Savannah's wedding—unless she cancels."

Savannah's voice came through the speaker. "I'm not canceling, Carly Sue! Here, let me talk to Emery." There was a muffled sound before Savannah got on the phone. "Good morning, Mornin' Glory. I bet you slept a lot better than I did. I didn't catch a wink with all the fussing." Before Emery could ask what fussing she was talking about, she continued. "So how was Rory Earhart in bed?

That was one thing that Lucy never wrote about, and something I'm dying to know." She lowered her voice to a whisper. "I hear that cowboys like it a little rough. Did Cole tie you up and spank you with his riding crop like an untrained pony?"

This wasn't the first time Savannah had brought up spanking in the bedroom, and Emery had to wonder if her friend didn't have a little S&M fetish.

"Uhh . . . no, it wasn't like that." She glanced back at Cole. He was still tented, but now he had a smile on his face as if he knew exactly what they were talking about.

"Oh." Savannah sounded terribly disappointed. "So it was just regular old sex?"

There had been nothing regular about it. It had been amazing. The best sex she'd ever had. Which worried her. Now that she had been with Cole, how could she ever go back to regular old sex?

"Give her a break, would you?" Carly came back on. "There's no need to recap now, Em. You can give us all the details later. For now, just enjoy. We'll call when we get to the airport."

"I'm sorry," she apologized again. "I realize this trip wasn't exactly the spring fling you and Savannah had hoped for."

"Mexico would've been more spring fling-ish. But I don't know if it would've been more fun. Not only did we get to see the little white chapel, but I got to cook in a cool old diner, learn about barbecuing on a smoker, and sleep with a hot cowboy. Because even if he is still wet behind ears, there's no denying Dirk is hot."

"You slept with Dirk?"

"The key word being 'slept.' Not that he didn't get a little frisky. It took me threatening to punch his lights out before he settled down and went to sleep." She paused. "I have to admit that I'll miss the little flirt. I tried to talk him into coming back with me to California and learning how to be my sous chef. I thought he would like the adventure of a different place and job, but he wouldn't do it." She paused. "Something is holding him here in Bliss."

"Maybe he likes Winnie more than he's letting on," Emery said.

"Doubtful. Just like his jobs, that cowboy could never settle for one woman."

Savannah's voice came through the receiver. "Hurry up, Carly Sue. I can't miss my flight. My cat sitter can't stay longer, and Miles will be devastated if I have to stay away from him for one more day."

Carly spoke in a low voice. "She really doesn't have a clue. That man will only be devastated if the stock market drops. But I better make sure she gets on her flight or I'll be worried about her wandering around the airport unsupervised on my trip home. Love you, Em."

"Love you too, Carly. I'll miss you."

Carly laughed. "No you won't. Not when you've got Rory Earhart to keep you company. Now go enjoy. We'll call you later." She hung up.

After Emery lowered the phone, she should've turned around. But now that she didn't have the distraction of talking with Carly, she suddenly felt a little shy. It was embarrassing to face a man in the bright light of a morning sun after everything you'd done in the dim light of a crescent moon.

So she glanced around for anything that would prolong the inevitable. The little alcove caught her eye. It was far enough away from Cole to help get her rioting emotions under control, and the floor-to-ceiling bookshelves the perfect distraction from the hard body that caused those rioting emotions.

Snapping the shirt, she walked over and examined the titles on the shelf. Since Cole slept in Lucy's room, Emery assumed that the books on the shelf would be old classics. And there were some classics—including first edition copies of the Tender Heart series. But most of the books were current bestselling suspense and mystery novels. The kind of books a man would read. And to prove it, an open novel rested face down on the arm of the chair in the corner.

Most women would think nothing of an opened book. But the sight made Emery's stomach take a dip. Up until this point, Cole had been a man she could admire. He was honest, hardworking, and caring of his sister. But now, he was more than just a man she could admire. Now he was a man who checked off every box on her list, including lovemaking and reading. The perfect man she could trust with her body and her heart.

Tears filled her eyes, and no amount of blinking could stop them from falling down her cheeks. Especially when two strong arms encircled her waist and pulled her back against a warm, hard body.

"I'm sorry you didn't get back in time to see your friends." He moved her hair and kissed his way along her neck. "But I'm not sorry that I got to wake up with such a beautiful woman."

She tried to keep her emotions in check, but a sob broke free. Cole's head immediately came up, and he turned her around. When he saw her tears, his eyes filled with fear and confusion. "What's wrong, baby? What happen—" He stopped and pulled her into his arms. "Aww, sweetheart, I didn't realize how much saying goodbye to your friends meant to you. Do you want to meet them at the airport? If we leave now, I could get you there before their flight leaves."

She sniffed and shook her head against his shoulder. "It's not that."

"Okay. Then if it's not about saying goodbye to your friends, what is it? Is it about what happened last night?"

Again she sniffed and shook her head.

Cole pulled back. "You gotta help me out here, Emery. Your tears are tearing me up."

She realized too late that she should've gone with her friends leaving as the reason behind her tears. The real reason made her look like exactly what she was—a book dork. Unfortunately, she couldn't think of another excuse so she had to tell the truth.

"You're a reader!"

She made the declaration a little louder than she intended, and Cole actually jumped. He studied her for a long moment before he hesitantly replied. "Yes . . . Ms. Marble taught me in first grade."

She swatted his bare chest. "No, I mean you love to read."

He squinted one eye. "And that makes you happy enough to cry?"

She nodded. "You'd be surprised at how many men don't enjoy reading. They would rather watch sports on television or flip through a magazine while in the bathroom. And even though my family reads, they read non-fiction and medical journals. They've always teased me for walking around with my nose in a novel."

"Just so you don't get the wrong idea about me," he said, "if I had cable, I'd watch sports. And there's an outdated *Pro-Rodeo Sports News* magazine on the back of the toilet. But I think I get where you're going with this. You love books, and you couldn't be happy with a man who didn't love them too." The tears welled again, and all she could do was nod. He smoothed back her hair. "Man, your family really did a number on you, didn't they? It's okay to love books, Emery. And it's okay to want to date a guy who loves them too. Now could you please stop crying? If you don't, you're gonna have me bawling like a baby."

She sniffed and wiped her eyes. "I bet you were a cute baby."

"Ugly as a mud fence."

She gave a watery laugh. "Well, you've made up for it now. Because you are one cute cowboy."

His thumbs brushed away the last of her tears as his smile faded. "And you're beautiful. The most beautiful woman I've ever met in my life." He kissed her, his lips sweet and tender. When he finally pulled back, she saw something in his blue eyes that nestled deep in her heart and took root.

"So I was thinking," he said. "Now that your friends are gone, that room at the motor lodge is going to be awfully lonely. What do you think about spending your last few days in Bliss with a cute cowboy? We could climb back in bed and . . . read."

How could Emery refuse?

"Rory didn't have time for love. He had a cattle empire to build. Unfortunately, love was like a down-and-out relative. Once it came to visit, there was no getting rid of it."

CHAPTER TWENTY-ONE

COLE WHISTLED AS HE STROLLED into the kitchen to rustle up some breakfast. When he saw Gracie sitting at the table, his whistling fizzled and his face heated. He didn't know why. It wasn't like he had *I just experienced an amazing night of sex* written on his forehead. Still, having to face your little sister after an amazing night of sex was an uncomfortable situation. Especially when your sister seemed to be in a sassy mood.

"My, but don't you sound happy this morning." Her eyes twinkled as she took a big bite of cereal and munched it. "This wouldn't have to do with the woman you snuck into your room last night, would it?"

Damn, and he thought they'd been so quiet.

Choosing to ignore the question, he moved to the coffeemaker. "You're up awfully early this morning." Early being a little after ten. Normally, Gracie didn't get up until noon. Which was why he'd thought he had plenty of time to figure out how to tell his little sister about inviting Emery to stay with them for a few days. Now he had no time. As soon as he filled the coffeemaker with coffee and water, Gracie started in.

"It's Emery, isn't it? Zane told Becky about you scooping her up like a Tender Heart hero and waltzing right out the door of the Watering Hole."

Cole cringed at the description. Not a hero as much as an idiot. It was a ridiculous thing to have done in front of a gossipy town. And if he had to do it over again—an image of Emery straddling his lap popped into his head—he'd do it the same exact way.

"Zane and Becky need to mind their own business." He pulled down two cups from the cupboard.

"We are their business, Cole. We're family. And no coffee for me, thanks. I've been having trouble sleeping."

He glanced at her. "That's because you stay up so late. If you tried going to bed at a decent hour, you'd sleep a lot better." Now that she knew about Emery, he figured he might as well jump into the subject with both feet. "And this cup isn't for you."

She sat up straighter, her eyes wide. "Emery's still here?"

"Yeah, and she might stay a few more nights. Just until we get the book contract ironed out."

He turned and waited for the coffee to perk before he poured it into the cups. As he poured, it hit him that he didn't even know if Emery liked coffee. Or what she liked to eat for breakfast. She'd been sleeping like a new baby foal when he'd left her, and he hadn't wanted to wake her up to ask. But he'd find out. He planned to hold her hostage in his room until he found out everything there was to know about Emery Wakefield.

He turned with the cups, intending to head back to his room and start his interrogation, but his sister's shocked face stopped him in mid-stride.

"The book contract?"

The question made him realized that he hadn't told Gracie about his decision to sell the book. He'd spent all day yesterday being pissed at Emery for lying to him. Then after talking to Zane, he'd headed to the Watering Hole. He hadn't even thought about telling his sister until now.

Damn, sometimes he was a complete asshole of a brother.

He set down one of the cups of coffee and moved to the table. Once seated across from Gracie, he got straight to the point. "I've decided to sell the book to Emery."

Her eyes widened. "But I thought you didn't believe the book was written by Lucy. And I thought it didn't even matter if it was, because we aren't going to get any money from it anyway. Which is why you tossed it in the trash."

Yep, he was an asshole. He cleared his throat. "I'm sorry about that." A thought struck him. "Shit, you didn't actually throw it away, did you?"

"Of course not. I spent way too much time ... searching for it."

He relaxed in the chair. "Good. It appears that I was wrong. Not only about the book, but also about the will. Emery is an expert on Tender Heart, and she's convinced that it's real. And Lucy's will says nothing about the proceeds of any long lost manuscripts. So Zane says that if it was found on this property, it belongs to our family." He took a sip of coffee. "I'm assuming you found it in the stuff Becky pulled down from the attic." He expected her to be a little more excited and got worried when she wasn't. "What's wrong? I thought since this was your plan, you'd be happy."

"I am. I'm just trying to absorb it. So what happens now?"

"Emery's publishing house will make us an offer. If we like it, we'll accept and sign a contract."

"And then they get the book?"

"Or you could give it to Emery now. I trust her."

Gracie studied him with a peculiar look on her face. "You love her."

He choked on the sip of coffee he'd just taken. Once he stopped coughing, he tried to disabuse Gracie of the notion. "I do not love Emery."

A smile spread over her face. "Yeah, you do. You're just too stubborn to see it. After what Mama did to Daddy, you've had trouble trusting women. And now suddenly you trust a New York editor that you've only known a few days—trust her enough to invite her to stay with us when you've never even had a girl spend the night before. If that's not love, I don't know what is."

The truth of her words was like a swift kick of reality. He didn't trust women, and yet he trusted Emery after only a few days. And he hadn't had a girl stay the night before. Not only because he lived with his sister, but also because he didn't want women getting the wrong idea. He wasn't ready to settle down. After watching what his mother's desertion did to his father, he didn't know if he would ever be ready. And yet here he sat, wanting nothing more than to be back in bed with Emery.

He could lie to himself and say it had to do with the night of amazing sex. But last night hadn't just been sex. It had been much more. But he wasn't ready to label it as love. Not yet. Maybe never. All he wanted was to enjoy the days he had left with Emery.

He got up. "I'm going to take Emery some coffee and find out what she wants for breakfast."

Gracie smiled a very knowing and annoying smile. "I bet I know what she wants for breakfast."

He rolled his eyes, then reached down and ruffled her hair. "Very cute, brat."

Her smiled faded as her gaze locked with his. "Does selling the book mean you've decided to keep the ranch?"

It was a good question. One he'd answered early that morning when he woke up to the view out the window of the sun cracking open the night. At the sight of the pink morning spreading over Arrington land, something inside of Cole had cracked open as well and his heart filled with hope—hope for Gracie, and the ranch, and himself. And hope is one of those things that you don't even know you lost until you find it. He didn't know if his newfound hope was due to finding the book or Emery. But it didn't matter. All that mattered was for the first time in a long time he felt happy.

"Yes," he said. "We're keeping the ranch."

A smile spread over Gracie's face, and she pushed back from the table and whirled her wheelchair around in a tight circle. "We're going to keep the ranch! We're going to keep the ranch!"

Her sheer joy was contagious, and he lifted her out of the chair. He spun her until they were both dizzy and laughing. When a blur of chestnut caught his eye, he stopped to find Emery standing in the doorway. The sight of her made him feel even dizzier. She looked sexy as hell wearing nothing but his snap-down western shirt with her hair all sleep-tousled.

"I didn't mean to interrupt," she said as she took a step back. "I'll just . . . go get dressed—"

"No!" Cole blurted the word a little too loudly. He blushed as he sat Gracie in her wheelchair. "I mean there's no need to get dressed. We're causal in the mornings here on the ranch. Isn't that right, Gracie?"

She flashed sparkling eyes at him before smiling at Emery. "Casual is definitely the word for our ranch. I hear you're going to be staying with us a few days."

Emery glanced at Cole. "I haven't really decided yet."

"Well, it only makes sense." Gracie gave Emery the

same wide-eyed look of innocence she gave him when she wanted something. "I can't let the book leave this house. So if you want to read it, you'll need to do it here."

Cole could've kissed his sister, bless her devious little heart. Unfortunately, Emery wasn't as big of a pushover as he was. Her eyes narrowed on Gracie before she turned them on him. "Really?"

He shrugged and widened his eyes. "It only makes sense."

Emery smiled. "Then I guess I'll just have to stay here a few days." She looked at Gracie. "When can I read the book?"

"Soon." Gracie rolled toward the door. "But right now I need to feed my chickens. And since we're keeping the ranch, I might ask Dirk if he wants to work here full time."

"Over my dead body," Cole said.

But Gracie acted like she didn't hear him as she rolled passed Emery. He might've gone after her if a beautiful woman in his shirt hadn't been blocking his way. Once the screen door slammed, he walked right over and did what he'd been wanting to do since he first saw Emery standing there. He backed her against the wall and kissed the daylights out of her. And she kissed him right back with enthusiasm—just one of the many things he liked about the woman.

Her hands came around his neck and her mouth opened beneath his like a flower to a bee. He wanted to jerk the snaps of her shirt open and dive into the warm softness of her body. But since he couldn't take her against the kitchen wall with Gracie and Dirk lurking around, he pulled back and smiled.

"Good mornin' . . . again."

It took a moment for her eyes to focus, which had him feeling cocky and happy. "Good morning," she said. "I didn't mean to run Gracie off."

"You didn't. She needs to get outside more, instead of being cooped up in here. And speaking of cooped, I probably should thank Dirk for those silly chickens. They seem to be the reason she's getting up earlier and spending more time outside."

A twinkle entered Emery's eyes that he couldn't read. "Yes, I'm sure it's the chickens. So what were you two celebrating?"

He stepped back and shrugged. "As stupid as it may be, I've decided to stay here and try to turn a worthless cattle ranch into a prosperous horse-breeding ranch."

He didn't know what he expected, but it wasn't her excitement. She flung her arms around his neck and hugged him tight. "That's wonderful, Cole. And it's not stupid. You belong here. This is your heritage."

It was his heritage. And for the first time, it didn't feel like a ball and chain. The winds of fate had changed in his favor, and all he wanted to do was enjoy it. He pressed his lips to the soft spot behind her ear and whispered. "So what do you want for breakfast, Miss Wakefield?"

"I would give anything for a cup of coffee."

"Hmm?" Cole hummed against her neck. "Anything?"

She pulled back. "Within reason."

He toyed with the top snap of her shirt. "How about we start with the shirt off your back?"

"The story Etta wrote wasn't the story she had intended to write about the unethical practice of purchasing wives. Instead, the story was about lonely cowboys and destitute women who were just looking for happiness and someone to share their lives with."

CHAPTER TWENTY-TWO

𝕮

"SO WHAT'S IN THE PACKAGE?" The post office clerk with the balding, sunburned head stared down at the legal-sized manila envelope Emery had placed on the counter. When he looked up, his eyes twinkled with a feverish light. "It's the final story in the Tender Heart series, isn't it?" His hand reverently touched the envelope. "Have you read it? Does Rory end up shooting that bastard Dax in a gunfight? Or does Duke do it?"

Emery wasn't surprised that the man knew about the book. It seemed that everyone in town knew Gracie had found the final novel and Emery was the "big city" editor who was going to publish it. For the last week, whenever she came to town, everyone tried to get her to leak information about what happened in the final book. And they weren't above using bribery.

The clerk leaned closer and spoke under his breath. "I'll ship it for free if you let me take a peek."

Emery smiled. "Sorry, but this isn't the book. It's just legal contracts."

"But I bet you've read the book and know how it all turns out."

"Actually, I haven't finished the book."

She hadn't even read the second chapter. Not only because Gracie was possessive with the book, but also because Emery just hadn't had time. Her time had been filled with Cole.

He had taken off a few days from fixing cars to show her around the hill country. The first day, they took a drive to enjoy the blooming bluebonnets, red Texas paintbrush, and bright pink winecup. They'd stopped in small German-named towns for beer and bratwurst and browsed through quaint little shops. The next day, Cole had taken her to Zane's and taught her how to ride a horse. Although she hadn't ridden so much as bounced along in the saddle holding on for dear life. They'd picnicked next to a creek with a small waterfall where Cole had told her all about his dream of owning a horse ranch and she had told him all about her dreams of publishing the Tender Heart book and proving to herself and everyone else that she had found her niche.

It was so easy to talk to Cole. He was a great listener . . . when he wasn't trying to kiss her. Not to say she didn't prefer his kisses to talking.

"So I bet Cole and Gracie are getting millions for the last book." The clerk's remark brought Emery out of her daydream.

Yes, Cole and Gracie were getting millions for the last book. Mostly because Emery had told Cole the amount he needed to hold out for. It wasn't exactly ethical, especially when she was sitting on the other side of the bargaining table. But she couldn't seem to stop herself. She cared about Cole and Gracie. Cared more than she dared to admit. Besides, it wasn't as if the book wouldn't make that amount back for her publishing house . . . and plenty more.

She nodded at the envelope. "Could you send this priority overnight?"

Once she'd sent the revised contract, she dropped Mrs. Crawley's diary off at the motor lodge. While she hadn't gotten a chance to read the last novel of Tender Heart, she had found the time to read Mrs. Crawley's great-grandmother's diary. For the last three nights, she'd read it aloud to Cole, who thought it was as fascinating as she did. She wanted to ask Mrs. Crawley some questions about the diary, but when she got to the office, the woman was busy checking a couple in. So Emery just dropped off the cookie tin and left. She was halfway back to her car when a little old woman in a Sunday bonnet and white gloves stopped her.

"Are you that editor who's publishing the new Tender Heart book?" When Emery nodded, she rammed a plastic-wrapped dish at Emery. "It's the best apple pie in the county. Won first place at the fair five years running."

"I bet it's delicious. But just so you know, I haven't read the book yet. So I can't tell you who shoots Dax or if Rory and Etta have a son or if Esther Reeves gets her just deserts for butting her nose into everyone's business."

The aged eyes beneath the brim of the hat twinkled. "I'm sure she does. That woman is the biggest busybody in Tender Heart."

Emery nodded. "She is, isn't she? I laughed hard when Etta knocked her into that horse's watering trough— totally an accident, of course."

The old woman laughed. "That's exactly what she deserved." She balanced the pie in one hand and held out the other. "Maybelline Marble. And I'm probably just as much of a busybody as Esther. That happens when you've lived in town for as long as I have."

Emery took her hand. "Are you the same Ms. Marble who made a chocolate cake for Cole and Gracie Arrington? I didn't get a chance to taste the cake, but my friend who is a chef said it was the best cake she'd ever had."

"Well, isn't that sweet?" She leaned closer. "So tell me . . . exactly how many chapters were found?"

It was an unusual question. But Emery figured it was Ms. Marble's way of getting any kind of information to gossip about. "I'm sorry, but I can't release any details until the book is published."

Ms. Marble nodded. "I figured as much, but it was worth a try." She held out the pie. "Take this anyway. I'm diabetic and can't have sugar." Her eyes twinkled. "I'm sure you can find a handsome cowboy to share it with. Maybe one who looks a little like Rory Earhart."

Emery took the pie and smiled. "I think I might be able to find someone who fits that description."

"I thought you might." She took Emery's arm as they walked down the street. "The mail-order bride who married Gus Arrington was one lucky woman. My grandmother was a mail-order bride as well. In her journal, she talks about stepping off the stagecoach and having a good fifty men waiting to help her down. The big, brawny blacksmith knocked the rest of the men out of the way and got to her first."

Emery turned to her. "I just got finished reading Mrs. Crawley's diary, and it was amazing what those women went through. And here I thought Lucy had made it all up."

"Most of the town thinks it was the Arringtons who started everything, but it was the brides who put Bliss on the map. And all you have to do is read one of the many mail-order-brides' diaries to prove it."

"Many? You mean there are more diaries than yours and Mrs. Crawley's?"

"Of course, there's more. Since there were over sixty brides in a ten-year span, I figure there must be dozens of journals lying around in people's attics."

Emery couldn't believe her luck. Not only had she found the last book in the Tender Heart series, but she had also found Lucy's research resource. Maybe she could put together a foreword to go with the last novel using a few excerpts from the diaries—or better yet, publish all the diaries in completely different book. She'd have to run it by her editor-in-chief.

"Do you think people would let me read their diaries?" she asked. "Would you?"

"Of course I would." Ms. Marble paused and shot a sly look at Emery. "If you give me first crack at Tender Heart."

Emery laughed. "You do drive a hard bargain. And while I can't divulge any secrets yet, I'll see if I can't get you an advance copy."

"Fair enough." Ms. Marble nodded at the grocery store. "For now, I need to get some sugar for the chocolate chips cookies I'm making for the church bake sale."

While Ms. Marble headed toward the grocery store, Emery headed to Emmett's gas station. To avoid any other Tender Heart fans, she kept her head down and race-walked. She was so intent on not being seen that she didn't notice Cole stepping in front of her until she ran into his broad chest. The pie plate slipped from her hands, but he caught it before it hit the ground.

He balanced the pie in one hand and tugged her close with the other, giving her a smile that melted her heart. "I just caught a pie and a beautiful woman. This must be my lucky day."

She wrapped her arms around his neck. "And mine." She kissed him. Kissing Cole had become as natural to her as breathing.

In the last few days, she had been trying to get her fill of him. It wasn't working. The more she tasted him, the more she wanted. And it seemed like he felt the same way. His arm tightened around her waist, and he pulled her up to her toes as he deepened the kiss. When he drew back, his eyes glittered with the same desire that made her dizzy with need.

"Do you want to go for a drive?" he said in a rough, sexy voice.

"I thought you had work to do."

"It can wait." He took her hand and pulled her along behind him. "Emmett! I'm taking my lunch break."

Emmett appeared in the doorway of the office. "You do realize that it's only ten thirty, right? And you got Virgil dropping off his tractor." He smiled at Emery. "But I can see how you'd lose track of time." He limped out of the office. For the first time, Emery noticed his prosthetic leg. She felt even guiltier for her rudeness when she'd first met him. But Emmett didn't seem to hold it against her. "So does Rory get a new hound dog after Flea Bit dies in the barn fire?" he asked. "It broke my heart when that dog died."

Cole cut in before she could answer. "Dang it, I forgot about Virgil bringing his tractor. Could you handle it, Emmett?"

"If it was anyone else but that ornery man, I'd gladly do it. But me and Virgil mix about as well as gasoline and fire."

Cole heaved a sigh and turned to Emery. "I guess I'll have to take a rain check on that drive." But instead of releasing her hand, he pulled her into the garage where he kissed her until the sound of a trailer being backed into the bay had him lifting his head.

"I can't think when I'm with you." He gave her another quick peck before he turned and waved at the man who climbed down from the truck. "Hey, Virgil! I'll be right with you." He walked over to the worktable and grabbed the worn backpack that sat on top. He brought it back and handed it to her.

"What's this?" she asked.

He grinned. "The book. I took it this morning while Gracie was sleeping."

Emery didn't know why she didn't feel more excited to finally have the book in her possession. Maybe because the book wasn't what she wanted most anymore. Maybe what she wanted most was standing there watching her with blue eyes the color of dreams.

"Go on," he said. "Go read it. I'll see you tonight."

She went, not because she was any hurry to read it, but because she knew if she stayed, Cole wouldn't get any work done. As she headed out of the garage, Virgil stopped her.

"What about Clyde Duda? Did he ever find that missing sow? I've been worried about that pig ever since I read the series."

Behind her, she heard Cole's laughter, and she couldn't help but smile at the farmer. "I don't know." She held up the backpack. "But I'm going to find out."

Once out of Bliss, the excitement of finally being able to read the last book in the series hit her. All the way back to the ranch, she kept looking over at the backpack that rested on the seat next to her. She had thought about reading it on the front porch, but when she saw Dirk working in the yard, she turned up the road that led to the chapel.

It seemed fitting that she would read the final Tender Heart book in the place where it had all started. She left the door open and scooted into a pew in the shaft of sunlight before taking out the manuscript. Since this was the original copy and the first draft, she wouldn't need her red pencil. It was doubtful that she would need it for the second and third edits either. If the first chapter was any indication, Lucy Arrington's writing was virtually mistake-free.

But Emery soon realized that the first chapter hadn't been a good indication of Lucy's writing. The second chapter had more than a few grammar and typing errors. As did the third. And the fourth. But it wasn't the grammar and typos that had Emery's stomach tightening with each word. It was the voice and style. While they were good, they were nothing like Lucy's.

Hoping she was mistaken, Emery read on. But by the tenth chapter, her stomach had grown so knotted that she felt as if she might throw up. She tried to make excuses for the differences. Maybe Lucy had been so weak from the cancer that her voice had changed. Maybe she'd been on hallucinogenic medications while writing it. Or maybe it was Emery who was hallucinating after too many of Cole's kisses.

She pulled her own tattered copy of the first Tender Heart novel from her purse and quickly read through the first two chapters. When she was finished, she let the novel slip from her hands and fall to the floor. She wasn't mistaken. While the first chapter of the last book was Lucy's, someone else had written the rest of the manuscript. Which meant that the stack of paper on her lap wasn't the final book in the Tender Heart series.

It was a hoax.

As the truth dawned, Emery felt like she'd been hit in the heart with a sledgehammer. All her dreams melted like the first New York City snowflakes. There would be no job promotion. No editorial awards. No bookstore windows filled with a *New York Times* Bestseller that she had edited. And there would be no parental pride or brotherly back pats when she finally proved herself to her family.

But as disappointed as she was over the loss of her own dreams, she was even more disappointed for Cole and Gracie. They would be devastated when they found out. And Emery didn't know how she was going to tell them. It would be like winning the Publishers Clearing House Sweepstakes, then having the guy grab the gigantic check back and say "Sorry, wrong house."

Suddenly, Emery wasn't sad so much as angry. Who would pull such a cruel trick? Whoever it was, they weren't going to get away with it. If they were still living, Emery would make sure they paid.

She carefully collected the pages of the manuscript and placed them back in the backpack before she stood and looked around. While she'd been reading, the morning had turned to afternoon. The late sun shining through the brilliant colors of the stained-glass windows made them look like framed Christmas lights. She would like to see the chapel at Christmas. Would like to see it decorated with evergreen garland and a fresh-cut pine from Arrington land.

But that wasn't likely. This would probably be the last time Emery stood in the chapel. Once she talked to Cole and Gracie, there would be no need for her to stay any longer or ever return. Her dream was over. And so was theirs.

With tears in her eyes, she walked out of the chapel and pulled the door closed behind her. She headed down

FALLING FOR TENDER HEART

the steps, but stopped when she saw Gracie sitting in her wheelchair on the cobblestone path.

"Gracie?" She glanced around. "How did you get here? Did you come from the house on your own?"

"I've been here before in my wheelchair. It just takes a while." Gracie rolled closer, her gaze going to the back-pack. "Is the book in there?"

"How did you know?"

"When I couldn't find it, I called Cole and he told me that you had it. That's his backpack." She lifted her gaze, and her eyes turned sad. "You read it, didn't you?"

Since there was no help for it, Emery nodded. "Yes. I read it. And I'm sorry to say that Lucy Arrington didn't write the entire book." She waited for Gracie's shock, but instead the young woman only nodded.

"I know. I wrote the other chapters using Lucy's type-writer that I found in the attic."

Emery's breath rushed out in shock. But she was only shocked for a moment before all the pieces fell together and made perfect sense. If Emery hadn't been so distracted by Cole, she would've figured it out much sooner.

"So that's why you didn't want me reading the entire manuscript."

Gracie nodded. "I'm not nearly as good a writer as Lucy."

Emery moved down the steps. "You're wrong. You're a good writer with a strong voice, Gracie. It's just not Lucy Arrington's voice. So where did you find the first chapter?"

Gracie glanced behind Emery. "Here, in the chapel." She paused. "I found it the night of the accident. I used to come here a lot." She shrugged her shoulders in a dejected way. "I guess I was hoping for some divine answer for why my mother left me. Renovations were still going on then. The outside was complete, but the workers had just started on the inside—patching the plaster and replacing some of the rotted oak planks in the floor. It was dark, and I tripped over some tools that had been left and dropped my flashlight. It rolled into one of the holes in the floor, and when I knelt in to get it, that's when I found the envelope. It was tucked back under the flooring and I wouldn't have seen it if the beam from the flashlight hadn't reflected off the metal closure. Inside was the chapter. Once I read it, I knew it was Lucy's. I wanted to show my father and Cole. But it had started to rain, and I couldn't chance getting the old paper wet. I left it here in its hiding place and hurried back to the house to tell Cole and Daddy." Her eyes turned sad. "I didn't get there, of course. While in the hospital, I called Becky and told her where to find the chapter. She got it and kept it safe until I got home. She's a good friend."

"So that's why she stopped the renovations and didn't want people in the chapel. She didn't want anyone else finding the rest of the book."

Gracie nodded. "I really thought we could find it by the time the letter reached you. Becky is tenacious, and she popped up every floorboard looking for the other chapters. But when you answered my letter, and we still hadn't found it, I started to get worried. That's when Becky had the idea for me to write the rest of the story using Lucy's typewriter. She doesn't understand about voice."

"But you know about voice, Gracie. How did you think you could fool readers?"

"I didn't think I could." Gracie met Emery's gaze. "I thought you could." She rolled closer, and her voice took on an excited edge. "You can do it, Em. I know you can. You're an expert on Lucy Arrington. You know her style and her voice. You could take my story and edit it to sound like Lucy and no one would be the wiser."

For a moment, Emery considered it. Not for her dream. But for Gracie's. For Cole's. Suddenly, she realized how much she had come to love this young girl. And how much she'd come to love Gracie's brother. There was nothing she wanted more than for Cole to stay on this ranch where he belonged. But no matter how much she wanted that for him, and for Gracie, she couldn't do it. Not just because it went against her morals as a human being and her professional ethics, but also because she couldn't do it to Tender Heart.

She couldn't do it to Lucy.

Gracie must've read the truth on her face because her excitement dwindled, and just that quickly, tears splashed down her face. "I just wanted to stay here. I just wanted to stay in the only place I ever called home." She wiped at her cheeks. "It doesn't matter if my mama never loved me, because here I have family who does love me. I guess I just thought that if we moved that might all change."

"Oh, Gracie," Emery knelt by her wheelchair and hugged her. "True family never stops loving you. No matter where you move—or what you do," Suddenly, she realized the truth in her words. There was a part of her that believed she needed to earn her family's love by prov- ing she was successful. But the truth was that she didn't need to prove anything. Her parents and brothers loved her regardless of what she did for a living. Like Gracie, her insecurities were self-imposed.

Gracie took a quivery breath and drew back. "So what now? I guess I'll go to jail like my uncle Raff."

Emery had been thinking the same thing mere moments ago, but that was when she'd been imagining a faceless culprit with deceit in his heart. That was when it wasn't a scared young woman in a wheelchair who only wanted love and happiness. The same things everyone else wanted.

She stood. "No one is going to jail." She grabbed the handles of the wheelchair and turned it toward her car. "I'm going to take you back to the house, and then I'm going to book a flight to New York so I can meet with my boss and explain that the subsequent chapters are fake. Since it will never be published, there's no need for any-one to know who wrote them."

"But what about Cole?"

"I don't think he needs to know anything more than he does."

Cole stepped out of the trees. "Too late."

"For once the stage was on time, despite Rory's prayers that it would be late. He wanted just a few more minutes with Etta . . . just a few more minutes to figure out how to say goodbye."

CHAPTER TWENTY-THREE

W HEN COLE LEFT WORK THAT afternoon, he'd had one thing on his mind: Getting home to Emery. He'd thought a lot about her while he worked on Virgil's tractor. He'd come to a realization that terrified him, and at the same time made him feel happier than he'd ever felt. He loved her. He didn't know if she felt the same way or if him telling her would stop her from leaving. All he knew was that he wanted her to know. When he'd arrived home and Dirk told him that he'd seen her heading to the chapel, he figured it was fate. The chapel was the perfect place to make his declaration.

It was also the place he was brought back to reality.

After overhearing Gracie and Emery's conversation, it looked like Cole wasn't destined for a happily-ever-after. There had been a glimmer of a chance that Emery might stay with the man who had helped her realize her dream of publishing the last Tender Heart book. But there wasn't a chance in hell that she would stay with a man who was responsible for making her look like a fool to her publishing house. It was Cole's fault. He'd known in his heart that the book wasn't real. He'd known, and yet he'd let greed and lust override his intuition.

And love. He couldn't forget love.

Even now, he couldn't take his eyes off Emery. Especially when he knew he only had her for a short time.

"Cole," Gracie said, her voice quivering with tears. "I'm so sorry. I didn't mean—"

Without taking his eyes off Emery, he cut his sister off. "Go back to the house, Gracie Lynn. You can explain yourself later."

There was a squeak of rubber against stone, then only silence. Cole didn't know how to fill it. Or maybe he didn't want to fill it. If they never spoke, he could just stay here looking into Emery's eyes forever. But words had to be spoken.

"I'm sorry," he said. It was the truth. He was sorry. Sorry the book was a fake. Sorry Gracie had lied. Sorry he couldn't hold on to Emery.

"I know what she did was wrong, Cole," Emery said. "But she did it to keep the ranch—to keep you."

"You can't keep people. She should know that." Cole certainly did. It was a lesson God seemed to be teaching him over and over again. And still, he wanted to hang on. Still, he wasn't ready to let go.

"So how much did you overhear?" she asked.

"Enough to know that we won't be rolling in money." He should've been more upset about losing millions. But it wasn't the loss of the money that made him feel like someone had opened him up and ripped out his insides. It was the loss of this woman.

He got it now. He understood why his father had taken his mother back. Why he had been willing to give her everything to make her stay. But Cole wasn't willing to give everything. He had to hold on to something—to some shred of self-respect. His entire body might be a gaping wound, but Emery didn't need to know that.

"So I guess you're leaving." His voice didn't sound like his own. It sounded distant, like it was coming from the deep tunnel of his despair. And hers didn't sound much better.

"I guess there's no reason for me to stay."

He paused for only a second before he nodded. "I guess not."

Emery stared at him for only a moment before she looked away. "Does this mean that you'll sell the ranch?"

He didn't give a shit about the ranch. "I don't know. Probably."

Without warning, she threw herself into his arms and buried her face in his chest. If he thought he'd felt gutted before, it was nothing compared to now. "Please don't sell, Cole," she whispered against his skin. "Please stay here in Bliss. An Arrington has no business living anywhere but Texas."

He swallowed hard. "Just like a big city girl has no business living anywhere but New York."

She lifted her head, her eyes heartbreaking pools of sadness. She started to say something, but then stopped. And as much as he wasn't through with her—as much as he would never be through with her—he knew he needed to be the one who brought an end to the torture.

He tried for a smile, but knew it fell far short. "I'm going to miss you, Emery Wakefield." Before any more tears rolled down her cheeks, he kissed her. It was the kind of desperate kiss that held more pain than desire. The kind of kiss that hurt because you knew it had to end, and when it did, you were going to be more than hurt. You were going to be devastated.

That's exactly how Cole felt when he pulled away. Devastated. But he didn't let the feeling stop him from releasing her. Since his truck was parked next to her car, he headed to the chapel. But he only got halfway up the path before he glanced back. He hoped to see her standing there looking as hurt as he felt. But she wasn't. She was walking away.

He felt like he was five all over again and watching from the porch as his mother drove away. And he had to fight like hell with his heart to keep from doing what he'd done then—run after her and beg her to stay. Luckily, knowing what the outcome would be gave him the strength he needed to turn and not look back again.

The sun had started to set, bathing the little white chapel in shades of pinks and tangerines. It was a beautiful sight that should've soothed Cole's tattered soul. Instead, it made him angry. God had no business showing off when it was His fault things had turned out this way. In fact, as he looked up at the tall spire, it looked like God was flipping him off.

Cole picked up a rock and hurled it at a window. It must've hit the lead casing because it pinged off without breaking the glass. So he hurled another one. And another. And another. Not one found its mark. Not a one. Now really pissed, he marched up the path and shoved the door open so hard it crashed against the wall.

"Fine! Take my mom. Take Gracie's legs. Take my dad. Take the ranch. And take Emery. Take it all." He looked around for something to throw at the windows. But all he found was a copy of a Tender Heart novel lying on the floor under a pew.

It would be appropriate if he broke a chapel window with the book. But when he turned to the first page, he couldn't bring himself to throw it. Just looking at Emery's name written so precisely on the top of the page made all the anger drain out of him. His knees gave out, and he sat down in the pew. He didn't know how long he stared at her looping handwriting before he turned the page and started to read.

As a kid, he'd thought the story was stupid and boring. As an adult, he realized there was nothing stupid or boring about it. It was a well-written, intriguing story. After the first chapter, he was hooked and had to read on. Around chapter eight, Gracie texted him with a long apology followed by two words *Emery left*. He ignored the pain in his heart and texted her back, telling her where he was and that he wouldn't be home for a while. A sad-faced emoji was her only reply.

It was getting too dark to read, but he wasn't ready to stop. He retrieved a flashlight from his truck and read on. He didn't know why he needed to finish the book. Maybe he wanted to find out why everyone loved it so much. Or maybe he just wanted to keep the pain of Emery leaving from consuming him. Either way, he kept reading until the end. Then he drove home and started the second book.

He woke the next morning in the chair of his reading nook with a kink in his neck and the second book on his lap. He hadn't finished it before he dozed off, but he'd read enough to realize that Tender Heart wasn't just a sappy romance. It was an epic story of western life—the trials and tribulations . . . and celebrations. Because no matter how hard life was, the characters always found something to celebrate. No matter how dark the rainclouds, they always looked for the silver lining. And maybe that's why everyone loved the series. They responded to strong people who refused to give up.

Cole had once thought the people in the Tender Heart series were just characters, but they weren't. His great-aunt had told the story of his ancestors—his history. Their strength and determination was in his blood. And it was about time he started acting like it.

The first thing he needed to do was talk to Gracie. The days of going easy on her because he felt guilty were over. It was time he started treating her like an adult rather than a kid.

He found her sitting at the kitchen table. But she wasn't eating her usual bowl of cereal. Instead, she watched Dirk, who stood at the counter with his back to Cole, cracking eggs in a bowl and chattering like a magpie. A know-it-all magpie.

"Now the key to perfect scrambled eggs is going low and slow."

"Low and slow?" Gracie said in a breathless voice like she'd been running a marathon.

"Yep." Dirk whisked the eggs and then poured them into the skillet that was heating on the stove. "Low heat and a slow stirring hand. Low and slow is the way to go."

Gracie released a long sigh that had Cole looking back at her. The look in her eyes was pure adoration—or more like lust. Cole gaze whipped to Dirk, and there was no way to describe the anger that boiled up inside him.

"You sonofabitch!" In four long strides, he had Dirk by his t-shirt and was whirling him around to punch him in the jaw. But Dirk was quick and ducked the punch as Gracie screamed.

"Cole!"

Cole only gave her a glance, but it was long enough for Dirk to jerk free and put the kitchen island between them. "Now, Cole, I was just making Gracie some breakfast."

"And seducing her," Cole said between his teeth. "How long has it been going on? Did you stay in the barn again last night? Did you lure her out there?"

"Stop it, Cole." Gracie rolled her wheelchair over. "He

didn't do anything."

Dirk held up his hands. "She's right. I swear. I don't think of Gracie like that. I got here this morning and was just making her breakfast because she spilled the milk and didn't have any for her cereal. But now that you're here, you can take over." He nodded at Gracie before quickly skirting around the counter and exiting out the side door.

When he was gone, Cole turned to his sister. "What the hell are you thinking, Gracie Lynn? First, you write a book and try to pass it off as Lucy Arrington's and then you fall for a no-account drifter."

Her chin came up. It reminded him so much of Emery that his chest constricted in pain. "Dirk is not a no-account drifter. He's a good human being and a perfect gentleman." She glanced down at her lap. "But you're right about the book. I shouldn't have written it. I just wanted us to stay here so badly." Before he could say anything, she held up a hand. "I know, now that we aren't going to be offered a million-dollar contract, we can't keep the ranch. And Dirk says I need to grow up and accept it—of course, he doesn't think I should follow you to Kentucky. He thinks I should go to a physical rehabilitation center and try to walk again."

It ticked Cole off to no end that Dirk was butting his nose into their business. "And I guess he's an expert on rehabilitation too."

"I wouldn't say he was an expert. He found the facility online and gave me their information. I emailed one of the therapists there about my injury. He emailed me back almost immediately and put me in touch with a young girl who had my exact same injury and surgery. After a few months at the center, she's now walking with a walker." She looked at him, her eyes hopeful. "Do you think I could do that? Do you think it's too late?"

Cole wanted to be hurt that Dirk was the one who had figured out a way to motivate Gracie. But he couldn't be hurt when his sister was finally hopeful. "Yes. I think you can. I think you can do anything you put your mind to. I always have."

She smiled. "And I've always believed you can do anything you set your mind to, which is why I can't understand why you let Emery go."

It was a sucker punch, and it took a second for Cole to recover enough to answer. "It wasn't my place to try and stop her."

"That is such bullcrap. Of course it was your place. If you love her, you should've figured out a way to make her stay."

He could've denied loving Emery, but what was the point. "We both know how well that works. Daddy tried to keep Mama here, but the more he held on, the more she wanted out. Now if you'll excuse me, I'm going to go fire Dirk."

Gracie blocked his path. "No, you're not. We've already been over this, Cole. I'm paying him. So he stays until I say he doesn't."

"If he stays longer, Gracie, it will only hurt you more when he leaves. Take my word for it."

Gracie studied him for a long moment before she spoke. "You're probably right. But I think the old adage *'tis better to have loved and lost than never to have loved at all* is right. I'm glad Dirk showed up. I'm glad I got to know his smile and his laughter. My life would've been so much duller without it. My heart would've been so much smaller."

"My heart feels pretty damned small right now."

"Because you didn't tell Emery that you loved her, did you?"

"It wouldn't have mattered."

"How do you know that unless you try?" She took his hand and squeezed it. "You realize that was Mama's biggest problem, right? She doesn't know how to express love. She just knows how to run from it. Let's not be like her, Cole. Let's be like Daddy. Let's love openly, freely, and completely. No matter the cost . . . no matter the pain. If you love Emery, then you need to love her one hundred percent."

"She won't leave her job in New York."

"Then you make the sacrifice."

His eyes widened. "You mean move to the Big Apple? What would I do there?"

Gracie thought for only a moment before she answered, "How about be her Tender Heart hero?"

"Silent tears tracked down Etta's cheeks as the stage took her further and further away from Tender Heart. She stopped crying when the driver pulled sharply on the reins, almost tossing her to the floor. 'There's a rider coming.'"

CHAPTER TWENTY-FOUR

"I REALIZE THAT NO ONE LOOKS good on Skype, but you really look like crap, Em." Carly's face got bigger on Emery's laptop that was sitting on the bed in the Bliss Motor Lodge "Are you still crying? I would've thought you'd have run out of tears by now. We couldn't even talk last night; you were sobbing so hysterically after saying goodbye to Cole."

Emery pushed the wadded up tissues behind her back. "My allergies are just acting up this morning."

Carly snorted. "You've never had allergies in your life. That's little Miss Savannah who can't look at a peanut without needing her EpiPen. She exploded like a blow-fish that time I forgot and used peanut oil for frying my wasabi wontons."

On the other side of the screen, Savannah scowled. "I don't think you forgot, Carly Sue. I think you did that on purpose to get back at me because the guy you were dating at the time was gawking at my girls."

"Why would I kill you over that? My hoes always come before my beaux, which is why I'm talking to you two instead of heading into the restaurant. But you really need to pull yourself together, Em."

"Emery has every right to fall apart." Savannah's Persian cat's fluffy tail swished across Emery's screen. "She just found out that the man she loves was only using her for sex."

Savannah's words shouldn't have hurt so much, especially when it was Emery who had given them to her. And it was the truth. If her relationship with Cole had been about something other than sex, he would've made an effort to stop her from leaving. But he hadn't raised even one objection. And she couldn't blame him. If she'd stayed, she'd only be a constant reminder of all the money he could've made if the book hadn't been a hoax.

"It's better that it was just about the sex to him." She sniffed. "If he loved me, it would be that much harder to leave. And I need to get back to work."

Carly moved away from her laptop, grabbed a whisk, and started whisking something in a bowl. She was always cooking when they Skyped. It was like watching the Food Network. "So what did your boss say about the other chapters being fake?"

"She was pretty upset, but she thinks we should contract with the publishing house that publishes Lucy's books and rerelease the old books in the series with the new chapter. If we do, at least Cole and Gracie would get some money." She paused. "But I hate the thought of that. I think Lucy would hate it too. I truly believe that the rest of the book is here somewhere and Lucy would want it published all together. Besides, releasing one chapter is too much of a tease. People will be ticked off there's not more—not to mention all the fortune hunters who will come to Bliss looking for the other chapters. Cole is a private man and I don't think he'll want to exchange his privacy for a little money."

Carly stopped whisking. "But won't you lose your job if you don't get them that first chapter?"

She had a good point. If Emery didn't get them the rights to the first chapter, there was little doubt that she'd be looking for a new job soon. Her head had already been on the chopping block before she came to Bliss. The ax started its downward swing when it turned out the rest of the book wasn't Lucy's. If she screwed up getting Cole to sign over the first chapter, her head was in the basket for sure.

Savannah pulled her cat onto her lap and stroked her fluffy fur. "Well, I, for one, don't know why Emery would care if she loses her job. She's never liked it anyway."

Emery stared at the screen. "What?"

"You've never liked your job. The most excited I've seen you was when you thought you'd found the last book in the Tender Heart series. Up until then, all you did was complain about how your boss is more worried about the bottom line than good literature. I thought you took the job because you wanted to live in New York. But the entire time you've lived there, you haven't gone to one tourist attraction, one Broadway show, or even to see the Rockettes—I mean, who doesn't want to go see the Rockettes?"

It took a while for Savannah's words to sink in. When they did, Emery recognized them as the truth. She didn't like her job. And she didn't like living in New York City. If she liked it, she would enjoy all that the city had to offer. But she'd had more fun in Bliss than she ever had in New York.

"You're right," she said. "I don't like living in New York. And I do hate my job." Once the words were out, it was like a huge weight had been lifted off her shoulders. She got up from the bed and started to pace in front of the window. "For the last few years, I tried so hard to live in reality. And I thought reality was working at a mundane job that didn't make me happy. But that's not reality, that's just stupidity."

She stopped pacing when she suddenly realized that she *had* been living in a fantasy. But the fantasy wasn't Tender Heart. The fantasy was her belief that she had something to prove and New York was the only place she could prove it. She thought if she could just become a successful editor she would finally fit in somewhere. But she had never belonged in New York. And she hadn't belonged in Los Angeles either. Because belonging and fitting in has nothing to do with finding the right place to live or the right job. It has to do with finding your true self.

Here in Bliss, Emery had found herself. She now knew who she was. And she wasn't a big-shot editor. Or a famous doctor. Or a brainy geek. She was just a woman who loved books. Flowers. Little white chapels. Small western towns...

And a blue-eyed cowboy who had helped her figure out how to belong.

"Oh, no," Carly said. "You're not going to start crying again, are you? Because I can't take any more boo-hoo-ing."

Emery turned to her laptop as the tears slid down her cheeks. "I'm staying."

Savannah lifted her hands. "Well, thank you, Sweet Baby Jesus. I've been praying that you would figure that out."

"Me too," Carly said. Emery's shock must've registered on her face because Carly held up her spatula. "What? You think I don't believe in prayer and God? I believe. I'm just not as vocal about it as Savannah."

"So why didn't you two tell me you thought I should

stay?" Emery asked.

Savannah laughed. "We tried to last night, but you're as stubborn as that cute cowboy of yours."

"I'm not stub—"

A strange noise cut her off.

"What was that?" Carly asked.

"That was a horse whinny if ever I heard one," Savannah said. "And I should know, since those animals scare me to death."

"A horse?" Emery walked to the window and drew back the curtains. What she saw made her breath catch and her heart thump in double time. It was like a page from her favorite book had come to life. But now she knew the difference between fantasy and reality. It wasn't Rory Earhart that sat astride the pretty chestnut mare. It was Cole Arrington. The real flesh-and-blood man she loved.

She watched as he gracefully swung down from the horse and tied the reins to the hitching post in front. The knock sounded on the door only seconds later.

Emery rushed over and glanced in the mirror above the dresser. Carly was right. She looked like hell. Her eyes were puffy and her cheeks were wet. But she only had time to wipe the tears away and pull her hair out of its ponytail before Cole knocked again.

Her hands shook so badly it took her forever to slide back the deadbolt and open the door. He wore his faded jeans and a black western shirt, the sleeves cuffed on his strong forearms. The brim of his black cowboy hat cast a shadow over his eyes, but not the blush on his cheeks. That blush melted her heart.

"You're still here," he said.

She nodded and prayed that he couldn't hear her heart knocking against her ribcage. "I'm still here." Her voice sounded breathless.

He studied her for only a moment before his eyes grew concerned. "You've been crying."

She didn't even try to deny it. "That happens when you're sad."

There was a moment when he started to reach for her, but then his hands dropped to his sides, and he exhaled. "I've been pretty sad myself. And I've done a lot of thinking . . . and a little reading." He pulled her Tender Heart book out of his back pocket. "You left something in the chapel." As happy as she was to have the book back, she hated that it was the reason he was there.

She took the book and stared down at the cover. "So that's why you came?"

There was a long pause, and when she glanced up, his eyes were intense. "I came because I want to be your hero, Emery." While tears gathered in her eyes, he continued in his deep, strong voice. "I want to be the kind of man you look up to. The kind of man who doesn't quit just because things get tough. I want to be the man you dream of—not only when you're sleeping, but when your eyes are wide open. A man who will fulfill all your fantasies and desires." He nodded at the book she held in her trembling hand. "I might not be as perfect a hero as Rory. But I promise you I will be. And I promise you that I'll never stop loving you. Never."

Emery placed a hand over her mouth to hold in her happiness. "Oh, Cole!" She threw herself in his arms. "You don't have to work to be my hero. You're my hero just as you are. You are everything I've ever dreamed of and more . . . so much more." She pulled back and took a quivery breath. "I love you. I'll always love you."

He kissed her. He kissed her like he had kissed her the very first time—with a hunger that consumed her with its heat. But along with the hunger was a tenderness that spoke of so much more than just passion. When he drew back, she had a hard time not slipping down to the floor in a puddle.

"I've been wanting to do that ever since I saw you standing there in my shirt," he said with a grin.

Emery glanced down. She'd been so wrapped up in Cole she'd forgotten what she had on.

"Are you blushing?" He reached out and touched her cheek. "And here I thought I was the one who blushed." His tone was teasing, but his eyes were serious. "Why did you take it, Em?"

She blinked back the tears. "Because I couldn't leave without something to remember our time together. But as it turned out, I didn't need the shirt. I think about you every second of every day."

"Same here," he said. "Which is why I think we need to get hitched."

Emery stared at him. "Hitched? As in married?"

"That would be the hitched I'm talking about. I'd ask you right now, but there are some things that come first. Like meeting your family and getting your daddy's permission, and figuring out what a cowboy is going to do when he moves to New York City."

It was all too much to take in. Cole loved her. He wanted to marry her. And he was willing to move to New York City to prove it. Tears dripped down her cheeks.

"He-e-ey." He cradled her face in his hands. "That's nothing to cry over. I promise I'll do my best not to embarrass you with your big city friends."

"You would never embarrass me, Cole. But like I said before, you don't belong anywhere but Texas. Anywhere but on the Arrington Ranch."

His smile faded. "Then that means you're not going to

marry me?"

It didn't take her any time at all to answer. "No, that means that I'll be the one doing the moving."

Cole let out a whoop, and then scooped her up in his arms and swung her around. She laughed and held tight. When he finally put her down, his eyes were serious. "As much as I want you to live here with me, I think it's only fair to warn you that it's not an easy life. While I'm struggling to start my horse ranch, I won't be able to afford a lot of extras. Or even a big wedding."

She looped her arms around his neck. "I don't need fancy things, Cole. In fact, I'd be quite content to go barefoot and wear my man's shirts for the rest of my life. And as for my wedding, I want it simple. My mother's wedding dress, a bouquet of wildflowers, and a little while chapel surrounded by my family and friends."

A look came into Cole's eyes. A look that was as easy to read as an open book. And this book told a story of love. And laughter. And a happily-ever-after. Emery's happily-ever-after. She rose up on her toes and prepared to give him a kiss to beat all kisses when Savannah butted in.

"That was the most beautiful proposal ever."

"What the hell?" Cole jumped back and looked around. "Are your friends here?"

"I was Skyping with them when you knocked." She sent her laptop an exasperated look. "But they should've had the decency to disconnect when they saw it was you at the door."

"Are you kidding?" Savannah sniffed. "I wouldn't have missed that for the world." She dabbed at her eyes.

Carly groaned. "Would you stop it? I can't take any more sniveling. Besides, this is cause for celebration, not tears. Or are you just crying because Emery might beat you to the altar?"

"I'm not going to beat her to altar," Emery said. "It will be months before we can even start to plan a wedding."

"Months?"

She looked at Cole to find him frowning. It made her happy to know that he didn't want to wait to make her his bride. "I have to give notice at my work and pack my apartment and figure out what I'm going to do here in Texas."

He pulled her into his arms. "That's easy. You're going to love me." He gave her a quick kiss. "As for the rest, two weeks is plenty of notice for leaving your job. Packing can't take more than a week. Which means we could get married in May—the exact month that Rory and Etta got married."

Emery's eyes widened. "You read the books?"

He smiled. "Not all, but I'm working on it. Now what do you say, Emery Wakefield? Is it going to be a Tender Heart wedding in May?"

"Rory Earhart had never planned on getting married. But as he stood in the little white chapel and watched his beautiful bride walk toward him, he figured that sometimes it was best to leave the planning to God."

CHAPTER TWENTY-FIVE

"THERE'S STILL TIME TO CHANGE your mind."
Cole turned from the mirror and found Zane standing in the doorway. He wore the same outfit as Cole: a gray western tux and matching Stetson. Except his tie was yellow not gray . . . and knotted correctly.

Cole pointed to the mess he'd made of his. "Do you think you could help me with this thing? I have a mind to toss it in the trash and leave my collar open."

Zane walked over. "I wouldn't do that if I were you. That little southern-fried friend of Emery's will have your hide. The woman is as nervous as a dog on bath day that this wedding won't turn out perfect." He untied Cole's tie. "I'm not sure why you wanted someone so high-strung as your wedding planner—keep your chin up."

Cole lifted his chin. "Because she's Emery's close friend. Not to mention the fact that she's free. Emery and I need to save as much money as possible so I can buy some good mares for that stud horse of Becky's."

"I thought before Emery left her publishing house she acquired a non-fiction book of the actual diaries of the mail-order brides."

"She did, but she's only getting paid for editing it. She wants the advance and royalties to go to the families who offered their diaries."

Zane glanced up from the tie. "You know I'll loan you whatever you need to get your stable started."

It wasn't easy, but Cole had decided to listen to his little sister and take help from his family. "I might take you up on that. But for now, you loaning me the stallion is enough."

Zane nodded. "Fair enough." Once he finished knotting the tie, he stepped back. "So you didn't answer my original question. Are you sure you want to go through with this? I mean I like Emery and all, but you've only known her for a little over a month. Marriage isn't easy. If I'd known how hard it was, I might've waited before I jumped into it."

"You knew Rachel for most of your life before you two got married. I wouldn't call that jumping into it, Zane." Cole studied him. "Everything's okay between you two, isn't it?"

Zane flicked at a piece of lint on his tux jacket. "Of course. What wouldn't be okay?" He lifted his gaze. "But as your best man, I just want to make sure you know what you're doing."

Cole smiled. "For the first time in my life, I know exactly what I'm doing."

"In that case, I'd better get you to the church on time." Zane herded him toward the door. "I don't want to get on the wrong side of Bridezilla Wedding Planner."

ZANE WASN'T WRONG ABOUT SAVANNAH. As soon as they stepped into the clearing the chapel doors opened and she appeared. "Sweet Baby Jesus," she said as she hurried down the cobblestone path in her frilly yellow bridesmaid dress. "Where have you been?" She hooked an arm through his and Zane's and pulled them along. "I need your help getting the rest of the chairs set up. I'm terrified that we're not going to have enough."

Dirk appeared in the doorway of the chapel. He wore the same dove gray tux as Zane and Cole, and Cole wasn't exactly happy about it. He still didn't like the guy, and yet Dirk had somehow weaseled his way into being one of his groomsman. Or more like Savannah had helped him weasel his way in. She had a thing about uneven attendants. Emery had Gracie as her maid of honor and Savannah and Carly as her bridesmaids. When Cole couldn't get ahold of Raff, that left him with two: Zane and Emmett. And Emery's two brothers would throw the entire balance off in the opposite direction.

So he was stuck with Know-it-all.

"No need to worry, Savannah," Dirk said with his big annoying smile. "I once worked at a hotel and helped out with the weddings. There are always people who say they're going to show up, but never do."

"I hope you're right, Dirk." Savannah's gaze lowered to his lapel. "Where in the world did you get that pink rose? Emery's colors are yellow and white. That's going to clash horribly."

Before Dirk could answer, Carly appeared. She looked more like a pixie fairy than usual in the yellow confection of a dress with the coronet of yellow wildflowers just as yellow as her spiky hair. Although her disposition was more grumpy dwarf than Disney fairy.

"We need a little clashing with these hideous dresses

you chose for us. And where do you want these, Miss Bossy Pants?" She nodded at the folding chairs she lugged in each arm.

"Here, let me help you with those," Zane hurried up the steps and took the chairs from Carly. If the look she gave him was any indication, his help wasn't needed or wanted. But Cole's cousin didn't seem to notice as he continued. "We can't have a little thing like you carrying such heavy chairs."

Carly's eyes narrowed. "A little thing like me? I'll have you know that I lift fifty pound bags of flour—"

Savannah cut her off. "Now Carly Sue, don't cause a fuss on Emery's wedding day." She glanced around. "And speaking of Emery, has anyone seen her? She's supposed to be in the back room getting ready. But when I peeked my head in to check, her mother said she'd disappeared."

"She went for a walk," Carly said.

"Sweet Baby Jesus, why would she go for a walk this close to the ceremony?"

Since Emery had declared her love, Cole had been doing much better with his trust issues. But the bride disappearing on her wedding day would make any groom a little nervous. Okay, he was more than a little nervous. He was scared shitless. He turned on a boot heel and strode down the cobbled path. "I'll go look for her."

"You can't see her before the wedding," Savannah called after him. "It's bad luck."

No, that wouldn't be bad luck. Bad luck would be if Emery decided to make a run for it. And since his life had been filled with bad luck, it was highly possible. It became even more likely when he couldn't find her after ten minutes of searching. He had about to get his truck to continue the search when he saw a flash of white in the cemetery behind the chapel. He opened the gate and walked around the simple wooden crosses and massive gravestones that marked the final resting place of his ancestors. When he saw which grave Emery was standing over, he smiled. He should've known where to find her.

The headstone wasn't as massive as some of the others, but it told the story of who was buried there. The stone was cut to resemble a book and engraved with the words *Lucy Arrington, a Tender Heart*. Beneath the words were the dates of his great-aunt's birth and death and the Earhart brand of a heart-encircled *E*. Cole used to think the brand was sappy. But after reading the entire series, he now thought it was pretty cool. Or maybe love had just changed his way of thinking. That love intensified as he looked upon his bride. The beautiful white gown hugged her slim body and the long, gauzy veil trailed down her back like closed angel wings.

She turned, and the way her eyes lit up made him feel like he'd just lassoed the moon and given it to her. No matter what happened to his dreams of a horse ranch, so long as he had this woman by his side, he'd be a happy man.

"Cole," she breathed.

He would never get tired of hearing her say his name with such love. He moved closer with every intention of kissing the daylights out of her. But before he could, Emery held up the piece of aged paper in her hand and started chattering with excitement.

"You aren't going to believe what I found. I was talking to my mother about how my great-aunt's grave almost got washed away in the last California rainstorm, and suddenly I thought about Lucy's grave and how I had never seen it. So I asked Becky and she told me about this gravesite. Why didn't you ever tell me about your family cemetery?" Before he could answer, she flapped a hand. "It doesn't matter. Because as I was standing here thanking Lucy for her stories and for getting us together, I noticed this on the ground."

Ignoring the piece of paper she held, he pulled her into his arms and kissed her. She melted against him for only a second before she pulled back. "Don't you want to know what it is?"

He kissed her nose. "From your reaction, I would say it's a page from Lucy's last book. A page you haven't read before."

She blinked. "Yes. But don't you see what it means? Somewhere in this cemetery the rest of the book could be buried."

He kissed each cheek. "And I promise we'll scouring the entire area . . . right after you become Mrs. Cole Arrington."

A dreamy smile tipped her mouth. "Mrs. Cole Arrington." The smile drooped. "What are you doing here? You're not supposed to see me until the wedding."

"What did you expect me to do when my bride went missing?"

Her eyebrows lifted in a sassy sort of way that made him grin. "Worried, were you?"

"Maybe just a little."

She immediately cuddled into his arms and rested her head on his chest. "I'm not going anywhere, Cole Arrington. I'm exactly where I was meant to be. Did you realize that technically I am a mail-order bride? Gracie sent a letter and here I am?"

His heart swelled, and he kissed the top of her head. "You are such a Tender Heart dweeb." He noticed the flowers resting against the base of his aunt's headstone. "Which explains why you know that pink roses were Lucy's favorite."

She pulled back and looked at the flowers. "I didn't bring the roses, but I probably should've. Maybe she would've given me more than one page." She glanced at the paper that rested on his shoulder. "But really, a page is enough. Now we know that she finished it."

"Maybe. But it doesn't really matter."

Her pretty green eyes widened. "Not matter? How can you say that? Now that you've read the story, don't you want to know if Rory and Etta live happily-ever-after?"

The wind hadn't been blowing the entire morning, but suddenly a warm breeze swept through the cemetery, lifting Emery's veil into a billow of ghostly white and ruffling the petals of the pink roses that lay on Lucy's grave. Cole didn't much believe in signs, but he hadn't believed in love either and the proof stood in his arms.

He smiled. "I have little doubt that they do."

ACKNOWLEDGMENTS

T HIS BOOK WOULDN'T HAVE HAPPENED without these amazing folks:
Roxanne St. Claire for starting me on this new adventure. God called you right when I needed you and I'm
glad you took the call. My editor Lauren Plude for keeping this pantser in check. Outlines would be easier on
everyone, but then what would we talk about during the
editorial calls? My copyeditor Rebecca Cremonese for
being so thorough and professional. You rock, girlfriend!
My proofreader Sandi Farmer for grading my work and
catching the little bloopers. My cover designer Kim Killion for putting up with a neurotic author who wanted
perfection. You gave it to me! As did my talented photog-
rapher Amanda Carras. Next time, we're doing shirtless
models and body oil. Lol! My beta readers Margie Hager
and Sue Boren who never fail to step up to the plate. And
my awesome Katie Krew and amazing readers for all their
reviews, support, and love. I love you right back.
Last, but never least, my family. My Jimmy who for-
gives me for all those scrambled egg dinners and late night
writing. My daughters who give me kudos when I need it
and call me out when I get too crazy. My son-in-laws for

listening to me go on and on and on about my characters. And my grandkids who remind me to take a break and smell the Play Dough.

Thank you, Lord, for putting all these wonderful people in my life. I am truly blessed.

A Sneak Peek at the next
TENDER HEART TEXAS
novel.

FALLING HEAD OVER BOOTS
out May 2017!

IMPOTENT?

He was NOT impotent. He was a strong, virile bull that just needed a little motivation. Yes, that was it. Motivation was keeping him from being the acclaimed stud everyone knew him to be. The female population didn't stir his blood. Didn't prime his juices. Didn't fill him with a raging desire to pursue and conquer.

Females could do that to a male. One second, they could make you feel like the king bull of the herd, and the next second, they could make you feel like a castrated steer.

Zane Arrington's hands tightened on the steering wheel, and he had the sudden urge to put his fist through the side window. Instead, he took a deep breath and tried to get control of his temper and his wayward thoughts. And if he was good at anything, it was control. He'd been controlling his emotions and thoughts for years.

Now, where was he? Oh, yes, he'd been thinking about Ferdinand, and why the prize bull he'd paid a half million dollars for wasn't doing his job of impregnating the herd. It couldn't be impotency. The bull had proven himself to be a damn good producer, which is why Zane had bought him. Ferdinand's prize bloodline was going to enrich the herd. That was if Zane could figure out what was wrong with the animal's libido. He had tried everything from vitamins to hormones, but the bull flat refused to mount one heifer. His sister Becky just thought the bull needed more time to adjust to his new environment. And maybe she was right. She did seem to know a lot about males. She had half the male population of Texas panting after her.

Which made absolutely no sense to Zane. He loved his sister, but she was the biggest pain in the butt this side of the Pecos. She was too opinionated, too controlling, and too competitive for her own good. He liked his women to be soft-spoken, reserved, and sweet. Just like . . .

He shook his head. No, sir, he wasn't going there.

Becky. He was thinking about his sister Becky and how he was going to kill her for not checking in like he'd asked her to if she was going to be late. But asking never worked with Becky. She was hardheaded just like their daddy. Zane was more easygoing like their mama. Which is exactly how he'd ended up babysitting his little sister. He should've flat refused to let her move back to the ranch after college. He should've sent her to Austin to live with Mama and Daddy so they could've been dragged out of their comfortable bed at all hours of the night. And he planned on reading his inconsiderate sister the riot act about that . . . as soon as he made sure she was okay.

Since Becky loved to dance, his first stop was the only bar in town. The Watering Hole was never busy. Not only because it had the worst food in Texas, but also because most folks were home by eight and in bed by nine. So he wasn't surprised to find only a few vehicles in the parking lot. And none were his sister's brand new half-ton pickup. He wheeled his own half-ton around and was about to look elsewhere when the owner and a regular of the bar came out the door. And in Bliss, folks never got away with just a wave.

Zane rolled down his window. "Hey, Hank. Hey, Jeb. How y'all doin'?"

"Fair to middlin'," Hank said. "Not as bad as most, but not as good as you." He grinned. "I saw that article about you in *Rancher's Life* magazine. I don't remember the exact words, but it was something about you being the perfect mix between the hardworking cowboys of the old west and the technically savvy ranchers of the future."

Zane adjusted his hat. "I don't know if I'd go that far." Especially when he'd wasted a fortune on a bull with no libido. Not that he was willing to spread that gossip around. He had yet to even tell his daddy. Even though his father was retired, he still considered the ranch his and would be pissed that Zane had wasted the money.

"Yep," Jeb said with a sloppy grin that pretty much said he'd had too much to drink, "you're done the Arrington name justice, and the town of Bliss proud."

The comment should've made him happy. He'd spent most of his life trying to do his family name justice and the town proud. But right now he didn't feel happy. He just felt confused about how his perfect life had gone to hell in a handcart so quickly.

"So what has you in town so late at night?" Hank asked. "You looking for Becky? She was in earlier, but she left around nine with Dale Foster. I thought she was dating Jake Holmes."

"That was last week," Jeb said with another sloppy grin. "This week it's Dale."

Obviously, the entire town was keeping up with his sister's speed dating. Not wanting to fuel the gossip, Zane told a little white lie. "Actually, I was looking for my foreman Jess. He wasn't answering his phone so I thought I'd see if he was here." He changed the subject. "You okay, Jeb. You need a ride home?"

Jeb shook his head. "I think I'll walk tonight. Maybe sober up a little before I get home." He winked. "You know how ticked wives can get when you've had a little too much to drink."

No, Zane didn't know about that. He'd never had a little too much to drink. Not only because he didn't like feeling out of control, but also because his daddy had taught him that a good husband never had more than the occasional beer. And Zane was a good husband. A damn good husband.

His hands tightened on the steering wheel. "Yeah, wives can sure get ticked at that. Y'all have a good night."

After leaving The Watering Hole, he headed down Main Street. The town was closed up tight. Not that there were a lot of businesses still opened in Bliss. Most of the buildings were vacant and had been for years. The only thing keeping Bliss on the map was the occasional tourist looking for Tender Heart.

Tender Heart was a fictional book series that Zane's great-aunt had written. It was based on the mail-order-brides who had come to Bliss in the eighteen hundreds and pretty much started the town. The series was considered a classic and had rabid fans that showed up sporadically looking for their favorite fictional characters and the little white chapel where all the brides had been wed. They were sadly disappointed when all they found were ordinary folks and a bunch of vacant buildings.

A flicker of light in one of those vacant buildings caught his attention, and he took his foot off the accelerator and slowed down to take a closer look.

The diner had been built in the late fifties when Bliss was experiencing its heyday. At the time, Texas was producing plenty of oil for all the gas-guzzling cars, cattle prices were high, and the Tender Heart books had just come out and were selling like hotcakes. The diner had closed when Zane was in high school, but he still remembered the hearty home-cooked meals you could get there. The kind of meal that warmed a man's belly and stuck to his ribs.

Nothing like the cheese sandwich Zane had made for his supper.

His mind started to go down the bad path again, but he reeled it in and concentrated on the flickering light in a diner. Was that a flashlight? Candlelight? Or maybe a fire? At the thought, he drove into the back alley and parked behind the diner. He wasted no time getting out and heading to the door. He shoved it open so hard that it ricocheted off the wall. He went to flip on the lights, but a distressed feminine shriek had him charging for the kitchen where he found a woman flapping at the flames of a small fire with a dishtowel.

He wasted no time scooping the woman up in his arms. Which wasn't that difficult. She was a tiny little thing. Although in her agitated state, she was a little difficult to hang on to.

"Put me down!" She wiggled and swatted at his shoulder.

"It's all right, ma'am. I got you. You're safe now."

"I'm not worried about my safety, you knucklehead. I'm worried about the book!"

The harmless swats turned into punches that stung a little. And did she just call him a knucklehead? Obviously, the woman wasn't a resident of Bliss. No one in town would ever call him a knucklehead. It was also obvious that the fire had made her a little delirious if she was worried about a book.

He tightened his hold and stepped out into the alleyway. "Now, don't be worrying yourself about a little ol' book. I'll buy you a new one. Let's just get you out of harm's way so I can call the fire department."

"I don't want a new one. I want that one!" She clipped him hard enough on the chin with her fist to knock his head back and his cowboy hat off. And Zane hated his hat touching the ground. He loosened his hold to pick it up, and she squirmed out of his arms and raced back to the diner. He caught up with her before she reached the door. He wasn't the type of cowboy to manhandle a female. But sometimes you had to take the bull by the horns. Especially if it was for its own good.

"Now that's about enough." He wrapped an arm around her waist and lifted her off her feet. "You can't go back in there. I don't care about your silly book."

"It's not a silly book." She kicked him in the shin, and he saw stars.

"Sonofa . . ." He bite back the cussword as he hauled her over to his truck. But once there, he wasn't sure what to do with her. If he let her go, he had little doubt that she would head back into the diner. And if she continued to kick like a mule, there was a good chance he wouldn't be fathering any children. So he did the only thing he could do: He turned her around and pinned her against his truck. He held her arms down so she couldn't hit and straddled her legs and clamped them tightly between his.

That seemed to shock her into silence. Of course, it shocked him into silence as well. It had been awhile since he'd gotten this close to a woman, and he'd forgotten how nice it felt. She really was a little bit of a thing. The top of her head barely reached the second snap on his western shirt. Although her moussed hair added another couple inches that brushed the underside of his chin. He expected the spikey, short hair to be prickly, but it was as soft as the feathers of a baby chick. And her hair wasn't the only thing that was soft. Two full breasts pillowed his ribcage, and her lower body conformed to his better than his Sealy Posturepedic.

Desire settled hot and heavy in his loins.

He wasn't surprised. He hadn't had sex in months. It was perfectly normal to feel a little randy after such a dry-spell. And maybe that was Ferdinand's problem. Maybe they'd been offering him too many heifers. Maybe he needed to be cut off from the herd for a few weeks so he would appreciate the selection he had.

Ignoring his reaction to her tempting body, Zane held her tight while he fished his cellphone out of his back pocket. It took awhile for Mike Wright to answer. He was the volunteer fire chief and rarely got called during the day for a fire. Let alone late at night.

"Hey, Mike, this is Zane Arrington." The woman in his arms stiffened up like a poker, and he couldn't help smiling. Obviously, she hadn't known who had come to her rescue. And that was his fault. He should've introduced himself before he started manhandling her. He loosened his hold.

"Hey, Zane," Mike said. "What's up, man?"

"We have a little fire at the diner."

"No, shit? I'll be right there."

After Mike hung up, Zane placed the phone back in his pocket. "So have you settled down enough that I can let you go without you racing back in to get your book?"

"It's too late," she grumbled. "It's probably burned to a cinder by now. And it's all your fault."

He drew back. "Excuse me? How is that my fault? I wasn't the one who started the fire."

"If you hadn't charged in like an insufferable super hero,

I wouldn't have jumped and knocked over the candle I was using to read."

The gall of woman amazed him. "And exactly why were you reading in the vacant diner in the first place? Last time I checked, breaking and entering is illegal."

She released her breath in an agitated huff. "Which is exactly why I was reading by candlelight. Now do you mind letting me go?"

Zane didn't know why he hesitated. Maybe because it had been so long since he held a woman that he was kind of enjoying it. Still, there was only one woman he should be holding. And it wasn't this woman. He released her and stepped back.

It was dark in the alley, but now that he had the chance to study her, there was something vaguely familiar about her spiky hair and pixie features.

"Do I know you?" Before she could answer, his brain finally clicked in. "Well, I'll be damned. If it isn't Little Carly Sue?"

DEAR READER,
Thank you so much for reading *Falling for Tender Heart*. I hope you enjoyed reading about Bliss, Texas, as much as I enjoyed writing about it. If you did, please help other readers to find this book by telling a friend or writing a review. Your support is greatly appreciated!

Katie

ABOUT THE AUTHOR

KATIE LANE IS A USA Today Bestselling author of the *Deep in the Heart of Texas, Hunk for the Holidays, Overnight Billionaires,* and *Tender Heart Texas* series. She lives in Albuquerque, New Mexico, with her cute cairn terrier Roo and her even cuter husband Jimmy.

For more info about her writing life or just to chat, check out Katie on Facebook www.facebook.com/katielaneauthor, Twitter www.twitter.com/katielanebook, and Instagram www.instagram.com/katielanebooks. And for upcoming releases and great giveaways, be sure to sign up for her mailing list at www.katielanebooks.com!

Printed in Great Britain
by Amazon

38091555R00145